Terracotta

C. L. Mawby

To my wife, Jacqueline,
who helped cast light when I was in darkness

Chapter 1

A late June evening in 2016, and a pitch-black sky from the electrical storm had raged over Chicago for most of the day, the horizontal rain beating against the taxi's windows like a drum. Dirk Davis turned the collar on his overcoat and readied himself as the taxi reached a measured stop outside the restaurant he'd been requested to attend at short notice by his fence, Garrick.

He paid the driver and stepped out onto the saturated sidewalk, feeling the heavy rain hit his face. A nearby canopy provided little cover from the weather, rattled in the ensuing wind, and rivers of water flowed through the streets, the ageing drains giving up long ago, allowing the system to drown in the sheer volume of water.

In a nearby alley, a homeless man with long dishevelled hair watched Dirk from the Dumpster he was using as a shelter, the lid propped partially open by a discarded pole.

He entered the restaurant just before 21:00, on time for his meeting. Standing by the door while waiting for a staff member to attend, he shook his overcoat before rolling up his cap and placing it into one of its pockets. It was a well-lit establishment that gave a warm, welcoming feeling from the wind and rain he'd just been through.

There were only a handful of customers in the restaurant: a small group of men sat to the right, while to the left, an older man in a grey suit sat alone with his back to Dirk, drinking red wine from an ornate, silver-rimmed glass, watching the world go by outside.

A waitress warmly welcomed Dirk, then asked, 'May I help you, sir?'

'Yes,' replied Dirk, 'I'm here to meet with a Mr Lombardi. Has he arrived yet?'

'Yes, sir. He's waiting for you in one of our private rooms. If I can take your coat, I'll take you to him.'

Chapter 2

Dirk stared over the rim of his coffee cup, thinking deeply about the job he'd been offered several minutes before. The waitress interrupted them as she brought the main course to the table. 'Will there be anything else?' she asked, smiling at them both.

Garrick Lombardi hadn't changed much in the twenty-five years since he and Dirk first met in New Jersey, just the added wrinkles and the now dyed black ponytailed hair that hid the ageing grey. His olive skin gave away his Italian heritage, while the expensive tailored suits he always wore over his tall, slender frame showed he had money. Dirk knew he had strong ties to the local Mafia, but Garrick always left him to his own devices, which he preferred.

'No, that will be all for now, thank you,' replied Garrick smiling back at the waitress, and he patiently waited for her to close the door to the private room before he continued. 'I presume you have questions?'

'How much are we getting this time?'

'You'll receive the usual cut for this type of job, but, if the team completes the job within half the time, then...' and he paused, 'you'll receive triple the payment.'

Dirk's eyebrows rose sharply, and he choked on the

coffee he'd just drunk. 'Triple?!' he spluttered before reaching for a napkin to wipe his chin.

'Yes, triple,' answered Garrick, grinning at the comedy timing.

Triple! No one paid triple! thought Dirk as he dabbed the coffee on his clothes. 'What's the catch?'

With his smile now diminished, Garrick's tone became serious. 'There's no payment if any of the pieces are physically damaged, and that's all I can tell you unless you accept the job.'

'That's a big catch.'

'I wouldn't have called you if I thought you and your team couldn't handle it, Dirk,' came Garrick's charming response as he started his meal.

For several minutes Dirk pondered his decision carefully. With this money, he could stop putting off his retirement, and he'd finally put all this behind him. But the nervousness of the past nagged at him, bringing a more sensible and measured approach. He'd been here before. Easy job with easy money, and everything went wrong. *Ignore the bonus, do it right, and live another day*, he began repeating to himself.

'Have you made a decision?' asked Garrick, disrupting Dirk's pangs of guilt that were beginning to surface.

Dirk put his coffee cup down. 'Yeah, I'm in.'

'Good. Let's get down to business.' Garrick took a mouthful of wine to cleanse his pallet before resuming. 'The client has heard about your reputation and wants you to do a job for him.' He lowered his glass and continued,

'The job is relatively simple. Steal two terracotta soldiers from the Chicago Field Museum of Natural History, on loan from a private collector. They're around two metres tall, weigh in the region of six hundred pounds each, and, as I've already mentioned, are to be undamaged upon delivery.' He produced a mobile phone from his suit pocket before placing it on the table and sliding it towards Dirk. 'This is a burner phone, with only one number in the contact list. That number is for when you've retrieved the artefacts. They'll then give you a time and place to hand over the goods.'

Dirk took the phone and slipped it into the inside pocket of his jacket.

Garrick continued, 'The exhibition with the statues opens this Saturday and will be on show for the next two months only. If the job is completed within a month, we get the aforementioned bonus. The client has also stressed that he wants the statues from the private collection, *not* from the official Terracotta exhibition in the same museum. Any mix-up, and again, no payment. Everything else is up to you.'

Dirk thought for a moment, before starting with the questions. 'What's the difference?'

'I don't know,' replied Garrick, 'and it's not my place to ask. He's particular like that.'

'What makes the client think it's the right time to acquire the goods?'

'He believes the museum security is easier than where they'd be housed normally.'

Dirk nodded; it made sense. 'Did you ask for an advance?'

'I did, and that's a no-go, I'm afraid. That's why there's a bonus. He believes in incentives, and this is usual for him.'

'How long will we need to sit on them until the arranged transfer time and date?'

'On previous jobs like this, he's always collected the same night. So, holding on to the items shouldn't be an issue.'

'What if we do damage the pieces?'

'Then it's down to you to get rid of them. Remember, you won't be paid if one piece is damaged. I don't know how easy it'll be to shift to another source if the statues are damaged. So, you might as well leave them. Plus, they'll become a hot potato at this point. If it does happen, I'll ask where I can and arrange another sale to recuperate some losses, but it won't be easy, and if my client finds out what I'm doing, he might think it's a double-cross, and I don't want to go down that route. They'll probably be worthless if they're badly damaged, but ancient artefacts are not my expertise. If you damage them, hope it's before you take them from the museum, so you can just leave. I don't know who the private collector is supplying the exhibition. But I'll ask some discreet questions. I don't want to raise any suspicions with the statues' owner either.'

'It seems our employer knows. How else would he know that the security is easier, and more importantly, what condition they're in?'

'That makes sense and a good point. I'll ask our client if he's willing to part with the information.'

'No, don't bother,' responded Dirk quickly, waving a hand. 'It's probably not a clever idea to ask him. As you rightly said, it makes us look like we're planning to fail or double-cross. We've our reputation to uphold after all.' Dirk drank some more coffee and thought for a moment. He'd have to ask Sharyn to help on this matter. Something didn't smell right. He didn't want to put Garrick at risk and wanted to know the potential comebacks if something went wrong. *If the client knows the owner, there must be a grudge or something. Why not just offer to buy them instead? And why does he want them so badly?*

'Any more questions?' spoke Garrick, snapping Dirk away from his thoughts.

'Well, you weren't kidding when you said man-sized earlier, were you,' stated Dirk with a wry smile while putting his coffee cup down. 'Let's see. We know the time frame, plus where and what the targets are. We also have a contact number for organising the handover point, and we've got the payment plan. The rest, as you said, is up to me. What about the contact number you've given me?'

'That'll also be for a burner phone, just for the handover. Of course, after the handover, the client's phone will undoubtedly be discarded, and I suggest you do the same. But I shouldn't need to tell you that.'

'I take it you've had dealings with this client before? As you said, he's particular.'

'You know better than that, Dirk. All I can say is, he's a

long-standing client, and I trust him. Of course, we're still using pseudonyms like we used for the first fifteen years of our professional relationship…' They both chuckled at that. 'But he likes his artefacts, and there's a professional respect between us, like between you and me.'

Trying to be tactful, Dirk responded, 'I simply want to ensure the client's request has the highest chance of success, so we all get the best possible outcome.'

But Garrick seemed to understand what Dirk was probing at, and his voice became stern.

'Don't go there, Dirk. That was twenty-five years ago. Let it go. You're letting your paranoia get away with you again. What happened, happened. The deal I brokered with the New Jersey syndicate still stands. They'll never touch you.' Garrick eased up on his tone. 'But I sense your concern, and as we've discussed retirement before, you're almost certainly treating this as your last job… again. You and your team are the most gifted people I know in our business. Just do what you do best, complete the task professionally and live another day. And if this is your swan song, send us a postcard, and for Christ's sake…' Garrick started to chuckle. 'Grab a partner, settle down and live a little. You're too much of a jobsworth.' He then gave a wink before continuing with the meal.

Dirk apologised, knowing Garrick was right. He had suddenly become nervous about the job, more than usual, and he didn't know why. But, knowing now that he couldn't back out, he shook his head slowly, putting it down to the chance of taking retirement. He gave a wry smile towards Garrick.

They decided to take a break from work, finishing the main course and discussing the news on TV. Shortly after, the waitress returned and took the empty plates, returning several minutes later with dessert. Garrick then requested more wine and coffee.

With dessert finished and the bowls cleared, they relaxed a little before Garrick brought attention back to the job. 'So, what do you think? Can it be done?'

'I can't see why not. It's not unlike any other job we've done before,' replied Dirk confidently. 'It's just in a museum instead of a mansion. I'll get my team together and take it from here. Is there anything else I need to be aware of?'

'I don't think so,' said Garrick, 'but I'll contact you in the usual way if I have more information.'

'Likewise. Am I good to go?' asked Dirk.

'Yeah, no problem. You go. I'll settle the bill.'

'Thanks, Garrick.' Dirk got up and took his overcoat from the coat rack. 'I'll be seeing you.' As he opened the door, Garrick regained his attention.

'Dirk…'

'Yeah?'

'Good luck, though I'm sure you won't be needing it.'

Chapter 3

Dirk put on his overcoat and cap and exited the main entrance onto the street outside. The rain had stopped, but there was still the blustery wind. It was 23:15 as he walked back towards the station at Adams and Wabash, deciding to catch the train home.

When the train arrived at the platform, Dirk entered a deserted carriage, sat down, turned his cap around, and picked up a paper someone had discarded on the seat next to him. He skimmed through it but struggled to concentrate on its contents, so he soon put it down. He was already rapidly thinking about the job and its potential problems and solutions but soon realised his thoughts were consuming him. He took long, deep breaths to dismiss his ideas, then closed his eyes to concentrate on the sounds and movement of the carriage, trying to stay relaxed.

When the train approached Paulina Station, he stood up and waited for it to stop. The doors opened, and he exited the carriage, making his way off the platform, down the stairs to the short path under the raised tracks to North Paulina Street, where he started the short walk home. It was quieter now; the only noises heard were his own footfalls and the trickling sound of rainwater entering the drains.

Dirk kept his senses keen on his way home just in case he was followed. His ordeal in New Jersey twenty-five years ago had seen to that.

He and his then team had entered a home, expecting the owners to be away, but when the couple were found watching TV, there was a confrontation that escalated very quickly. It was Dirk who shot and killed them both, feeling there was no other way out. The New Jersey syndicate, however, wasn't impressed. The couple had friends in high places, and it brought a lot of heat into the city. The syndicate were going to make an example of Dirk, fearing he knew too much about their operations, breaking the omertà if he was caught. If it wasn't for a timely intervention from a visiting Garrick, Dirk believed he'd be at the bottom of the Hudson.

The situation severely knocked his confidence, leading him to make the conscious decision to no longer use guns during jobs, and even though he'd been thriving ever since, the effects suffered meant he now lived with OCD and bouts of brain fogging. All the while, bottling up his emotions. Frustration crept in from time to time, mainly from others' lack of respect.

Sharyn knew how he felt and kept telling him not to keep it within and talk, but he was nervous, he didn't want history to repeat itself, and above all, he didn't want to lose his friends. Only Garrick knew what had happened, and helped Dirk move to Chicago. His current team were the lucky ones. They'd had some close calls, but he always managed to steer them through.

It took ten minutes for him to walk home through the empty streets, and once indoors, he took off his boots and clothes before heading to the bathroom to refresh himself before bed. Dirk inspected his face in the mirror, using the flats of his fingers to massage his cheeks, feeling the stubble already beginning to protrude through his skin as he did so. Bags had formed under his eyes from the recent late nights, but other than that, he thought he looked OK. And as he continued to stare at his reflection, there was that nagging feeling in the back of his mind that these jobs seemed to be getting more challenging with age, even if his mind felt more than willing to accomplish them. Dirk then ran his fingers quickly and roughly through his hair before making some notes to empty his mind before going to sleep.

Chapter 4

I t was just after 09:00 the following day, and Sharyn Shepherd had just sat at the breakfast bar in her apartment. She'd already been up for several hours; she'd been jogging, had breakfast, and was now resting with a cup of tea while reading the local paper online. It detailed problems caused by the storm, with flash flooding reported in several parts of the city, and her local hospital reporting a delay in starting up its backup generators when a power cut hit the area. Once caught up, she'd finished her tea and begun her work.

She was lucky enough to start using modern technology at an early age and kept on top of the new tech as it appeared. Though it hadn't been an easy road, having to put up with the sexist and racist comments all the way through childhood. And even when she silenced these critics with her talent, Sharyn still couldn't get a scholarship, and could only put it down to the fact she was black.

Sharyn started hacking for extra cash on the side, improving her knowledge and capability vastly, but eventually, it led to a brush with the law. Her lawyer managed to play down her abilities significantly, putting it down to the newly coined 'Script Kiddie' craze at the time, where unskilled individuals were using the programmes of others to attack the still evolving internet. As a result, Sharyn was sentenced to six months in prison in her home city of New Orleans, halting any ambition for a scholarship.

Finding it hard to get a steady job for five arduous years, Sharyn had to settle for a string of waitressing roles to earn a living and soon became frustrated and bored, knowing she could offer a lot more with her potential.

It then seemed her infamy became her saviour when she was approached by a tech firm, offering her a position within the company. Her role was to help prevent and catch other hackers by getting into other companies' systems and searching for potential flaws within the security of a client's computers through vulnerability assessments and penetration tests. 'To set a thief to catch a thief,' as the man quaintly put it. The only problem they had foreseen was that she'd have to relocate to Chicago. Sharyn snatched the chance of a fresh start with both hands and never looked back. As she saw it, becoming a 'white hat' was much better than waiting on tables.

Since moving seventeen years ago, Sharyn had worked hard to build a good network of contacts, which enabled her to set up her successful website design, security and PR business eight years ago. However, at forty-seven, the one remaining problem was the vice for taking risks. So, when Sharyn needed 'a fix', she did some hacking on the side, telling herself it was only to update herself with the new tech. In the long run, this was how she encountered Dirk, and they soon became close friends.

At 11:30, Sharyn decided to take a break from work and have a light lunch, and just as she finished her last mouthful, her mobile rang. Her heart raced when she saw it was Dirk.

'Hi Dirk, what can I do for you?' She twirled her hair around her finger.

'Hi, Sharyn. I hope I haven't disturbed you. I need help with a new promotion on my website and wondered if you'd give me a hand? You know me and technology,' he said, chuckling.

Knowing that Dirk was more than capable of dealing with the website promotion himself, Sharyn instantly knew this was his way of saying, 'I've got a job. Are you interested?' Sharyn felt a tingle in the back of her neck, that knowing sensation; she was becoming excited with the prospect of danger. 'OK, Dirk, when do you want me to pop round and discuss what you need? Though it can't be this afternoon, as I'm seeing another client.'

'Tomorrow, if that's all right, say around 10:30?'

'That'll be fine. See you then.'

'Thanks, Sharyn. It's appreciated.'

With the call ended, she put the phone to her lips and smiled, unable to contain her excitement. The possible risks enhanced her emotional state like a drug surging through her veins.

Chapter 5

On Friday, Dirk entered his official workplace at 09:30, an auto repair shop three blocks away from where he lived, enjoying a good reputation within the neighbourhood and constantly busy. He used it to cover some of his tracks when dealing with his non-legitimate work.

When he entered the building, his two employees, Cody and Willkie, had already been there for several hours. They gave a sarcastic 'afternoon, boss' behind cheerful grins and grease-streaked faces, the local radio playing in the background.

'Morning, guys.' Dirk grinned. 'Hope you've been busy. How's Mr Devlin's Lexus coming along?'

'Finished this morning while you were still in bed,' Willkie cheekily replied. 'And I've already called him to say he can pick it up. He'll be in later to settle the bill.'

'And Mrs Simm's station wagon is also finished,' stated Cody beaming. 'She's already paid and collected it, just in time for her school run.'

'Great guys, let's keep the reputation going as always.' Dirk headed towards his office but stopped just before the door and turned around. 'By the way, Sharyn will be here at 10:30, so if you two could close the shop for an 'early lunch' and join us around 11…' He paused briefly, then added, 'Oh, and if either of you wants to stay behind and help me with the accounts after work? Just let me know.' Dirk smiled, and before either of them could respond, he entered his office and closed the door gently behind him.

There was great camaraderie between the three of them; they had all known and worked with each other for a while now, so all forms of banter were perfectly acceptable, but Dirk just liked to remind them occasionally that he was still the boss.

Cody Ruskin stood at six feet tall, with a short blond flat top, and even though he was thirty-three, he looked younger. Nevertheless, he kept himself in shape at the gym and seemed to ooze confidence, often coming across as a lady's man. Originally from the Bergen-Lafayette area of Jersey City, where Dirk was also raised, they first met ten years ago, during an art theft for one of Garrick's clients. Cody was pulled in as the getaway driver, as Dirk's regular driver had suddenly become ill, and they hit it off straight away. There was no doubt that he had skill, and when his regular driver retired a couple of years later, Dirk offered Cody the chance to take the spot, which he gladly accepted.

Willkie Boone was forty-one, Chicago born, and immensely proud of his Native American ancestry. He traced his lineage back to the Potawatomi tribe of the Bear Clan, or Makwa Doodem, as Willkie called it. They were indigenous to these parts when the Europeans first settled in the Chicago area. The tribe was relocated to the state

17

of Nebraska when the United States took land from the Native Americans in 1833. Before he was born, his parents moved back to Chicago, deciding to lay down roots in their ancestral homeland.

Dirk met Willkie on the streets when he first moved to Chicago, roughing up people on the whim of others. However, they both found a common liking for engineering, so Dirk took him under his wing until he became established in the city, both with the auto repair shop and his new team.

Compared to Cody, Willkie was shorter but broader in stature, with shoulder-length jet-black hair laced with grey, but was notably the team's muscle, which often led to competitive streaks at the gym, which Cody often lost.

When Sharyn arrived just before 10:30, Cody was dealing with a customer.

'Hi, Cody, where's Dirk?'

'Hi, Shaz. It's been a while,' Cody replied, pleased to see her, and then pointed to one of the vehicle pits, where a beat-up blue Pinto resided, before returning to his customer.

Sharyn responded bluntly with, 'Thanks,' trying to ignore the term 'Shaz', which she loathed, and walked over to the Pinto before looking into the pit underneath. She soon forgot Cody's comment when she saw Dirk with Willkie standing under the car, talking about the problem with a lamp in hand.

'Anyone home?' she asked. Dirk stopped talking and smiled at her, acknowledging her presence, before turning back to Willkie and quickly finishing their discussion about the Pinto.

Dirk walked out of the pit, grabbed a nearby rag to clean the grime off his hands, and leant towards Sharyn to give her a welcoming peck, but then abruptly stopped when Sharyn whipped the rag out of his hands and wiped his face with it.

'Oh no, you don't.' She laughed. 'You've muck on your face as well.'

He smiled and apologised, then went over to the sink to wash. After he'd dried himself, Dirk offered his hand, which Sharyn responded to, and they both headed into his office and closed the door.

'Sorry about that. I didn't notice the time. I would've cleaned up earlier if I'd realised.'

Sharyn smiled and sat down. 'There's no need to apologise. Now, what have you got for me? I presume it's got nothing to do with a promotion.' She then generally pointed through the window before asking, 'Should we wait for the guys to come in?'

He smiled again. 'The guys will be in around 11:00. And you're right. It's not about a promotion. Though if you could add one to my website, I'd be grateful to keep up the pretence.'

While Sharyn took out her laptop to start work, he continued, 'I wanted to chat with you first, as I want some information gathering for this new job. The guys don't need to know this bit yet.' He paused, making a coffee for himself and a tea for Sharyn while she tapped away.

'What do you want to use? Tyres?'

'Nah, let's say exhausts. It's been a while since we've done those. Fifteen per cent off our normal price should do the trick.'

'OK, no problem.'

As he handed her the mug of tea, he continued, 'The job involves taking two artefacts from a museum. I'll give more details when the guys are in, but for now, I've no info on who owns these artefacts, other than they're on loan from a private collector to the museum. The client claims they'll be easier to take from there.' He took a mouthful of his coffee. 'To be that particular with the information, the client and the owner must know each other. Now I've no call to know the client, that's normal, but—'

'But you want to know who you're up against in case things go south,' interrupted Sharyn.

'Well yeah,' replied Dirk. 'It just seems to be a little odd, that's all. Why does he need the pieces so badly? And why not buy them from the collector? Why steal them?'

'OK, I'll see what I can do.' She nodded, smiling towards the door.

Dirk turned his head to see Cody and Willkie grinning through the glass and beckoning them in. Willkie spoke as he opened the door. 'We've put a sign up outside that we'll be back in an hour, and we've locked the unit doors.'

'Thanks, Willkie. Grab a coffee, both of you, and we'll make a start.'

'Where's it this time?' Cody asked. 'A nice little number in someplace hot? I could do with a beach holiday.'

'No, quite the opposite,' replied Dirk. 'This time, it's a local job. And hopefully an in and out one.'

Once everyone had settled, Dirk continued, 'We're to take two statues from the Chicago Field Museum of Natural History that are on loan from a private collector. We've got a two-month window to take the items, but it's triple the regular payment for an added incentive if completed within a month.'

There was a momentary pause as they all looked at each other in surprise; even Sharyn stopped typing. Cody was the first to break the silence. 'Triple?' The hint of disbelief was obvious.

Dirk smiled. 'That's what I said when I first heard it, though I was less professional and choked on my coffee.' This made the rest of the team chuckle, breaking the silence as quickly as it had arrived.

Dirk took another mouthful of coffee before continuing, his tone now serious. 'At this point, I want to add: just because we've got a bonus target date, it doesn't mean we've to complete it by then. We've been at this game for a while now and we're not starting any rush jobs. Our reputation's more important to me than the money. Let's see if it's feasible before making any rash decisions.'

Dirk placed his mug on the desk. 'Now for the detail. The pieces weigh in the region of six hundred pounds each and are both around two metres tall. Willkie, the task I'm giving you is how we will remove the statues from the museum and then transport them safely to the drop point.' Willkie nodded, and Dirk turned to Cody. 'Cody, with

Willkie's recommendations, organise the vehicle we will use. But, again, remember the weight we're transporting, and we'll need to be able to load and remove them quickly and safely at the drop point.'

'OK,' replied Cody.

Dirk turned to Sharyn. 'Sharyn, as usual, I need your tech skills to tell us the type of security we'll be up against, plus any building schematics. I'll be taking a trip to the museum this weekend when the exhibition has its grand opening. I'll be looking at what I can see and start working out a route in and out of the building.'

Sharyn looked up from her laptop and nodded. 'I can't see that being too much of a problem. I'll also see what the transport authority are up to over the next two months. We don't want to run into any unexpected road closures, do we?'

'Thanks, Shaz,' grinned Cody. 'That'll make my job easier.'

Sharyn stared at Cody; her tone became sharp. 'You're welcome, honey... but call me 'Shaz' again, and I'll use your bank account to fund my next holiday.'

That quickly wiped the grin off Cody's face while Willkie started laughing. Cody responded by punching his arm firmly. Sharyn smirked before going back to her typing.

Dirk halted the proceedings sternly. 'Great idea Sharyn, but now to the serious points about the job.'

'The first and most important thing about this job is that the pieces cannot be damaged, otherwise, we don't get paid. If damaged, I'll call 'walk away' and leave the pieces where they are. I'm serious about this point, and it appears that our client knows the targets very well, so it wouldn't be wise to lie to him. I want no cover-up because we don't want any come-back. Cody, your driving skill is going to be tested on this job, so make sure you get the route right. Secondly, there is no upfront payment this time, so we need to spend money wisely, and the standard protocols apply to prevent tracing.'

'Where's the drop-off point, boss?' Willkie asked.

'As of yet, we don't know, but do the usual and take a couple of trips around the area to work out escape routes, etc., just in case.' Dirk placed the phone Garrick had given him on his desk and continued, 'When, and *only* when we've taken the artefacts, we contact the number on this phone. The client will tell us where we need to take the statues, which should be on the same night. According to our fence, this is his normal manner of operating.'

'What are the statues of?' Sharyn then asked.

'I was coming to that,' replied Dirk. 'Terracotta Soldiers. But I want to add that there's also an official exhibition with Terracotta Soldiers in a different hall. And we won't get paid if we take these instead.'

'Why those specific ones, if there is an official exhibition in the same museum?' enquired Cody.

'That's a question I also asked, but it appears we may never know,' said Dirk.

'I'll do some digging while I investigate the security,' interjected Sharyn.

Expecting her response, Dirk smiled at Sharyn. 'That covers about everything. I think our next meeting should be in the evening and on my boat at the harbour in three days. I want no discussions in the workplace in case someone walks in at the wrong moment. And save any questions for the next meeting unless you think it's important.'

He paused before asking, 'Any questions?'

Before looking back at Dirk, the team all looked at each other and shook their heads.

'OK, if there's nothing else, thank you for your time. Cody, Willkie, grab your lunch and then go back to work. I'll finish off this promotion with Sharyn.' And with that, the guys got up and left, closing the door behind them.

Sharyn then spoke to Dirk. 'How do you want me to give you my information about the target?'

'We'll get to the boat early if that's OK. I'll put the guys on an errand, so it delays them. As I said, they don't need to know yet. I need them to focus on their given tasks.

Once we have the full facts, I'll let them know.'

'OK, no problem.' She turned her laptop to show Dirk the completed website promotion. 'How's that for your needs?'

'Perfect,' said Dirk.

'Good, that's me finished then.' She shut down her laptop before giving Dirk a wry smile and adding, 'I'll send you the invoice for the usual cost. After all, we must keep up with the pretence, mustn't we?' She put the laptop in her bag and stood up, placing her bag over her shoulder. They kissed their goodbyes, and Dirk showed her out of the repair shop.

The rest of the day went by peacefully enough, though Cody kept being ribbed about Sharyn's put-down.

After work, the guys went to the local bar to socialise and unwind. It was their favourite watering hole, a bit old-fashioned in some respects, with moody lighting and an old jukebox continuously playing dated music, but they liked it like that. It was always busy, and there was always a chance to play a couple of racks of pool.

However, things were different tonight. They were oblivious that they were being watched from one of the many dark recesses in the bar. Numerous eyes watched them intently, moving around unseen, detailing their every move. Dirk was only there for a couple of hours before leaving Cody and Willkie to it and headed home.

The eyes followed Dirk as he left the building before refocusing their attention on Cody and Willkie. At the end of the night, they walked down the walls and stealthily followed the two men home.

Chapter 6

A little after 09:00 the next day, Dirk looked out the window, a glorious Saturday with clear blue skies, a vast difference from the storm several days ago. After grabbing a bite for breakfast, he headed out the door and ate as he walked to his auto repair shop.

In the years Dirk had lived in Chicago, he'd put some of his ill-gotten gains into the area through anonymous means. Yes, he was trying to retire, but it never seemed like the right time. Garrick told him this was driven by guilt, or he was a fool and should keep what he earned instead of being a 'new age Robin Hood', as he called it. But Dirk didn't see it like that. He was never flash with his cash and wasn't the type to make himself look good; he left that to the likes of Garrick. Instead, Dirk wanted to give something back to benefit the less fortunate. He didn't care no one around him knew, and he didn't feel the need to shout it from the highest skyscraper. Besides, many companies and rich people were making enough noise already, so they took all the attention he didn't want.

However, this new contract had given him a new focus on his future, as jobs that paid this good were few and far between. If they completed the job to obtain the bonus, he would think seriously about calling it a day. Garrick was right with what he said at the meeting. He'd never settled down, mainly because of the trust issues with his illicit activities, but all that could change if he just retired.

Dirk strolled along the streets and was about half a block away from the repair shop when he was torn away from his thoughts whirling around, as he heard a man boom a joyful, 'Morning.' There was a slight delay in Dirk's response, as he also noticed someone else was following him. Finally, he turned back around as if he'd seen nothing and continued his way to work.

The man following was roughly fifty yards behind him and was not someone he recognised from the neighbourhood. His mind went into overdrive. *Perhaps a detective or a government agent?* Dirk pulled out his mobile and activated the video to record before placing it next to his ear. He then started having an imaginary conversation as if he were answering a call, periodically turning his head before crossing the road or standing still for several moments while dealing with the invented car problem. Finally, when he thought he had enough footage, he stopped filming and put the phone back in his pocket. From what he could see, the guy looked amateurish at shadowing.

Dirk got to the main gates of his repair shop, and as he unlocked the padlock, he casually looked around before opening the gate. Unfortunately, his shadow was still there, making a poor attempt to hide around the corner. He closed the gate behind him, made his way into the building, switched off the central alarm, and ensured the various surveillance cameras were still recording. Dirk prepared himself before this person walked in, quickly uploading the video footage he'd just taken to his cloud before placing his paperwork on the desk and turning on the coffee machine while keeping an eye on the security monitor for the main gate.

It was about half an hour later, and Dirk thought he would be left alone when he noticed his newfound admirer walking through the main gate. He knew it took thirty seconds to walk across the parking lot to the main door, so he studied the monitor for ten seconds more: the man was still alone. He switched the channel on the monitor to view the internal camera in the office; to ensure they were recording before turning the monitor off. Knowing the man would walk through the door any moment, Dirk sat back down, pretending to be absorbed with his paperwork.

There was a longer than expected delay before the man came through the main entrance, so Dirk established that the man was nervous and wasn't confident in his approach. He then pretended to have just noticed the man, who was now looking around to see if anybody else was within the building. He could see him clearly now. Young, wearing a stylish, fitted three-piece suit with shiny shoes. They didn't look cheap. His black hair and olive skin were in pristine condition.

Dirk asked, 'Hello, can I help you?'

'Erm… yes… I hope so,' replied the young man, cautiously walking towards the office. 'My name is Kirby. My peers have been told about your work by an associate in the city and they have given me the task to approach you with a lucrative job offer. I must admit it's a pleasure to finally meet you in person, I'm looking forward to working with you Bruce.'

Kirby's mannerisms made Dirk believe he had a decent education and upbringing, though he did come across as a little naïve. And Bruce was Dirk's handle for his criminal activities, though it was more given to him than by choice. He always thought it was because he was from New Jersey, like Springsteen. He wasn't overkeen on it, but it had stuck.

Dirk responded with a weak chuckle. 'You make me sound like a criminal or something, but I am afraid you've got the wrong man, Mr Kirby—'

'No,' the young man interrupted. 'Not Mr Kirby. Just Kirby. We don't believe in having surnames.'

'OK… Kirby.' Dirk thought this odd but rolled with it. 'As I said, you've got the wrong man. I'm the repair shop owner here like it states on the sign outside, and I've no one called Bruce here. But if you're after some repairs or a custom job on your vehicle, let me see what we can do to help.'

Kirby looked and then sounded perplexed as he answered but seemed to be talking to himself as if searching for reassurance.

'I was certain you were the person I was looking for. You matched the description given to me perfectly. The associate said you were the man to go to, to acquire a pair of statues for my mast…' Kirby suddenly stopped in his tracks before rewording his following sentence. 'For my guardian.'

'And who is this associate who led you to me?' inquired Dirk.

'Mr Mbundu. He said—'

'Stop right there,' Dirk interrupted and quickly stood up with anger in his tone. 'I'm not the person you want, and I don't want to know any more. If the police come around here asking questions, I don't want to know anything that puts me or my business at risk. I see and read the news and know all too well about Mbundu and what he deals in. So, I suggest you stay away from him as well. Kindly leave my premises before I call the police.' There was a pause, but Kirby looked confused and had frozen to the spot.

'*Now!*' shouted Dirk. And that shocked Kirby into moving towards the door, shaking his head in disbelief.

Feeling guilty for shouting, Dirk took a deep breath to calm his anger and spoke again. 'Look, Kirby. You look too much of a nice guy to get mixed up with someone like Mbundu. Whatever you are up to, get out, and get out as fast as possible.'

Kirby looked at him and nodded. 'My apologies for disturbing you in this way today.' And with that, Kirby left the building.

Dirk sat in his chair and quickly switched the monitor back on to recheck the parking lot. Seeing Kirby leave, he relaxed into the back of his chair and looked up to the ceiling with some relief, but he soon found himself rapidly thinking. His thought process began to repeatedly churn through Kirby's remarks. *Two statues. Are these the two statues I've been tasked to go after? Why did Kirby need to get involved with Algernon Mbundu?* It was the reason Dirk had become angered and interrupted Kirby. Dirk never had direct dealings with drug dealers, especially the Jamaican posse. He disliked drug use and its trappings, so he tried his best to avoid that side of the criminal fraternity.

Dirk continued to think. *Surely there's a better, more accessible option than going to a Jamaican drug lord first to hire a thief. And Mbundu's ethics are questionable at best.* There was a lot of talk on the street that he dealt with black magic, though Dirk didn't believe it himself. To him, Mbundu used other people's beliefs in a controlling manner to scare and intimidate anyone to get what he wanted. Had Kirby gone to other parties as well? If so, this meant that the job could get messy.

Dirk then decided to lock the main gate, keeping an eagle eye out as he walked across the lot as he did so. There were no urgent vehicles to be repaired, so the guys weren't due in today, and he didn't want any more interruptions while he was alone.

He tried to get back to his paperwork, but his mind was still buzzing after talking to Kirby. He then remembered the slip-up Kirby had made. He'd said, *mast…* before correcting himself to guardian. *Was that short for master?* Dirk couldn't think of any other explanation. *If so, what's this guardian a master of? Or does it mean that Kirby is a servant or even enslaved? And if so, what hold does this guardian have over him?*

Setting the paperwork to one side, Dirk started separate communiqué's to Garrick and Sharyn, asking for their assistance, going through a system that Sharyn had set up for him, making emails harder to trace by outside sources.

But as he continued, he was aware that one question kept going around in his head. *Why go to Mbundu?* He found it hard to believe that Kirby would go to a prominent drugs and arms dealer, when the Mafia were not only renowned historically in the area but were also the stronger force, having their fingers in a lot more pies. *Had Kirby visited the Mafia as well? Or does he or this guardian have a poor reputation with them?* He put that query to Garrick before adding a still of Kirby from his film footage to the messages before sending them. Feeling free from mental distractions, he continued with his paperwork.

It was early evening when Dirk left the repair shop. The paperwork had taken longer than he wanted, and the meeting with Kirby hadn't helped his frame of mind. Instead, he'd become concerned about the job and hoped Garrick or Sharyn could shed more light on his anxieties.

Chapter 7

At 19:30 on the same day, Sharyn was relaxing in her loungewear after a day out with friends. Once she'd spent an hour or so on social media and eating dinner, she turned off her laptop, headed over to her utility cupboard, and opened a well-concealed cubby-hole. Inside were two purpose-built personal computers, a wireless keyboard and other equipment used for her illegal activities. Dirk and Willkie had thought of everything for the cubby-hole when making it: it was near the access panel for the utilities, but the electrics were carefully rewired in a way that created the illusion that the hideaway was part of the construction of the building. They had even made it fully insulated and, under Sharyn's guidance, inserted a water coolant system for the computers to keep them cool while in the confined space.

There was only one thing with the cupboard she didn't like, and as if on cue, a hairy house spider, about the size of a dollar coin, ran out of its hiding place within the cupboard, heading straight towards Sharyn. She leapt quickly to her feet before rapidly stamping them and started to squeal in a high-pitched manner, flapping, brushing her body with her hands vigorously, fearful that an unseen cluster of spiders was swarming over her clothes. This only heightened the situation, making her skin crawl with anticipated terror. Her breathing became rapid, the squealing becoming warbled, as a steady stream of tears began to roll down her cheeks from her widened and fearful eyes.

The spider stopped in its tracks suddenly, looked up briefly at Sharyn, and then seemingly had second thoughts about its situation before running in a new direction, quickly escaping to find another hiding place where it hopefully wouldn't be disturbed.

Sharyn waited for her heart to stop pounding before setting up the vacuum cleaner, then hastily cleaned the cupboard and the immediate surrounding furniture: her built-in safety mechanism, trying to remove any more spiders lurking, waiting to jump out at her.

Once satisfied that no more remained, she switched off the vacuum cleaner, dried her eyes with her sleeve and made a fresh cup of tea while taking more deep breaths to calm down.

Fifteen minutes later, and after another blast with the vacuum cleaner, just to make sure, she connected the setup wirelessly to her wall-mounted television and started work on what Dirk had requested. It took a while for the encryptions to kick in, but when it was up and running, Sharyn started to hunt for what she was after.

She started with what was known in the trade as a meta-search engine on one computer. It used all the online search engines, then amassed the information and collated what was found, optimising her time. It wasn't difficult for Sharyn to add the parameters she wanted to start her analysis: searching for the security and blueprints on the museum, and then another about the private exhibition that contained the statues. She let that run in the background while undertaking other questions. It wouldn't give her all the information she wanted, but it gave her a starting point, which would provide her with possible targets to hack if required. The road closures were the easy part of the investigation. She went to the City of Chicago website, printed off a list of the roads to be closed, and gave a start and finish date, plus the reason for the closures. Not just for roadworks but also for upcoming block parties and neighbourhood festivals.

Sharyn then noticed the email from Dirk in her inbox. It was addressed to Domino, her handle when dealing with illegality online. She liked the ambiguous feel of her pseudonym; it made her feel comfortable.

Opening it, it read:

Hi Domino
    Had a visitor today (please see attachments). Can you find out anything about him?
    He gave the name Kirby, I don't think he is from Chicago, so I hope he's on recent travel manifests.
    Let me know what you find when we meet.
    Bruce

Sharyn sat back and watched the security footage, listening intently to what was being said, writing notes about Kirby and what he said. She then used the still Dirk had taken and set up another meta-search, along with facial recognition software for Kirby.

Eventually, when the information came through the search engines, the real work began. Her second computer was lean, making it fast; it didn't use the traditional search engines that tracked and recorded websites visited. If the computer was seized, it would be difficult to find where Sharyn had been looking. She ensured there were no problems with her encryptions before linking a trail of servers and satellites to hide her tracks while hacking and implementing remote access trojans (RATs).

This was a problematic hack, as the information needed would be on more secure servers than normal, taking hours to complete. Several times, she had to close the net. Mainly to establish new connections to stop being discovered, but also to take a break. This was the only time Sharyn drank coffee to keep that buzz while hacking and stay awake.

In the end, the tiredness got to her, and she called it quits in the early hours. Giving herself a five-hour window, she put some smooth jazz on low volume to empty her mind before drifting off to sleep.

When she awoke, it was 10:27. Sharyn got dressed and went for a run to wake herself up. When she returned, she made breakfast and a mug of coffee. Now feeling fully refreshed, she continued to gather the information needed.

It took her the best part of the day to collect all the required information. Some of the RATs had done their job, which still surprised her after all these years. People were still not tech-savvy enough to keep their information safe in this technological age. Yes, they would protect their computers, tablets, mobiles and the like, but there was always a back door, with items linked through the wi-fi but not associated with hacking, like fitness trackers, or one example she remembered where she found a corporation had a large flashy fish tank in their foyer. It was linked to their server via wi-fi, so it could be monitored. Obviously, no information was stored on the fish tank's computer, but it gave a convenient and unprotected back door to enter the central system.

When finished, she spent a couple of hours creating a presentable dossier for Dirk and the guys, making it easier to digest the information. Sharyn then placed the data onto an encrypted memory stick and tucked it away, ready for tomorrow night, before putting her equipment away, cautiously looking for eight-legged beasts.

Chapter 8

It was a pleasant Sunday morning, the sun was out, and a nice refreshing breeze was coming off Lake Michigan. Dirk was on the train to the Chicago Field Museum of Natural History, but it took longer than he'd liked to get to his destination. After Kirby's visit yesterday, he was paranoid and wanted no more surprises. He had changed lines at Fullerton Station, stopping for a coffee. And once satisfied he wasn't being shadowed, he boarded another train and continued his journey to the museum via Roosevelt Station and the number one-four-six bus.

When Dirk exited the bus, it was a little after midday, and he immediately started to make mental notes of his surroundings. Looking towards the marble steps at the south entrance, he moved anticlockwise around the building, then stopped at the hot dog stall in the southeast corner by the museum, his paranoia nibbling at his mind, checking for tails. Once he'd eaten his hot dog, he proceeded to climb the steps to the south entrance, where he produced his ticket, purchased a guidebook, and entered the museum's sizeable central hall.

Looking at the guidebook, he noted where the private and Terracotta Warrior exhibitions were, then walked around the entire museum before seeing the exhibit. He took note of displays, carefully placing exits, stairs, visible security and elevators into the frame. Then made mental notes of the layout against the guidebook.

Dirk thought it wasn't looking too bad; the personnel and cameras were expected. He noted several points where beams were placed that no doubt would be switched on when the museum closed. It was nothing they hadn't dealt with before, though he'd have to wait to see what Sharyn had found before deciding on a plan. It was the scale he was concerned about. They'd only done private residences before, and while some of these were mansions, there were no wide-open spaces like there were here, and with another floor overlooking the main hall, it was going to be a challenge. He stopped for another bite to eat and a coffee in the Field Bistro, just off the main entrance, giving his racing mind time to empty and rest from his investigation.

Feeling refreshed from his late lunch, he walked across the main hall, past Sue, the museum's skeletal Tyrannosaurus Rex, towards Levin Hall, where the private collection was being shown. And while moving under the arches of the main hall, he considered the cover they would give during the heist. Then, when he noticed the elevator next to the exhibition entrance in the main hall, he looked at his guide map and made another mental note.

He entered Levin Hall and immediately saw the security shutter primed at the top of the doorway, waiting to shut at a moment's notice if the alarm was triggered. He feigned interest in the other pieces, only giving the written descriptions a courteous read. His main interest was the security measures he could spot throughout the room.

There was another entrance at the far end on the right, and Dirk decided to begin looking on the left-hand side of the room and work his way round in a clockwise direction, starting with pieces from Europe.

The first piece he came across was a fifteenth-century German sallet helmet. It was on a stand and encased in glass; the age of the piece showed in its wear and tear. Dirk slowly made his way through the collection, making mental notes of what he saw along the way. Finally, he passed a Scottish claymore sword and a small selection of sixteenth and seventeenth century wigs on stands, upon a Chippendale desk.

The theme then changed to North America, showing war-torn Confederate and Union flags from the battle of Gettysburg that were mounted, crossing each other upon the wall. A complete Union officer's uniform on a mannequin stood before them, including a sabre. Alongside were pieces of local Native American artefacts and trade goods from several tribes, which Dirk noted incorporated Willkie's own.

Then came the Asian section of the collection, and straight away, the Terracotta Warriors were the first thing Dirk saw. Now he was seeing them physically, and this close, he was in awe of the detail and their near-perfect condition. He could see no cracks on the statues. Of course, they were weathered, but you would expect that of pieces with age. There were tiny amounts of what looked like paint, which meant they must have been decorated. Both were standing warriors in roughly the same pose and looked like they should be holding a spear or something. Their armour was sculpted into two-inch square plates, joined together with what looked like a sculpted cord. This covered their chest, abdomen and shoulders. They had a thick high collar that Dirk imagined was for neck protection. The rest of their clothing looked like some form of robes and boots.

Looking between the two, there were slight variances in stature. The one on the right looked broader, and the armoured plates seemed slightly more prominent, probably because of their larger frame, while their hands showed a marginal difference in shape. The only noticeable difference Dirk could see was their facial features, and where both were mottled grey in colour, the one on the right was virtually covered in a light coating of fine black powder, from the left knee and right-hand side of the waist, running upwards. Dirk then spotted on the floor a framed notice between the two warriors.

It read:

Terracotta Warriors

These statues are based on the heavy infantry soldiers from the Terracotta Army.

The warrior on the right has been damaged by smoke from an intense fire, leaving the statue stained with a thin covering of soot.

At the point of purchase, the owner of these two warriors believed they were authentic Terracotta Warriors from the burial mound of the First Emperor of China.

However, the Chinese government states that there is only one perfect statue, a kneeling archer, which now resides in China's Qin Shi Huang Terracotta Warriors and Horses Museum.

This means that the owner had unfortunately bought counterfeit statues, but we would like to stress that these are the only two counterfeit items in this exhibition.

The owner has now classified the statues as counterfeit, so the Chinese government has spared these items from destruction. But the owner still wanted to include them in the exhibition as an example: to show that even experts get things wrong from time to time.

Please visit the official Holleb Hall exhibition for more information about the Terracotta Army, which has extended its visit due to popular demand and will be here until January next year.

Dirk reread the notice, but he'd become puzzled, and questions started jumping through his head. *Why would anybody want a pair of fake statues? Perhaps the client didn't know they were fakes.* But it read as though the owner had known about this for a while. *Does the client know? Or had the owner fallen out with the client before the owner knew they were fakes?*

Pausing his thoughts, he then kicked his focus back on what needed to be done.

He surreptitiously started to look for any security around the pieces. They were standing on a new piece of scarlet carpet tile, but he saw no wires running under them as he looked further. This suggested there were no pressure plates, which Dirk thought was strange. Perhaps the museum thought they were too heavy for someone to take. Plus, why take fakes? It still didn't make sense to him. He decided to continue with the rest of the exhibition, to focus his mind elsewhere and wait for Sharyn's investigation.

The collection continued with Persian statuettes, more like the size Dirk usually dealt with on his jobs. But the life-sized stone statue of what looked like a sitting bull mastiff dog caught his eye. While not as detailed as the Terracotta Warriors, it was still impressive, to say the least.

Dirk came to a section of pieces from Japan with small intricate carvings: while most were made of jade or ivory, one was an eggshell that had been worked to show a coastal scene. A light situated behind this piece highlighted the detail that must have taken weeks, if not months, to complete. Then came what the collection guide stated was the star of the show. A complete set of Samurai swords: tanto, wakizashi and katana, made by Hikoshirō Sadamune, a famous Japanese swordsmith of the early fourteenth century. They were on a unique stand within a glass case and standing alongside them was an original set of Samurai armour from the fifteenth century.

On all other available wall spaces, in between the show's

artefacts, were pieces of art by various artists. A banjo that belonged to Vess Ossman was also on display, who played ragtime in the late nineteenth century. A small section on Africa showed a wall-mounted Zulu shield and spears, with a Kpinga throwing blade in a glass case, a strange-looking weapon with multiple angled edges.

Overall, it was an impressive collection, to say the least, thought Dirk, and according to the guide, this was only a fraction of it. He then concluded that the collector had more money than sense. Most collectors he knew accumulated specific items from a particular person or period, like American postage stamps or art by Andy Warhol. This seemed more like a mixture of expensive things the owner saw and had to have rather than a devoted collection. But who was he to judge? He just stole to order.

Dirk scanned the collection again, looking for any pieces of security he'd missed, and then started making his mental notes. Two static security cameras were in the hall, one at each end, while working out from the fittings in the wall, two security beams were running at different heights in front of the displays, with the tell-tale signs of pressure sensors on various smaller items and glass cabinets. And while these weren't the items they were taking, they would need to avoid them when moving the statues. There was also another security shutter on the other door that led to the North American Indian section of the museum.

He left by the entrance he originally entered before walking to the next hall to look at the official Terracotta Warriors exhibition.

Chapter 9

He casually walked up to Holleb Hall to find a small queue of five people and joined the line. When he reached the front of the queue, he was stopped by a female guard at a desk set up by the entrance.

'Good afternoon, sir. I'm afraid no photography is permitted within this exhibition, so if you could please place any smartphones and cameras into this box. You'll be able to collect your belongings when you leave. Thank you.'

'Sure. Why's this?' he asked as he placed his phone and camera into the box.

'Unfortunately, it's part of the conditions to hold the exhibition from their owners,' replied the guard as she locked the box and gave a numbered card to Dirk. 'This'll enable you to collect your personal belongings when you've finished. Please wait next to the door. The next guard will show you in when they're ready. Enjoy the exhibition.' She said before turning to receive the couple behind him.

Dirk didn't have to wait long before a male guard came through the door and beckoned him into a partitioned space. 'Can you hold up your arms to the side, sir?' he asked. As Dirk raised his arms, the guard pulled out a security wand and moved it around his body.

'Seems a lot of protection just for some statues. Can't exactly tuck them under your arm,' joked Dirk, as the wand beeped when it reached his right hip pocket. Dirk pulled out a set of keys, and the guard continued with his check.

'It's to help prevent counterfeit copies being made, sir,' replied the guard. 'You may now enter the exhibition, sir. Enjoy.' And he let Dirk pass and enter the hall.

Dirk expected to see several rows of soldiers, like the ones he'd just visited, and was pleasantly surprised and intrigued when there weren't, so decided to take his time around the exhibition.

It detailed the rise of the Terracotta Army, with how, why and where they were created. There was a map and a miniature model of the First Emperor of China's tomb showing where the pieces were found. Dirk was surprised at the scale of production and size of the site. Before this, he'd just seen the pictures of the rows and rows of soldiers and thought that was all there was to it.

He continued to the next exhibit, a chariot with four horses. This sculpture seemed to be scaled to half the size of what it should be, as the chariot was too small to house anybody, and he first thought it was another model of some kind, a replica. But when he read the accompanying notice, he was surprised to find out it was real. The detail was awe-inspiring; the chariot was made entirely of bronze with what looked like an oversized roof. Three sides had a window, the fourth, at the rear, had a door, all decorated with what the notice described as clouds, which, according to the statement, would have been initially a brilliant white and blue and designed for the emperor to tour his empire in his afterlife. At the front of the chariot, protected by the roof, sat its driver, also made in bronze. The four bronze horses, four abreast, each showed braided tails with bronze harnesses that connected them to the chariot and were all adorned with gold and silver.

Then, Dirk lost his train of thought as he felt someone watching him. He looked over his left shoulder and jumped slightly when he noticed a young woman standing just behind him.

'My apologies. I didn't mean to startle you,' she stated.

Dirk took an awkward second glance and hoped she hadn't noticed, as she was attractive. He gathered his thoughts and said, 'Sorry, you caught me unawares,' then quickly averted his eyes to the carriage.

'So I see,' she said smiling. Her English was near perfect, with hardly an accent.

'My name is Lin Shi,' she said, offering her hand as an introduction. Dirk looked back and, after slightly hesitating, accepted her hand and shook it gently. Lin was a slim East-Asian woman with shoulder-length raven-black hair, standing a little under Dirk's height. She was dressed in a smart, light grey business suit with a skirt, a white-collared blouse, and black and white high-heeled shoes.

Lin continued. 'What do you think of the exhibition?'

Dirk felt foolish and sighed with a wry smile before relaxing and answering. 'Actually, I'm pleasantly surprised. I imagined rows of the same thing I've seen on TV. But all this—' he looked around and gestured with his hand — 'well, it's truly remarkable. My name is Dirk, Dirk Davis.'

'I find that pleasing to hear Mr Davis.' Lin smiled. 'It's what we intended to do. Educate the world about the pieces. But, unfortunately, the popular view of where we go is often the same as yours. And it's proven such a triumph in Chicago, so we have extended our stay until January.'

Dirk's eyes widened in surprise before stating, 'You're part of the exhibition?' but then paused when he realised how stupid he must have sounded and began to stammer. 'I mean… err… so, you're part of the team who brought the statues here?'

Lin laughed. 'I'm glad you rephrased that sentence, but yes, I did help bring the Terracotta Warriors here to Chicago. Why? Does that surprise you?'

Dirk began to feel the flowing warmth of embarrassment rise in his body. 'Well…' He paused again, hoping he wouldn't make any more slip-ups. 'You don't seem to be the type…'

Lin raised an eyebrow at that comment and interrupted. 'The type? Be careful, Mr Davis. We don't want a diplomatic incident, do we?' She began to chuckle again.

Dirk then produced another wry smile. He calmed his nerves with a deep intake of breath before continuing. 'I normally associate this with boring old men, who wear tweed jackets with leather patches on the elbows, wear glasses, and use pen protectors. Not with a young, and yes, attractive lady such as yourself. There… I said it, now slap me round the face and get it over with.'

48

Lin just stood there and smiled before replying, 'Thank you for your honesty. I will take that the way it was intended, Mr Davis, as a compliment.'

'Thank you, but please, call me Dirk,' he replied.

'OK. Dirk. Yes, an unusual name, but one I'm familiar with.' Lin nodded before gently moving her hair behind her right ear with her hand.

'I think my mother had a thing for Dirk Bogarde before I was born.'

'I was thinking more of Dirk Benedict,' replied Lin, and they both began to chuckle. 'Well, it has been a pleasure meeting you, Dirk.' Lin offered her hand again. 'Will you be coming here again?'

'I don't know,' replied Dirk, as he gently shook her hand once more.

'It would be a shame to rush through the exhibition before closing,' countered Lin, before adding, 'I can tell you more about the pieces if you'd like?'

Dirk looked at his watch. It was an hour before closing, and he turned to look at what he had left to see. He then thought that the information might come in handy for the job. 'I suppose you're right. OK, I'll purchase another ticket and come back in a couple of days.'

'No need. I'm free on Wednesday at 10am, if that's OK?' replied Lin.

'Sure, it shouldn't be a problem,' Dirk replied, not believing his luck.

'Good, then let me show you out.'

'Thank you,' he replied as he was led out of the exhibition.

As he picked up his belongings from security, he thanked Lin again and began to walk off. He turned to look at her, but she'd already moved back into the exhibition, so he carried on. He then stopped and thought. *Wait, was she hitting on me?* He looked back one more time. Then, smiling, he decided to have another coffee in the Field Bistro before heading home, viewing the main hall with 'Sue' the T-Rex.

While he slowly drank his coffee, he started asking himself questions about the statues, both the targets and the authentic ones, mainly trying to think of how to move the figures without being seen by the internal security. But he was also puzzled by the two exhibits: the notice by the fake statues said that there was only one perfect statue, and that was back in China. Yet there were at least three he thought he saw in the authentic exhibition. And it was still bugging him why the client wanted the fakes. Not that he was complaining, the security seemed manageable. But it still didn't sit right with him: an unanswered question, slowly nibbling away in the back of his mind.

After finishing his coffee, Dirk stood up, walked out of the Field Bistro, and left the building through the north entrance. He continued his anticlockwise walk that he'd started earlier in the day, surveying the area as he walked. As he approached the southwest corner of the building, he noticed the security gatehouse letting a small delivery vehicle through the barriers. Before reversing down a vehicle ramp, it stopped alongside Dirk before the beeps sounded. The ramp started in front of Dirk and headed down to his left, to two bay doors. *That might come in handy*, thought Dirk, before crossing the road and carrying on to the bus stop to head home.

Chapter 10

Dirk used his car to get to his repair shop early the next day. Before Willkie and Cody arrived, he quickly settled into his paperwork while giving the booking log a once over. *Perfect*, he thought. No work was booked for tomorrow and just the expected delivery around 15:00.

Cody entered first and was followed five minutes later by Willkie. Both had a shocked look on their faces as they noticed their boss already at his desk. Dirk smiled, and once they were ready for work, he beckoned them into the office.

'Everything OK, boss?' asked Willkie.

'Everything's fine, replied Dirk. 'Are you both ready for tonight?'

'Pretty much,' stated Willkie.

'Not started yet,' Cody began, almost sheepish in his answer, and half expecting Dirk to become irritated; he quickly added, 'But when we pick up the supplies, we'll take a look tonight.'

Dirk looked at Cody before replying with no sign of the annoyance Cody was expecting. 'Just give us something to fish with, and don't forget the beers.' He paused briefly before continuing, 'I don't want you to take on any new bookings for tomorrow. Any jobs that you're working on, try and finish today. And if you know you're not going to complete them, phone the owners and apologise for the delay. But we should be back in time for the parts delivery at three, so we could finish any vehicles for desperate owners after that. I hope to cast off around nine tonight, so make sure you arrive about an hour before. I'm serving bolognese. Also, watch for any followers. I had a surprise on Saturday, which I'll tell you more about later. I'll go in a couple of hours to get organised and pick up Sharyn. But give me ten minutes, and I'll roll up my sleeves and give you guys a hand.' Dirk then stood up. 'Any questions?'

Both Willkie and Cody shook their heads and replied reassuringly, 'No.'

'Right then,' said Dirk, 'let's get to work.'

The rest of the morning passed quickly, with no hitches for the men. Dirk left mid-afternoon and let Willkie and Cody continue their workload. After freshening up at his apartment, he collected his overnight bag and drove to Sharyn's to pick her up.

When he stopped the car, she opened the door and jumped into the passenger seat, placing her bags behind her. They both smiled, and Dirk continued driving to Belmont Harbour.

Chapter 11

Dirk had purchased the boat second-hand from a local two years ago – a power catamaran – thinking it would be a suitable place for when he retired to relax and unwind, and he was right; he'd just never quite got around to the retiring part.

Despite being relatively new, it was in a sorry state when he first viewed the vessel. The previous owner had decided to lease it out to a man who wanted to surprise his girlfriend by proposing to her, but it turned out to be a scam. They found the boat trashed and deserted along the north shore three days later. It looked like a group had used it to party in and they'd wrecked most of the interior. In addition, they somehow managed to ruin the engine, which needed a rebuild. All this damage worked in Dirk's favour. With no one else wanting to touch it and the insurers refusing to pay out to the owner, he managed to obtain it for below the asking price.

Today, apart from the décor, the boat was mostly finished. The tools were neatly stored in one cabin, but the other three were habitable; it just meant Cody and Willkie must share for a night on this trip. The guys had helped where they could, especially with the engine, which was a huge learning curve for all three of them, but once they'd finished it, they took it out on several weekends for trials and to do some fishing.

While Sharyn was in her cabin, Dirk prepared dinner in the galley kitchen. The radio was on in the background, with the local newsreader talking to an expert. They were discussing deaths being investigated at the hospital that had had the power cut last week. It had been the top news story all day and was becoming too repetitive. While he had every sympathy for what had happened, he turned the radio off to keep the mood light.

Dirk had just placed the fried beef mince into a bowl and added the chopped onions into the pan with the remaining meat juices when Sharyn climbed the steps next to the kitchen.

'How's your cabin?' inquired Dirk.

'Nice, but I'll let you know in the morning. I've never slept on a boat before,' she replied, and smiled warmly.

Dirk chuckled. 'Don't worry, you're next to the bathroom if you need to…'

Sharyn nudged him firmly and scowled, not allowing him to finish the sentence, making Dirk chuckle.

'Where's your wine Mr Davis?' Sharyn responded with a dry smile.

Still amused, he replied, 'The white is in the fridge there,' motioning with his head towards a cupboard in the galley while stirring the onions. 'If you want red, it's directly behind me on the counter. But if you could pass me the red anyway, please, as I need to add it to the bolognese.'

Sharyn poured herself a small glass of red before passing the bottle to Dirk. 'Thanks,' he responded and proceeded to pour in an estimated glass measure of the red wine, which instantly sizzled with the already present juices as the pan deglazed. He quickly added the rest of the ingredients before tossing the beef back into the pan, turning down the heat before covering with a lid. Dirk then grabbed himself a beer and sat down near Sharyn. 'I'll boil the pasta when the guys arrive.'

'Food smells lovely. What's for dessert?' asked Sharyn.

'Hopefully, the guys will bring us something… Crap.' He quickly put down his bottle before jumping up and heading to the fridge.

'What's wrong?' Sharyn was slightly shocked when he had unexpectedly moved.

'I forgot to add something to the bolognese.' He took a small package out of the fridge and emptied its contents onto a clean chopping board.

'What's that?' replied Sharyn quizzically.

'Blood sausage,' responded Dirk, and he started to break it apart to a crumb consistency before adding it to the pan and stirring it in.

'Really?!' There was a repulsed tone in her response.

Dirk replaced the lid and sat back down. 'Yes, really,' he replied. 'I guess that's what you get with a mixed Irish and Italian heritage.' He then picked up his beer before continuing. 'The story goes that my Italian grandfather loved his bolognese how his mother used to make it and included chicken livers. But my Irish grandmother found

56

that chicken livers in her mother-in-law's bolognese were too strong for her taste. So when they married and got their own place, she changed the recipe slightly. Instead of adding the chicken livers, she added crumbled blood sausage. She'd blended the Irish and Italian together like their marriage. The family legend goes that my grandfather preferred it to his mother's but never had the guts to tell her. And apparently, she got the seal of approval from my great-grandmother too.' Dirk then finished in a Hollywood Italian accent. "But it's not as good as mamas."

Sharyn chuckled. After sipping her wine, she asked, 'Do you miss New Jersey?'

Dirk became uncomfortable with the question and was hesitant before he replied. 'Yeah, the early years. Both my parents died when I was young. They got caught in a drive-by, so never really got the chance to learn an authentic bolognese.' He briefly raised his eyebrows and continued with remorse in his voice. 'I miss them. We were close. I couldn't cope and went off the rails afterwards.' Dirk fell silent and stared into his bottle, sadness in his eyes.

Sharyn noted the change in mood and decided to change the subject quickly, so she looked around at the saloon section of the boat from her seat. 'I like what you've done with the boat. It's a vast improvement since I last visited.'

Dirk blinked a couple of times, snapping out of his thoughts. He sat back and also looked around before answering. 'Yeah, it's been a labour of love and learning. Luckily, besides the engine, most of the damage was cosmetic,' replied Dirk. 'Common sense told me that I'd have to reregister the boat and prove its seaworthiness. But I must admit, I was surprised by how helpful the original boat builders and the community were, showing me where the best place was for the needed parts, and the guys helped too. The course on how to handle her safely, before I could get insurance, was straightforward enough. But she's been a joy to work on.'

'You didn't want a sailing boat then?' replied Sharyn.

'Nah, not for me. I prefer the sound of engines, you know that.' Dirk gave a wry smile before changing the subject. 'Do you want a top-up? And we'll crack on with the information before the guys arrive.'

'Oh, and we were having so much fun,' replied Sharyn, disappointed that they would now discuss work. She liked Dirk a lot but wished he'd open up more about himself. So, while Dirk stirred the bolognese, she got her laptop ready.

Chapter 12

They'd been travelling the city's road network for over an hour. Cody was driving his much-loved first-generation Eagle Talon, while alongside him, Willkie was taking notes for him, researching the possible drop-off points and testing the roads. Without knowing the client's delivery point, guesswork was being applied, so at least a plan was in place. Both were confident because they knew the city well. When Cody thought he'd done enough for the evening, they headed to the nearest store, and once the provisions were loaded into the car, they proceeded to drive on to the harbour.

They travelled a quiet side street towards Addams/Medill Park, which they'd earmarked as a possible drop-off point. They were looking for potential hideaways along the street when they noticed someone starting to walk out into the middle of the road, less than a hundred metres ahead.

Cody expected the person to continue crossing the road but was surprised when the figure stopped and turned to face them. He quickly applied the brakes, and within moments, they started to skid. But still, the figure remained, motionless, steadfast, while the car screeched forever closer. Cody then released the brake and tried to steer around the figure, but he just sidestepped purposely to get in the way, leaving Cody with no other option but to start pumping the brakes, trying to slow the car down in time. He was thinking ABS would've been great at this moment in time.

Both men in the car could now smell the heated rubber flooding their nostrils and, tensing their muscles, prepared for the inevitable collision. In a last-ditch attempt to avoid the man, Cody applied the handbrake firmly but gradually, then steered, making the car slowly spin in a controlled manner. The man just watched as Cody's side of the Talon presented its broadside. As the vehicle came to a halt, Cody instinctively let go of the steering wheel to shield his face with his arms.

The figure took one confident step back as the Talon slid just in front of him to a stop. Then, he raised and pulled back his right arm, clenched his fist, and punched straight through the driver's side door window in one fluid motion.

Cody was caught off guard; he was just beginning to lower his arms from the impact he'd expected sooner. Then he reactively raised them again and looked away, trying to defend himself from the shattered glass showering him.

As the window smashed, Willkie tried to react, fumbling to release his seatbelt, but stopped suddenly when he heard the unmistakable sound of a handgun being primed. He looked to his left to see a semi-automatic with a silencer being held in his left hand, now pointing through the shattered window, inches from Cody's head. Seeing this,

Willkie submitted and slowly raised his hands.

Cody had heard the cocking action too, and upon seeing Willkie raising his hands, he slowly turned around, placing his hands in the air. The gun's muzzle was pressed against his temple as his face came into view. The hair on Cody's neck stood on end as he felt his skin begin to crawl in fear. He then hesitated, giving a moment to compose himself without moving his head as much as possible, before allowing his eyes to continue with the task. First, following the contour of the left arm, up to the assailant's shoulder, then moving to the face before finally locking on to their attacker's eyes.

Only Cody could see the face of the man who stood before him. He was in his mid-twenties, slim, with short, pitch-black hair and stylish clothes. The facial features were unmistakably East-Asian, and there was a menace in the man's eyes as he began to speak angrily, in a heavily accented pidgin English. 'Tell your boss, stay away from statues. They're ours. We make lots of trouble for him and you.' He quickly turned the handgun and fired a round into the wall of the front tyre before turning it just as quickly back to Cody's face. 'You understand?' The man smiled a little, evidently enjoying their discomfort.

Cody nodded slowly, but Willkie didn't respond; he was transfixed by something else he'd seen in the shaded recesses of the buildings ahead of the Talon.

The man took a step back and brashly spoke again, evidently wanting a response from Willkie. 'You there… red man, you understand?' That snapped Willkie back to the here and now, and he turned to face their assailant with anger etched across his face. Cody knew their antagonist was trying to goad them, and he quickly interrupted to defuse the situation. 'OK, OK… We understand… We'll let our boss know. OK?'

The man's wry smile disappeared before he snappily replied, 'Good.'

He took a few steps back, looking at them both, lowered his handgun, and ran behind the car. Cody tried to look where he went, but the man seemed to vanish into the long shadows of the evening's setting sun. He looked around to speak to Willkie but found him looking ahead, staring intently.

'You OK?' said Cody, concerned. Willkie blinked a couple of times before turning to face him.

'Yeah, I'm fine. Just a little shook up, that's all.'

Cody took a deep breath before getting out of the car. 'Let's change the wheel before any cops arrive.' Willkie looked into the shadows once more, as if searching for something, but shook his head before getting out to help Cody.

With the wheel soon changed, Cody opened the driver's door and, using his spider wrench, knocked out the remaining broken glass before getting in and driving off.

Willkie had said nothing while they'd worked on the wheel, which Cody put down to getting the job done. But during the drive to the harbour, he was still silent and seemed distant. He was staring out of the passenger window for the entire journey, despite Cody's best efforts to strike up a conversation. Having never seen Willkie this way before, Cody became concerned. He decided to speak to Dirk about it.

The breeze from the broken window was almost refreshing after the adrenalin-fuelled attack. The evening air was warm and laden with the scent of the city, while the sound of the vehicles on the main streets was a cacophony. Cody continually checked his mirrors for any tails and headed directly to the harbour.

Chapter 13

hile Willkie and Cody were dealing with their aggressor, on Dirk's boat, he and Sharyn reviewed the data she'd accumulated for the meeting.

'I'll leave the information about the building, security, etc., until the guys arrive. I don't want to go through it or answer questions twice. But we'll go through the other stuff you requested before they turn up,' initiated Sharyn.

'Fine by me. What did you find?' replied Dirk.

'I have to say, it's all rather interesting. I initially found all the relative information about what's in the exhibition.' Sharyn opened a file, showing a catalogue of the pieces being loaned to the museum, plus some details about the artefacts. Dirk leant closer and looked at the list intently, slowly running the back of his index finger down the edge of the screen. Sharyn scrolled down the list for Dirk, noticing he was nodding at every piece. Stopping at the statues, they paused and lightly tapped the monitor twice before continuing until they reached the end. There was a slightly puzzled look on his face when he'd finished.

'Problem?' inquired Sharyn.

'Two things,' replied Dirk, and he continued. 'At the

base of the statues, a sign stated they were fakes. The owner knows this, but there's no mention of that here. Also, on your list, it mentions a wall imp. But I don't remember seeing it at the museum.'

'Oh, that last point's easy,' responded Sharyn, and she opened another file, showing a delivery document. 'That's arriving on a later date, see—'

'OK, but I'm still concerned about the statues. It's just something that keeps preying on my mind,' Dirk interrupted.

'Well, Mr Davis, I was getting to that part next if you'd let me finish.' And she gave him a firm but friendly nudge with her elbow before continuing. 'The information on the owner was difficult to find at first because there was no reference to a name anywhere on the museum's computers that I could hack. So, I had to rethink the problem from a different angle. I decided to use the delivery note I've just shown you. The PDF file shows a photocopy of the actual driver's delivery documentation for the load.' Sharyn pointed to the top right of the document on the screen. 'See, the address of the delivery company is here.' She traced her finger down the document before adding, 'And this is the consignment list. As you can see, these are the artefacts from the exhibition.' Sharyn repositioned her finger again. 'Now, if I go back to the top of the document and note the order number here, and I then went into the delivery company's servers.' Sharyn switched files. 'That order number gives me the address where they collected the consignment from.' She guided Dirk to the address, a storage facility near O'Hara Airport. 'Repeating the same thing, I traced it back to this address and, using the usual means, tracked down the owner of the address, A Ms A Jenson—'

'Amanda Jenson, the business mogul!' interrupted Dirk again. 'But—'

'But what has this to do with the validity of the statues?' It was Sharyn's turn to interrupt. 'Well, investigating further, I found that the warehouse near O'Hara is a subsidiary company of Ms Jenson's, whose manager happens to be an old friend of hers. Now. Going into their accounts, I found an email trail between the warehouse manager and the museum's curator, discussing the legality of the statues.' Sharyn revealed copies of the email trail for Dirk's perusal. 'Plus, a correspondence between the manager and Ms Jenson's lawyers about dealing with the problem.' She then showed the secondary email trail. Again, Dirk read through the information.

Sharyn continued, 'Now, Ms Jenson's name is not implicated in the emails, but given the evidence of her address as a collection point and the other links of a friend, business and her lawyers, it squarely puts her name strongly into the frame.'

Sharyn then pointed towards the emails Dirk was reading. 'The lawyers state that their client wants to claim them as fakes. Then it instructs the manager to inform the curator.'

'Rather elaborate! Why not have the curator deal directly with the lawyers?' replied Dirk.

'I don't know for sure, but her business website states that Ms Jenson wants to crack the Chinese market, so perhaps she doesn't want to jeopardise that plan. Plus, using an unknown middleman, well, a woman in this case, and not the lawyers directly, who are well known to be linked with Ms Jenson, gives her that extra level of anonymity, I suppose,' stated Sharyn.

'This would mean that Ms Jenson believes they're legitimate statues, not fakes, which makes more sense as to why our client wants them. But why not wait until the Chinese exhibition has finished?' He suddenly remembered what Lin Shi had told him, answering his question. 'No, I remember, the Chinese exhibition should have left by now, but they extended the dates to January next year. But I bet, by the time Ms Jenson realised this, the deal with the museum had already been signed, so there was no way of backing out.'

Dirk leant back in his chair, looking more relaxed before he continued. 'That makes more sense now, plus it gets rid of some nagging questions in my head. Right, what do we know about Ms Jenson?'

'Well, by looking at her online personal profile, she's immensely proud of her family history. The original family name was Jensen, and they were from a Scandinavian background, though it's a bit vague regarding the country they came from. A forefather was an officer in the Germanic army, who helped fight for independence against the British, and later settled in Fort Dearborn, the forerunner to Chicago. The family later went into a mixture of business and politics, which they've continued to the present. So, I suppose they've helped shape and create what we see around us in Chicago today.'

Sharyn took a sip of wine to moisten her lips before casually holding the glass in her left hand while using her right hand to scroll through her files on the laptop. 'Ms Jenson is thirty-seven years old, an only child, who's been married twice, hence the Ms. She has a ten-year-old son called Henry from the first marriage, who attends one of the finest boarding schools in the area. She has a reputation for hostile takeovers, especially if you get on the wrong side of her. And get this, she lost out so badly in the divorce to the second husband that she used the rest of her assets to legally buy out and crush his business to get most of her wealth and reputation back. So yes, extraordinarily rich and with a ruthless business manner to match.'

'So, a person we don't want to tangle with,' Dirk said looking at Sharyn.

Sharyn shook her head slowly. 'Not really, no. And I can see why our client thinks it would be a promising idea to take the statues from the museum instead of her home. I tried to get into her home security system and failed. Probably state-of-the-art. And while digging elsewhere, I found that she has an armed security team with dogs. Though I'll try—'

'OK,' Dirk interrupted again. 'I think I've heard enough.' And with that, he got up and headed over to the stove to stir the bolognese in silence.

To Sharyn, he looked deep in thought, but Dirk was

focusing on his cooking, trying hard to stop his mind from racing ahead with the new information.

After a couple of minutes of feeling settled, he turned back to Sharyn and spoke. 'What did you find out about this Kirby character?'

Sharyn closed the current files and opened another set. 'Oh, you'll like this one.' And with that, Dirk covered the bolognese again, sitting back down next to Sharyn.

'I used your idea of the travel manifests, and straight away, I found him. A week ago, he took a Delta flight from Hong Kong to O'Hare International Airport, with a transfer point in Seattle. It also looks like he booked an open ticket, so no return date planned, and he's currently residing in the Hilton Chicago on an upper floor overlooking the lake.'

'I bet his room overlooks the museum,' Dirk added, before taking a mouthful of beer.

Sharyn selected another group of files and opened them. 'Now we get to the interesting part. During my searches, his name came up in another field. And after a cross-reference check, to make sure it was the same person, we had a match… on Interpol.'

'Interpol!' repeated Dirk.

'Now, don't get too excited, he's not a wanted criminal, but he's on a watch list, what Interpol call a Blue Notice. Our Kirby apparently has links to a cult, which has ties to theft, smuggling of animal parts and organ legging, which according to Google, *is the removal, preservation and use of human organs and tissue from the bodies of the recently deceased.* So, in short, gross. With the Blue Notice, Interpol essentially asks for the public's help for any information. In this case, in conjunction with the Hong Kong police.'

'What type of cult?'

'Well...' Sharyn opened a copy of his Interpol profile. 'As you can see by reading the profile here, Kirby's guardian is a man called Quillon Goddard, a French national who studied at Oxford University in the UK. He's the leader of a cult called the Jade Dawn. According to the Hong Kong police, this Jade Dawn is a death cult. Their motto is *Nihil Obstat*, Latin for *Nothing Stands in the Way*. They believe that the end of the world is nigh.'

'Nut jobs then?! They sound like a *Bond* villain,' smirked Dirk.

'Researching further online, I came up with nothing. But with the help of the dark web, I found out their websites were shut down immediately due to their content, so the cult doesn't bother with them anymore. They're *very* well-funded, though, which has led to the assumption that they're either into a lot more than just theft and organ legging, or they've rich backers. The organ legging is apparently true, and that's the only thing I can think of that ties him to Algernon Mbundu, as voodoo also deals with dead bodies, zombies, ritual sacrifice and the like.' Sharyn paused to take another sip of wine. 'The thefts are linked to art and artefacts and most likely another avenue of providing funding for their organisation. Or as one dark web user stated, even artefacts that have links with their version of Armageddon, how to survive it and come to power.'

'What does that mean?' asked Dirk.

'Well, according to the source, it appears that with the cult's beliefs of world doom – which by the way, they don't state how, but they blame corruption, politics and anything else that sounds good for the cause – when this happens, they believe they're going to be the new world order, and some of these artefacts are status symbols in some form, even magical. This would enable them to show they're the chosen ones, once their impending apocalypse comes.'

'Really? So, we've gone from *Bond* villain to *Indiana Jones* in minutes.'

Sharyn couldn't help but smile. 'The unwelcome news is, don't cross them. There have been reports of bodies being found, people who've got on the wrong side of them, and their organs missing in Jack the Ripper-style murders. Of course, nothing has ever been proven by the law, so it could be nothing more than just scare tactics. This leads me to Quillon, the cult leader.' Sharyn opened another file, showing a picture of him. 'He keeps a high profile, while owning an expensive estate on the outskirts of Hong Kong. This I find strange due to the accusations levelled against him, but he doesn't mind being seen in public. Apparently, he's more than willing to preach openly about the end of times and how they'll come to power. This has got him into hot water now and then with the Hong Kong and Chinese authorities, but it's never amounted to anything, leading again to the presumption that he's highly connected.'

Sharyn then returned to the file that showed Kirby's hotel reservation and pointed at the screen. 'One thing I noticed with the reservation, though, is the room is for two people, but no secondary names are mentioned. Now I thought Quillon would join him later, but revisiting the travel manifest shows that Kirby was travelling with a female called Anita Narang. I can't find any information on this Anita, and according to the manifest, she's originally from India, but I can find no evidence that Kirby is married. So far, that's it regarding the information you wanted. The rest is for when the guys join us.'

'Fellow cultist maybe, either way, it sounds like competition. Something we're not used to,' replied Dirk. 'Thanks, Sharyn, helpful as ever.'

Sharyn looked at him. 'You're welcome, honey.' She finished her glass of wine.

Dirk noticed headlights sweeping across the harbour next to his boat, and he got up to look out of the stern. 'Yes, it's Cody's car. They're just parking up now. I'll put the spaghetti on and the garlic bread in the oven. We can then eat.'

'Great,' replied Sharyn. 'I'm famished.'

It took several minutes before the guys came down the steps and onto the stern of the boat while carrying the cool boxes. Cody slid the rear door open. 'Permission to come aboard?' though his voice sounded suppressed.

Dirk instantly looked at the two of them, knowing something was wrong. 'What's happened?'

Chapter 14

Cody placed the cool box with the foodstuff on the table without saying a word. Then proceeded to unpack it before making a start at putting it away. Willkie, likewise, carried the cool box with the bait inside towards the boat's bow, then replaced the ice packs with fresh ones. There was an uneasy silence between them, which was evident to see.

'Is someone going to answer me?' stated Dirk in a raised voice, his tone now becoming that of a scolding parent. Willkie and Cody looked at each other, and Willkie broke the silence. 'I'll let you tell him what happened. I need some fresh air.' With that, Willkie went through the sliding door to the forward sunbathing deck before closing it firmly behind him.

Dirk saw the dejection on Willkie's face and then reviewed the tone he'd used. He went to the fridge, pulled out a cold beer, took off the top of the bottle before handing it to Cody.

'Sit down, tell me about it,' requested Dirk while gesturing to the chair next to him as he sat down.

Sharyn stood up. 'I'll finish putting this lot away and sort out the dinner.'

'Thanks, Sharyn,' replied Cody, who took a swig from his bottle, savouring the refreshing coolness of the liquid, before swallowing it and starting the account of what had happened.

Sharyn could tell Dirk was listening intently to every word spoken during Cody's account. He never interrupted and knew his mind was continually figuring out how all this fit into what she'd told him earlier. As if he was figuring out a Rubik's Cube in his head.

When Cody had finished, he added, 'You know, boss, I've been with this team for a while now, and nothing like this has happened before. He caught us off guard, and I want to say that I'm not put off by the attack, nor by the job, and I'll follow you, whatever the decision.'

Deep in thought, Dirk sat back in his chair, slowly nodding before he replied, 'I can sense a but coming.'

Cody continued, his tone marked with concern. 'What I'm worried about is Willkie. Whatever happened, it's affected him a lot. I've never known him to be like this after any situation. Something happened, but he didn't want to talk about it on the way here.'

'OK,' said Dirk. 'I'll go talk to him now.' And with that, Dirk stood up and gave Cody several supportive pats on his back before walking to the fridge. This time, he pulled out and opened two bottles of beer. One for himself and one for Willkie, before heading to the forward sunbathing deck.

He slid the door open and saw Willkie sitting on the left-hand side of the bow, staring at the Chicago skyline, backlit by the setting sun in all its glory. The boat gently rocked, and there was a soft sound of the waves lapping around the twin hull of the catamaran.

'Beer?' asked Dirk, resting one of the bottles on Willkie's right shoulder. Willkie turned his head to face the bottle.

'Thanks,' he said sombrely and took it from Dirk's hand before looking back at the cityscape.

'Cody told me what happened. It would've unnerved me too. Are you OK?' Dirk sat down next to him, to his right.

'I'm fine,' said Willkie, and took his first gulp of beer from the bottle.

'You sure?' replied Dirk. 'You seem to be quieter since the confrontation, so much so that your buddy's concerned. Well… I would say concerned, but I think he's feeling he's now in with a chance at finally beating you at the next gym session.'

This was a white lie on Dirk's part, a strategy to get Willkie talking, and it worked.

'Fat chance of that,' replied Willkie rapidly, before smiling. He turned to face Dirk again. 'To tell you the truth, it wasn't the attack that bothered me.'

'Oh,' replied Dirk, surprised by the response. 'Then what's on your mind?'

'During the attack, I saw something… something else.' Even as he thought of what he saw, Willkie could feel the hairs on the back of his neck and arms stand on end.

'OK, what did you see?' asked Dirk. But there was a lengthy pause before Willkie committed to a response.

'I couldn't make out its shape. The shadows of the surrounding buildings and bushes distorted it. But it looked large, and those eyes… those eyes were looking at us, unblinking, watching every move we made.'

'Eyes?' asked Dirk.

Willkie paused again. 'They were vivid green as if it were a predator, ready to strike for its next meal.' He turned back to look at the city and took a swig of his beer.

'Did Cody see these eyes?' asked Dirk.

'I don't think so,' said Willkie. 'But it noticed me looking at it, and at that point, I felt its eyes boring into me like it was piercing, searching my soul for something. I was distracted then by our attacker's comments, and when they'd left, I looked back to see the eyes still looking at me before they slowly blinked, then turned and faded away. At that point, Cody snapped me back out of it, and I helped him to replace the tyre.' Willkie now looked down into the water, subconsciously picking at the label on the side of his bottle.

'Do you think it was working with the attacker?' asked Dirk.

Willkie pondered Dirk's question before answering. 'I don't know.'

'Was there any way of knowing where you would be at that time?'

'That's been puzzling us as well. We made the routes up on the spot. So, there was no way they could've known where we would be. Cody was non-stop jabbering about it, venting his frustration on the way here. He talks a lot when he's stressed.'

'OK.' said Dirk. 'But I've known you long enough to know that you go quiet in the same situation. And I've also known you long enough to tell when there's something else going through your mind.'

Willkie turned to face Dirk but was hesitant before he began to speak. 'When I was young, there were stories told to me by my parents. Stories from the old country, from our ancestry.'

Dirk knew that this was a matter of importance to Willkie. Anything about his heritage was not to be sniffed at. He sat quietly, ready to listen to what Willkie had to say.

'The stories were about how the first dog came to this world and how it protected the tribal people against the wendigo. Wendigos are creatures of deceit who hunt and eat man. The stories say that the wendigo were once men like us, but they were punished for their greed and gluttonous nature. They were cursed and changed into monstrous giants of ice with frozen hearts and an insatiable cannibalistic hunger to eat men who were also too greedy and selfish. Their eyes always search men's souls, sensing their sins, and see if it satisfied their thirst for flesh.'

Dirk thought for a moment before speaking, hoping he wouldn't offend. 'Are you saying that you're being hunted by this wendigo?'

'It's the only way I can explain how it felt,' replied Willkie.

Dirk leant forward slightly. 'OK, if you believe that, I won't insult your ancestry and beliefs. But *if* this… wendigo is after you, then I don't think you've too much to worry about.'

Willkie looked puzzled and responded, 'Why do you say that?'

Dirk stood up, placed his left hand on Willkie's shoulder, and spoke firmly but gently.

'Take a look at the world around you, Willkie,' Dirk gestured his right hand while holding his beer towards the cityscape. 'This city… No, this entire world is full of people who are full of gluttony and selfishness, an entire smorgasbord for this wendigo you've just told me about, which makes you positively anorexic in comparison. So why would it hunt you when there are much richer pickings to be had? Plus, if you think you're selfish and greedy, that's not the Willkie I know and whom I'm currently looking at.' Dirk took a deep breath. 'Look. We were all dealt a bad hand during our early years. That's why we're involved in these jobs in the first place. We were herded into a corner with no way out. The problem is it also became a drug. It became addictive. You're feeling remorse over past actions, and I get that. Even I get pangs of guilt. But the remorse and guilt make us human, and that's why we've been giving something back to our local community. I dare say that if this wendigo is lurking around the streets of Chicago, then I'll put money on it that he's put on this earth to hunt those with no remorse or guilt first and people like us near last.'

Dirk walked towards the door to the cabin but turned around and spoke before he opened the cabin door. 'There're only two questions I now want answers to.'

Willkie turned his head to face him.

'The first is, do you still want in on the job? I understand if you say no, and I'll never, *ever* hold it against you. And second.' He smiled. 'Are you coming in for the bolognese?' Dirk slid open the door, entered the cabin and closed the door again, giving Willkie some time alone to think.

Sharyn was by the stove, serving dinner. Cody was grating cheese to garnish it. Sharyn looked up when she heard the door slide open. 'Just in time. I had to make more spaghetti, as the first batch was ruined. I managed to save the garlic bread, though. Is everything OK with Willkie?'

Her smile was warming and reassuring to Dirk, and he couldn't help but smile back. He sat at the table before answering. 'He just needs a moment to think, that's all.'

Sharyn and Cody brought the food and drink to the table and served them. There was an uneasy silence as they started to eat until the sliding of the bow door opening broke the tension.

Willkie entered the cabin and sat at the table, placing his beer next to his bowl of bolognese before picking up his cutlery. 'I'm in.'

'Thank God for that,' responded Dirk smiling. 'I thought I'd have to let you guys win at fishing, just to make you happy.'

That instantly started a debate between Cody and Willkie on who was the better fisherman, while Sharyn smiled at Dirk, slowly shaking her head.

'What now, Dirk?' said Sharyn.

Talking across the banter between Willkie and Cody,

he replied, 'Let's enjoy this quality food first, then we'll cast off and discuss it later when we've relaxed.' He looked between Willkie and Cody, shook his head and chuckled.

Chapter 15

With dinner finished, Dirk went with Cody to his car to give it a quick once over. When they'd finished, Dirk said, 'If you and Willkie prepare to cast off, I'll go and chat with the harbour master.'

'Sure.' Cody walked back to the boat, leaving Dirk to make his way to the harbour master's office alone. Once there, he asked them to keep an eye on the car while they were on the lake. Dirk knew the car would be secure within the harbour, but there was no harm in asking them to keep an eye on it. He told them a false story, which they seemed to believe, which also meant that if anybody else started to ask any questions, someone was at hand to answer them.

While walking back to the boat, Dirk's mind began to wander again, asking himself questions about how the guys were found and attacked. The longer he kept mulling it over, the more it boiled down to just one answer: a tracking device.

When he returned to Cody's car, Dirk put his hand through the broken window, opened the door, leant in further, and popped the hood. Then, walking to the front, he lifted it and propped it open. Dirk could never understand Cody's choice of vehicles. He preferred the traditional classic cars: Mustang, Shelby, old-style Ferrari and the E-Type Jaguar. They may be challenging to drive in some people's eyes, but if you didn't respect the car and the power it gave, then you deserved what you got. But to Dirk, his style of car also seemed more tactile. In a sense, pure.

Dirk set about the task in hand, taking out his phone and using the torch to look at the engine. He started talking to himself, going through the simple motions to clear and focus his mind. 'Where would I put a tracking device?' Pausing, he surveyed the car for more than a minute before continuing to speak. 'It would have to be somewhere easily accessible and magnetic. Perhaps strong adhesive, but magnetic would be the logical choice.' He closed the hood, got down onto his knees and shone the phone's light under the vehicle.

Lots of places to hide under here, but where? he thought. It would have to be in easy reach for an arm... unless they used a delivery device of some kind. That would mean taking the car onto the ramps to have a decent look. But he didn't have time for that.

Dirk decided to look at the wheel arches before returning to the boat. While the body shell was made of composite material, the main framework wasn't, perfect for a magnetic tracker. He chose the offside first, as that was a natural starting point in his mind: easier for someone to sneak something onto the car, away from the kerb and without being seen. He lay on his back, gently putting his phone on the floor to give him some light and started to feel around where the composite was connected to the chassis.

He touched something that he knew wasn't part of the car on the second arch, and with a forceful twist, it came off. Dirk rolled out from under the car, grabbed his phone and looked at what he'd found. A tracking device.

He stood up, but his frustration took over. He then dropped it on the floor and stamped on it continuously until it finally broke. Then, he picked it back up and proceeded toward the boat.

By the time Dirk got back, everything was ready to go. Willkie had already started the engines and was at the helm of the upper deck, and as Dirk got on the boat, Cody untied the mooring ropes.

Dirk shouted up to the upper deck, 'Take her out, Willkie. I'll be there shortly.' He entered the main cabin, where he caught Sharyn's attention and gently lobbed the device towards her, and while he washed his hands and arms to remove the grime from his investigation, Sharyn examined the tracker. Both felt the boat begin to move, and when Dirk was drying himself, Sharyn began to speak.

'Basic tracking device, probably fifty dollars from any internet site. I take it you didn't find it like this?'

'No. I'm hoping you'll tell me it's no longer working.'

'Not like this, no. This type of device will only monitor when it's moving. The tracker's owner can use a simple app to monitor where it is.'

'So, they'll know it ended up here at the harbour?' quickly stated Dirk.

'Most likely. Yes,' replied Sharyn.

Dirk went quiet for a minute, obviously thinking, before talking again. 'Is there any way you can find out who owns it?'

'Not from here. It'll also depend on the damage to the device. All I'll say is, don't get your hopes up.'

'OK, thanks, Sharyn.' Feeling a little despondent and annoyed at himself for breaking it, Dirk headed to the upper deck and took charge of the boat.

He took the craft out of the harbour, heading north, about half a mile off the coastline for about an hour, and anchored the boat on a calm Lake Michigan just before dusk.

They sat around the table on the stern, drinking and chatting. The available light shimmered and flickered on the gently rolling water, creating a dancing effect across its surface, while a soft and refreshing breeze came off the lake, accompanied by the sound of the water caressing the twin hulls. Later they adjourned inside to discuss the job.

Chapter 16

Once the laptop was ready, everybody assembled around the main cabin table.

'OK, let's get the ball rolling with the easy stuff.' Reaching into her shoulder bag, Sharyn pulled out a manila folder and placed it in front of Cody. 'That's the list of all road closures over the next two months. I'll keep you up to date with any changes.'

Cody looked briefly at the paperwork. 'Thanks, Sharyn. I'll look in detail when we've finished.' He put the paperwork to one side and picked up his beer, preparing to pay attention to the rest of the briefing.

Dirk leant forward and gave Sharyn a memory stick, which she placed into her laptop USB port. It contained photos from his visit to the museum. Dirk started with his opening speech, as a picture of the statues appeared on the screen. 'These, my friends, are the statues we'll be taking. But for now, we'll focus on the museum's security.' Upon Dirk's request, Sharyn started a slideshow of pictures from the museum, with the exhibition room first where the statues were situated.

'Right then, remember, we're only after the statues. The usual rules still stand; the rest of the exhibits are off limits. We don't run any risks, no matter how small or tempting.'

Willkie butted in, smiling, 'Must we go through this with every job, boss? We always stick to the rules.'

Sharyn leapt to Dirk's defence. 'Leave him be. You guys have been with him long enough to know he's got a structured routine to every—'

'OK, thank you,' Dirk interrupted firmly before anything else was said. 'I know I can trust you guys, but I see no harm in asserting our approach pattern. So, if we can all stay focused. Thank you.' A calm came to the room once more, and Dirk continued. 'This is the Levin Hall, situated on the main level, where the statues are displayed.' Dirk pointed at the screen while talking. 'As we can see, there're only two entrances to the room. The air vents in the ceiling here are useless to our needs, and the security is visually standard.' He waited for the next slide to appear before continuing. 'You can see here the obvious markers for security beams. While here, you can see that these items have pressure sensors. We're lucky. Our targets don't appear to have pressure sensors. I can only presume that the museum thought nobody would take them or that the sensors won't cope with the weight of them.'

Dirk turned to Willkie. 'Have you looked at transport at all?'

'Yeah. We'll have to use a class two utility van. A class one will take the weight, but I'd be concerned about the ease of access to the vehicle, and we'd have to sit on top of them. A pick-up truck is too open, and anything bigger would be too slow, increasing the risk of getting caught. My main concern is moving them from the exhibition to the vehicle. I'll need more info about the floor layout of the museum. Looking at what you've shown so far, we can't just drive up to them, and even with our physique, Cody and I won't be able to carry them far without the risk of damage.'

'OK, thanks, Willkie,' responded Dirk. 'I'll come to the moving of them later. What about you, Cody? How did you get on with the routes?'

'It's tough without an exact plan. Most of it's currently in my head. Willkie and I drove some of the possible routes tonight, before…' with a noticeable intake of breath, 'before we were interrupted. But now I've got the information from Sharyn, I can plan a little more, and I'll take it from there.'

'I understand,' replied Dirk. 'What do you think of Willkie's vehicle choice?'

'That shouldn't be a problem. I wouldn't mind some practice though,' stated Cody.

'OK. On Thursday, under Willkie's supervision, hire a class two for a week or two for practice. Go collect any orders we need in the Chicago area for parts instead of having them delivered. Also, take boxes of spare parts in the vehicle, roughly our targets' combined weight, and drive the routes you're looking into. That way, you'll get the practice you want. Is that OK?'

'Cool, I can live with that,' answered Cody.

'As this is in our own backyard, we'll most likely steal one on the night. I also need both of you to turn down the vehicle bookings a notch. That way, it'll give us the breathing space you'll need to deal with what I've given you.'

Both Cody and Willkie responded slightly out of sync with a 'Yeah,' but their assurance was evident.

'Good.' Dirk slowly rubbed his hands together before picking up his beer. 'Let's get back to the security.' He wetted his drying mouth with a gulp of beer before starting again. 'Levin Hall has security doors on each of the exits. So, it's an educated guess that the shutters come down when an alarm is triggered in the room. The rest of the building's security is visually much the same, pressure plates on exhibits, security beams in walkways, guards and shutter doors. Though, looking at the shutter doors to the main hall, these are stronger than those for Levin Hall. And as expected, cameras are situated around the entire building, so we need to find a way around them. I managed to speak to one of the official Terracotta Warrior exhibition curators during my visit, and she's invited me to come back in a couple of days to tell me more about them.'

'She?' stated Cody, beaming. Though Sharyn's face had become sullen.

'Pack it in, Cody,' replied Dirk, not looking impressed. 'I'll get the information on how to move the exhibits safely from her. Then, once I know, I'll let you know, Willkie. OK?'

'Fine by me, boss,' confirmed Willkie.

Sharyn, is there anything you want to add?'

'Loads,' came the reactive response from Sharyn, trying to compose herself.

'Then we're all ears,' said Dirk smiling back, gesturing an open-palmed hand to the computer.

'Thanks, Dirk,' and she inserted an encrypted memory stick into the laptop's USB port before opening a file marked as *security*.

'Right then. All that Dirk mentioned is correct, but I want to elaborate. The shutters that Dirk mentioned for Levin Hall are roller shutters made of quarter-inch grade steel, and the mechanism for the doors is built into the wooden door surround—'

'So flexible enough to reduce the force of ramming from either side of the door, and the only way to get out is with jackhammers, cutting torch or explosive. Which are all too noisy for our operation and too bulky to lug around. So—'

'So, we don't want to get caught inside,' interrupted Sharyn, finishing the sentence for him and giving him a stern look, making Dirk realise that he should've kept quiet.

Sharyn then continued. 'Security guards are twenty-four-seven, three-hundred-and-sixty-five days a year. Shifts are 05:00 to 13:00 hours and 13:00 to 21:00 hours, with four guards on each shift, while a further six guards work the opening hours of nine to five. In addition, there is a night shift, with three guards working from 21:00 to 05:00. They're on continuous patrol, carrying radios, mace sprays and extendable night sticks. The security hub's situated near the two delivery bays on the lower level. And all the alarms and security cameras in and around the building are linked to this. It's operated by two guards during the day and one on the night shift. There's also a kitchenette, toilet and small armoury in this room, where handguns and two shotguns are stored. Other staff, curators, caterers, etc., during the day. Cleaners must finish by ten each night, so the security is turned on in full, and rarely does anyone else work at night unless there's a private function.

'Regarding the security. Dirk has already mentioned most of the security devices. The beams across the corridors are situated off the patrol routes, so the guards don't trip them. There are sensors in all the glass windows, including the glass ceiling in the main hall. If they're lifted or smashed, they're triggered. There's also a type of sensor on more expensive exhibits, where a beam is directly pointed at the item. If the beam's broken or the piece is moved, even by millimetres, the alarm is triggered. While some objects in the museum have trackers, our targets don't appear to have any of these attached. I currently don't know whether the owner has brought in their own security measures, so I'll have to do more digging.

'Going back to the guards. The museum contracts extra security during busier times or for special exhibits. And the Terracotta Exhibition next door to our targets is a prime example.

'The alarm system is also linked to the first police precinct. The precinct is twelve minutes away by car, but they have a reported five-minute response time if an alarm is triggered, either by the exhibit alarm or a panic button in the security hub.

'Before I continue, are there any questions?'

Willkie and Cody looked at each other and shook their heads before looking at Dirk. He was either pondering what to say or absorbing the information; it was hard to gauge. In the end, he said, 'Are there any external cameras?'

'Sorry, yes,' responded Sharyn before quickly going back through her notes. 'There are seven cameras linked to the security hub, and two traffic cameras overlook the area, though they're at some distance.'

'Thanks,' said Dirk, who then went quiet again. His right index finger was now slowly and gently tapping the tabletop while his left hand rested against his mouth, the elbow on the table.

'OK. Ready for part two?' smiled Sharyn, and after seeing the nods from the guys, she continued. 'I want to start with some good news, as it seems we have a window of opportunity.'

Dirk moved his eyes to meet Sharyn's own. 'Go on,' he replied, though he sounded sceptical in his tone.

'I managed to hack several office computers at the museum and managed to find several email trails. They stated that they're having a security upgrade in the last week of July.'

'The week we have the last chance to earn our bonus,' Cody stated.

'Stay focused,' came the swift response from Dirk without even looking at him.

'Correct,' said Sharyn hesitantly.

'And this is good because?' asked Dirk.

'Well, during this week, while they're having these security checks and upgrades, the system will be turned off repeatedly, giving us an edge when trying to remove the items. The police have been informed of the changes and will only respond if called. Or if the alarm has been going for ten minutes.' Sharyn looked at Dirk for some form of acknowledgement.

'I see. So, what you're saying is, if the alarm is turned off or triggered, then the outside world won't know if it's a ghost or a bug in the system, so to speak.' Dirk still didn't seem impressed.

'Correct,' replied Sharyn.

Dirk continued. 'It seems a bit of a rush job to me. I would expect system bugs to be looked at over several weeks, not just one. Especially for a building of that size.'

'Again, correct, and this was the museum's plan also. However, they're busy at night for the two weeks after, as they have two fundraising nights, and there are five nights where groups of children have been invited to sleep over. So, they're hoping to install and iron out the bulk of the problems in the first week and use the next two weeks to complete the checks while elements of the museum will be busy.'

'OK, that's at least seven days we can wipe off the calendar. But let's try and keep this in some form of perspective. I want more information before I commit to a date. Does this mean there're more people onsite, for example? Remember, I don't want to risk everything to get the extra buck. I want the job done right, or not at all.'

Silence descended on the room, giving Dirk's response a grounding effect on the rest of the team, but it wasn't long before he re-engaged their thoughts, attempting to keep the meeting flowing. 'Do you have anything else, Sharyn?'

'Er, yes, several more pieces of information.' She opened another file on her laptop. 'Here's the blueprints you wanted of the museum. I'll add a copy to your memory stick to look over.'

'Thanks,' replied Dirk.

Sharyn continued, 'When I first moved here, I remembered looking up the local history and stumbled across information about the tunnel network that runs for miles underneath the city. So, investigating further, I discovered that one of these tunnels runs under the museum. Now don't get your hopes up too much, I'll need to do more research before I can see if this is helpful to us.' She closed her folders before speaking again. 'That's all I can give you for now. Do you want to go through what we discussed earlier, Dirk?'

'Yes, please.' While Sharyn prepared the information for Dirk, he began to speak to the guys. 'I want to talk about something that happened at the weekend, which may or may not have any bearing on what happened earlier tonight.' His tone was firm but also showed some concern.

'Ready, Dirk,' stated Sharyn. Her smile towards him was reassuring.

Willkie and Cody looked at each other puzzled, before looking back at Dirk. 'What are you talking about, boss?' asked Cody.

'I was at the repair shop on Saturday and had a visit from some guy called Kirby. He was looking for Bruce and offered me a job to steal some statues—'

'Our statues?' interrupted Willkie.

'I think so, but I also thought I'd done enough to persuade him that he had the wrong guy.'

Sharyn opened a file, showing a snapshot of Kirby, and Dirk looked and pointed towards the screen. 'This is Kirby. Have you guys seen him?' But both shook their heads, their expressions baffled.

'Now, I don't know whether this meeting had anything to do with your encounter. But my guess is it does, and this Kirby didn't believe me, so we've now been targeted.'

'What do we do now?' replied Cody.

'Tread carefully,' quickly replied Dirk. 'This is the first time we've knowingly had competition for the same item. We need to ensure we're not followed at every step, so we must check our vehicles continuously. If any of us find a device, sneak it onto another vehicle and tell us where and when you found it. I didn't tell you earlier because I wanted Sharyn to investigate this Kirby further.'

'What did you find, Sharyn?' asked Cody.

Sharyn put down her empty glass and brought up Kirby's Interpol file on the screen. 'As I told Dirk earlier, this guy is part of a cult that believes that Armageddon is coming and is collecting artefacts for funding or some form of status symbol. Now Kirby mentioned Algernon Mbundu...'

'The posse leader? What the hell?' replied Willkie, his eyes widening slightly while his head jerked backwards, caught off guard by Sharyn's statement.

'I think the link between Mbundu and Kirby is purely coincidental,' Dirk said. 'The cult and the posse have a common interest in organ legging.' Dirk folded his arms and leant back in his seat. 'I think the cult sends Kirby to hire and uses the posse for recommendations. This is where I'm mentioned. Unfortunately, it's just bad timing that we've already accepted the job. Otherwise, we could've been working for Kirby right now.'

'And what about this other team?' inquired Cody.

Dirk took a deep breath before answering. 'As I said, it's only a presumption. Your description doesn't ring any bells with anybody local to me, but as Kirby resides in Hong Kong, it may be enough to link him to your assailant. I'll ask around to see what I can find, but we'll have to be wary from now on.' He then sat forward before speaking again. 'I found a tracker on Cody's car before we cast off. Which explains how they knew where you were before they struck.'

Cody's surprise could clearly be seen, but Dirk continued. 'There's no blame here. As I said before, this is unfamiliar territory for us, and we've been caught off guard. We just must find a way back to an even footing, which is why Sharyn's going to study the device.' He put down his empty bottle. 'I think we'll leave it there for the night. It's a lot of information to take in, so let's tidy up before hitting the sack. I want to be up early to start fishing, and we'll discuss more about an ongoing plan when we head back around midday.'

Chapter 17

They arrived back at the harbour a little before 14:00, where they moored up and began to disembark with their overnight bags towards their cars. Dirk noticed that several people were loitering around and relaxed when he discerned that they were all holidaymakers, hiring neighbouring boat captains to do some fishing: easily recognisable with their brand-new fishing equipment. One of the owners caught Dirk's attention as they walked past his boat. 'How's the fishing, Dirk?'

'Great, John,' replied Dirk smiling. 'Caught no end. Willkie won, though. I have to let them win sometimes.' Dirk broke into a chuckle, but it was short-lived, as he felt an agonising sharp pain in his neck, proceeded by the feeling of being suddenly pulled backwards as the pain continued. 'Arrrrgggghhhhhh!'

Everyone looked around in shock, items were heard to be dropped, and a couple of people began running to Dirk's aid during the ongoing commotion, including his team. John shouted to someone behind him. 'Look what ya doing with that tackle, ya idiot.'

Dirk was being helped slowly to the ground, and he grimaced as he looked round to see one of the holidaymakers placing his rod on the floor and rushing over, shock etched in his face and apologetic with every word. He could see that the fishing line traversed from the rod to him, then presumed correctly that a fishhook had been embedded in his neck. An agonising couple of seconds later, Willkie had removed the hook; luckily, it was barbless.

'And that's why we buy cases ya muppets,' shouted John to anyone passing. 'Now go on. Leave the man in peace.' He began muttering obscenities under his breath before speaking directly to Dirk's team. 'Bring him aboard, and let's 'ave a look at him.'

'I can help,' said the holidaymaker quickly, almost stammering. 'I'm a doctor. I have my bag with me,' and he rushed back to his luggage.

'Jeez, heaven help us,' grumbled John as he boarded his boat, closely followed by Dirk, Willkie and Sharyn, who sat on the seating, while Cody remained next to their baggage on the promenade. The doctor promptly returned and placed his bag on the table beside Dirk.

'I'm really sorry about this,' he stated apologetically while opening his bag. 'It's only my second time fishing. I only took it up because a patient suggested it was a good way to relax and unwind. How wrong they were,' he said, smiling awkwardly.

'Do you take your bag with you everywhere you go?' Dirk asked the man while holding his neck.

'Occupational hazard, I'm afraid. I used to be a boy scout, who just happens to have a bad case of OCD, so a bad combination as you can imagine.' Again, he chuckled nervously before looking at Sharyn. 'Can you get me a bowl of hot water, soap and a facecloth, please?'

Sharyn looked at John, who responded with, 'Come this way. I'll give you a hand.'

The doctor continued. 'My name's Liam. What's yours?'

'Dirk.'

'Well, Dirk. I will give you a small dose of antibiotics before cleaning the wound when the soap and water arrives. I don't want to take any chances.' He started to prepare a needle. 'Again, I'm deeply sorry about this. I don't think fishing and I are cut out for one another.'

'I wouldn't give up too soon, doc,' replied Willkie. 'We've all done something similar when we first started. So, don't beat yourself up over it.'

'You're too kind. I just didn't imagine being the cause of an accident.' He then turned and faced Dirk. 'Now, you'll feel a little prick in your upper left arm.'

The cabin door reopened as Sharyn and John walked through with the requested items. It distracted Dirk briefly as he felt the needle go into his arm.

'OW!' Dirk looked at Liam and scowled.

'Sorry,' replied the doctor, and his eyes widened slightly in fear of Dirk's response. 'You moved slightly as you noticed your friend.' He pressed a small cotton pad as he withdrew the syringe. 'Please hold here,' he continued. Dirk obliged while Liam dealt with the needle.

The bowl was placed on the table between Dirk and Liam, who cleaned the puncture wound caused by the hook. When he'd finished, he positioned a Band-Aid over it before drying his hands on a towel that John had also supplied. 'Right then. That's me finished. It shouldn't cause you any problems but keep an eye on it, and if you have any issues, don't hesitate to contact your local health clinic.'

'Thanks, doc,' said Dirk.

'No thanks required,' Liam stated solemnly. 'It wouldn't have happened if I weren't here.'

'No hard feelings, doc. Accidents happen.'

'Thanks, Dirk. I'll leave you to enjoy the rest of your day. And again, my apologies.' Liam acknowledged everyone else and returned to his belongings before going out of sight.

Willkie and Cody began to chuckle. Dirk looked at them both. 'What!' he snapped.

John and Sharyn also began to snigger, Sharyn covering her mouth with her hand in a weak attempt to hide her grin. Dirk looked at them and shook his head slowly before a wry smile began to expand across his face. Before long, they were all in fits of giggles.

Chapter 18

I t was just after 10:00 on Wednesday morning when Dirk strolled through the museum's main doors. He saw Lin standing in the centre of the main hall, evidently waiting for him. As he walked towards her, he ignored his surroundings, now having the time to appreciate her without the awkwardness of when they first met.

Lin stood there as if she were a model striking a pose for a camera. Her black trouser suit and high heels framed the electric blue blouse she wore, adding a complementary element to her figure. Her shiny black hair highlighted the smooth complexions of her face, while her lips were decorated with a deep, dark red lipstick. As they locked on to each other's gaze, he noticed her eyes: hazel in colour, framed with eyeliner. Both were captivated by each other's presence, evident in their smiles as they came together in the hall.

'Good morning, Mr Davis,' Lin said, offering her hand to him, palm down, suggesting to Dirk that she wanted him to kiss the back of her hand, and while he thought this was refreshingly old-fashioned for a younger woman, he obliged gently, smelling the mildest hint of pleasant perfume as he did so.

'Good morning,' Dirk replied, as he stood upright.

Lin smiled, used her other hand to place one side of her hair behind her ear, and looked at Dirk. 'I must admit that I don't usually do this type of thing, as I'm heavily involved with the exhibition behind the scenes, without much time for socialising or sightseeing. But as we're staying for several more months, I find I've more spare time on my hands than usual. You've made an uplifting change for me, showing a keen interest in the figures. You were not pouring over the items like a scientist looking for answers, and you weren't like most tourists just gawking at their wonder. Correct me if I'm wrong, but you seem taken aback by the whole aspect of the army.'

Dirk nodded; she was right, and there was no doubting it. But while he was in awe of the Terracotta Army, he also knew that the main reason for this interest was gathering information to steal the items from the next room. And he was now beginning to feel pangs of guilt for taking advantage of Lin.

Dirk looked briefly towards the ceiling to reframe his focus before looking directly at her. 'I must admit that this isn't normal for me either. Shall we start over? Let's put that awkwardness to one side and see how we get on. Is that a deal?' He offered a hand in friendship, which gladly Lin took while responding.

'Dú mù bù chéng lín, dān xián bù chéng yīn'

'Pardon?' enquired a surprised Dirk.

'Sorry, it's an old Chinese proverb. It means: *a single tree does not make a forest; a single string cannot make music*.' But looking into Dirk's eyes, she knew he was still confused and added, 'Many things require people to work together to achieve an end.'

Dirk smiled and nodded as the acknowledgement lifted in his head. He offered his arm, which Lin accepted, and they walked towards Holleb Hall.

Upon reaching the hall, they walked in unhindered by security, and Lin directed Dirk by the hand to the centre of the exhibition. He looked around; no other soul was in the hall, making it eerily quiet.

Lin let go of his arm and looked towards the ceiling. Then after a moment, she spoke.

'What do you see?'

Dirk looked up to the banners that Lin was gesturing to, evenly spaced across the ceiling, each showing a terracotta statue's face. He looked at several of them before answering. 'Each face is unique.'

'Correct,' Lin responded. 'And that's not just in this room, but across the entire complex in China. All ninety-eight square kilometres of it.' She looked at Dirk, wandering several yards away, still looking upwards. Lin resumed but now also continued looking at each banner in turn. 'Think of what it took to make an individual warrior. Not just the number of craftsmen creating each piece, but the communication and scrutineering, which was vital to ensure that no two pieces were alike. Each man needed to pour their heart and soul into every piece they made, so they were perfect for the emperor's needs. And this was not just mentally but also physically as well. As a result, many lives were lost, creating his new vision of a new unified China.'

Dirk stopped and turned to look at Lin. He hadn't thought of it like that. First, he was in awe of the sheer scale required but now imagined hundreds of workers breaking their backs over each piece, churning them out day after day. Now, seeing it through Lin's eyes made the experience more profound.

Lin looked at Dirk and smiled as if seeing his mind awaken.

'Now look at the pieces around you and see them through new eyes.'

Lin took hold of Dirk's hand and slowly guided him to the piece where they first met several days ago, positioning him directly in front of the statue.

'Do you see a difference?' she whispered to him as they stood there looking at the statue.

Dirk was quiet before responding with a slow and meaningful tone. 'Yes, yes I do.'

He looked at the statue using the technique he practised with his mindfulness and began shutting out all other senses, concentrating only on sight. He noticed the individual marks on several areas of the statue, where simple tools and hands, made by long-dead artisans, had etched and moulded the unique details that could be seen, almost making the figure come to life. It became fascinating, almost bewitching.

He didn't know how long he'd stared at the statue, but as the rest of his senses returned to the fore, he began to smell the hint of Lin's perfume and the gentle caress of her fingers across the back of his hands. He then blinked rapidly as if being awoken from a dream.

Lin leant forward and turned around to face him, keeping her body close. 'Are you OK?' she asked tenderly.

'Yeah. I feel great,' said Dirk looking at her. 'Thank you.'

They continued ambling around the hall, their bodies periodically touching, caressing each other like a moth drawn to a light. Lin spoke about each figure and its part in the emperor's grand plan for his afterlife. Dirk was fascinated throughout their walk of the collection, not just with what he was learning about the statues and how they came into existence but also with Lin's passion for them. It was captivating to watch her express herself about something she loved.

He'd been asking questions, and Lin obliged by answering them in fine detail, but after a while, he remembered that he was here to do a job and had to ask those questions too. He turned to face Lin again. 'I'm confused. The notice in the hall next door states that the only perfect figure is in China. But several of the figures here look pristine.'

Lin chuckled. 'Then our restoration team have done an excellent job, and I'll pass on your compliments.'

'I see,' replied Dirk, feeling a little stupid for asking the question.

'We think the terracotta figures broke due to seismic

activity. Though investigations have shown that there was also some form of vandalism and fire at some point. We think the archer survived because of its low centre of gravity.'

Dirk asked another question, hoping it wasn't as trivial as the last. 'But they must be difficult to move. Do you have an army of people or special equipment to move the statues here? How do you manage it?'

'No, not an army,' replied Lin. 'We use the museum's equipment to move it from the vehicle bay to the lift outside before proceeding into the room here. The trickiest part is placing them in and out of their crates.'

'How so?' queried Dirk.

'Well, before we pack each piece, their condition is checked, and then they're wrapped in Tyvek bandages and cling film before being placed into their wooden crates. The crates are secured to help prevent damage in transit, where they are kept horizontally, travelling on their backs before being loaded in specially conditioned tail-lift air-ride vehicles. Once in the gallery, the crates are moved into the upright position. And finally, the pieces are lifted by hand or a portable gantry onto their display plinths.'

'I see. A lot of work then,' replied Dirk, trying to keep a mental note of everything he was being told.

'It can be,' answered Lin. 'But some places are harder than others.'

'Really? How difficult can it be handling ancient artefacts?' exclaimed Dirk.

'Oh, you have no idea what lengths a museum will go to, to try to get people through their doors. For example, here, in Chicago, it was relatively straightforward. But when we were at the British Museum, the exhibition was placed on a specially designed mezzanine floor in their library, above the bookcases. While it was being constructed, great care was taken to not damage the bookcases underneath the flooring. But we then had to consider the weight distribution while placing the pieces onto the floor and once the exhibition was open, limit the number of people in the room at any one time due to the weight restrictions. The hall was decorated with draped black cloth as a backdrop, and the main lights were turned off. Each piece was nicely spotlighted, giving a picturesque, if not haunting, view of the exhibits.'

'Wow, that's taking things a bit far.'

'Not really. We're used to it,' replied Lin with a wry smile. 'They're a great wonder and deserve the attention given to them.'

Dirk moved towards Lin and held her hands. 'How can I repay you for a wonderful morning?'

Lin looked into Dirk's eyes. She squeezed his hand tighter and subconsciously started to raise her left foot off the floor before tenderly speaking. 'Well. You could be my tour guide. Perhaps even dinner.' Her smile was warming to look at, and as if sensing his thoughts, she raised herself and gently placed her lips on Dirk's. He reciprocated her touch, and when they stopped, he caressed her cheek softly.

'I think I can manage that. Where and when would you like me to pick you up?' replied Dirk.

'Shall we say eleven o'clock in two weeks, on Saturday morning?' She almost purred in response.

'I can't see why not. Eleven o'clock it is then.' And they gently kissed again.

Lin eased away from Dirk's arms, but lingered their touch with their fingertips, then looked at her watch before saying, 'I should go now, I have things to do.'

Her hands were clasped together, and her left foot shuffled around on the floor.

They both stood there, smiling at each other, and he became hesitant before he finally turned to leave. As he walked away, he kept looking back. Lin stood there watching him for a while, smiling, before heading back into the exhibition.

Dirk headed straight to the Field Bistro and purchased a coffee before sitting in front of the window, overlooking the main hall. While slowly drinking, he began to feel hot under the collar, and his thoughts began running riot around his head. He tried to keep it together, knowing he still had a job to do, so quickly messaged Willkie about the truck information Lin had mentioned before using his mindfulness to calm down and rest.

He was just finishing his cold coffee when he froze seing a familiar face walking across the main hall towards the north entrance; it was Kirby. It looked like he'd come from the exhibition in Levin Hall. Dirk kept his coffee cup beside his mouth in what he later thought was a vain attempt to hide and watched Kirby leave through the doors.

Dirk put the coffee cup down and followed him. As he exited through the north doors, he could see Kirby heading around the building. He continued walking to keep him in sight but came to a complete stop when someone abruptly stopped in front of him.

'Sorry, mate. I know you must be busy, but I need a hand trying to find this place.' An open museum pamphlet was shoved in front of Dirk. He was about to politely tell the man to go away when the tourist whispered, 'You're in danger. Please, get in the car, sir.'

Dirk looked up at the man, who gestured at the pamphlet in a way he was actually pointing towards the white Chrysler 300 with blacked-out windows pulling up alongside them.

Dirk hesitated. His heart began to race, and he was deciding whether to run or fight, but as the rear passenger car door opened, he saw a familiar face.

'Hello, Dirk… Get in.'

It was Garrick.

'Thanks for the help, mate,' and the man choreographed Dirk into the car next to Garrick. The door was shut behind him, and the car pulled away. In the front seats were the driver and passenger, both dressed in expensive-looking suits.

'That was a close call,' said Garrick, before asking the driver, 'To the Hilton Hotel, please, Al. And Frank, connect me to Jonny.'

Both responded with a, 'Yes, Mr Lombardi.'

Dirk then looked at Garrick, his heart still thumping in his chest. 'How was I in danger, exactly?'

Garrick simply responded, 'Patience, Dirk.'

Chapter 19

Once Frank connected to Jonny, he passed the phone to Garrick, who gave Dirk an electronic tablet and gestured to turn it on while Garrick started a discussion on the phone. Dirk couldn't hear the other side of the conversation but got the gist of what was said.

'Hi Jonny, almost finished? Good. Did you get what we were after? Brilliant. We'll be passing in ten minutes. Be sure you're ready... Great Jonny, and thanks.' Garrick ended the call and passed the phone back to Frank. 'Cheers, Frank.'

Garrick gestured for the tablet, which Dirk obliged, and Garrick opened a file and selected a photo to open while speaking. 'I presume you've had a background check done on this guy you messaged me about?'

'Yep,' responded Dirk. 'Apart from wanting the statues, he's part of some cult who thinks the world is ending and he's on a watch list for Interpol. What have you found out?'

'Funny that you mentioned Interpol. Have you seen this guy?' said Garrick, passing the tablet back to Dirk.

Dirk looked at the photo in depth; it showed a tall, stocky man in an ill-fitting beige suit, with part of his shirt hanging over his belt. He surmised from the chiselled facial features and greasy greying blond hair that the man was a little older than himself. After a moment, Dirk responded to Garrick's question and handed back the tablet.

'No, should I have?'

'Well, that, my friend is the face of Interpol. His name is Semyon Pavlovsky, a Russian national. He's been tailing your guy for the past couple of days. He was also in the museum back there, keeping tabs on him. As were you, it appears. That's why I picked you up. The last thing we need is you being picked up on an Interpol witch hunt.'

'I see. Thanks,' replied Dirk. 'I spotted Kirby leaving when I was in the bistro and decided to follow. To see what he was up to.'

'Let us keep tabs on Kirby. You concentrate on the job. OK?'

Dirk nodded.

Garrick smiled before handing back the tablet, showing a photo of a young Indian lady dressed in a green, yellow and gold sari. 'How about this woman?'

Dirk quickly responded. 'No. But I presume this is the woman we learned about who travelled with Kirby from Hong Kong?'

'Correct,' said Garrick. 'With what we can make out, she's his personal assistant. Goes most places with Kirby, but today she took a taxi half an hour before Kirby left the hotel.'

'Where to?' replied Dirk.

'Don't know yet. We're still working on that one.'

Dirk repositioned himself in his seat and sat quietly

for several minutes, staring out of the window, feeling frustrated. Without realising it, his fist was clenched while thinking. *Why does it have to be so difficult? Why can't it just run smoothly?* He looked towards Garrick and spoke again. 'So why are we going to the hotel Kirby's staying at?'

'It's an opportune time to enter his room and look through stuff. Besides, your email about Kirby said he'd gone to the Jamaicans. Well, let's just say it ruffled some feathers. So, we've gone to snoop around to see what's going on. Jonny, who I spoke to a moment ago has gained entry to Kirby's room to see what he can discover for us, and we're on our way to collect his findings.'

'I see,' stated Dirk. Showing frustration, he thoughtlessly forgot where he was and blurted out, 'And here's me thinking the mob was all wide-brimmed hats, Tommy guns and knuckle dusters.'

'Careful, Dirk,' grinned Garrick. 'Some people may take that as an insult.'

Dirk's mouth became dry as he realised what he'd just said. 'Sorry… I didn't mean to offend.' In vain, Dirk smiled as if it was intended as a joke.

'None taken,' replied Frank from the front seat.

The cynical smile was wiped off Dirk's face at that remark, which amused Garrick for the next several minutes. By the time Dirk regained his composure, they had arrived at the hotel.

The car slowed, pulling alongside the sidewalk. Frank opened his window a couple of inches, and a figure came alongside and dropped a folded newspaper into his lap, who then closed his window. The driver seamlessly pulled away.

Frank pulled an envelope from inside the newspaper, and passed it to Garrick, who opened it and pulled out a memory card, which he placed into a card reader adaptor and connected to the tablet.

'Jonny uses a bodycam, like the ones the cops are trying out. We've used him several times on jobs like this. It normally avoids the need of the brass knuckles and Tommy guns you mentioned earlier.' The grin on Garrick's face was more annoying than ever. 'Let's see what he's given us, shall we?' He started to play the file.

The film started with a hotel room door opening, with the commentary from Jonny. 'Room service,' and with no response, 'right, we're in.' The footage showed him moving in and taking a good look around before shutting the door behind him, placing a cleaning trolley in front of it, evidently to cause an obstacle if someone did come in. He then started his search.

Jonny's search was extensive, taking his time looking over everything, carefully looking with gloved hands, before placing items back exactly where he'd found them. It was obvious he didn't know what he was looking for, as he commented on everything he found; clothes, fridge contents, various tourist pamphlets, and most of what Dirk and Garrick were seeing didn't seem that important. It wasn't until Jonny found four brand-new briefcases and what looked like a vanity case that it became interesting. The footage became obscured as Jonny fiddled with the locking mechanism, but once opened, the view showed the full contents of each one.

Inside the first two were clear and labelled sealed bags, which Jonny dutifully read out for the camera. 'Eagle feathers, bird beaks, a pack of white chalk, six white candles, six black candles, six red candles, a packet of French centimes, white sand and a couple of vanilla pods.' Jonny then joked, 'I'm half expecting wing of bat and eye of newt.'

At that point, Dirk quickly spoke up. 'Wait. Stop. Back it up to where the fridge was shown.'

'What for?!' said Garrick, slightly caught off guard by the interruption.

'Just realised. Those two cases don't look full. What if the stuff in the fridge is from these cases? When Jonny mentioned vanilla pods and wing of bat, it just occurred to me that this could be a list of ingredients. And look at what he's mentioned so far: candles, chalk, feathers. Don't you see?'

Garrick looked puzzled. 'No, I don't.'

'I think these are all related to witchcraft. And what does the Jamaican posse do to scare their followers? They use witchcraft, or as they call it, voodoo.'

The penny seemed to drop for Garrick. 'OK, let's go back.' He did what Dirk requested before continuing from the point of the fridges while Dirk prepared to take notes.

'Looking in the fridge, we have a selection of berries, fresh herbs and eggs, with some separated into containers of yolk and whites.' As that was the last item in the fridge,

Garrick stopped the film and moved it forward, adding, 'I can see your point, but ingredients for what?!'

'I don't know,' replied Dirk, his voice trailing off, unsure of his thoughts.

'Let's move on, shall we?'

'Yeah, sure,' Dirk despondently replied, his hand now rubbing his chin in thought. He then looked out of the window before refocusing back on the tablet screen.

The film was restarted as Jonny opened the third briefcase, containing shaped foam to protect what was within. 'What have we got here? Talk about the bizarre. I hope you're getting a clear view of this. We've got an engraved dagger, a set of hatpins,' Jonny hesitated as he picked up and unfolded the next item, 'and what looks like a small, basic sack doll that needs stuffing.' He neatly refolded the doll before putting it back into the case, re-locking it, and moving on to the fourth. 'Let's see what surprises we can find in here.'

It was opened to reveal shaped foam protecting two containers; one was the size of a small test tube, and the other was roughly the size of a jar of coffee. Both showed a yellow and black warning label. 'OK. What do we have here?' Jonny delicately picked up the small phial first, which was filled with powder. 'The label reads 'TTX'. I haven't got a clue what that is. And forgive me if I don't open it due to the lovely label of black skull and crossbones on a yellow background.' He put it back as he found it and picked up the last container. 'Right, this looks like it contains some dried flowers. It has the same pretty yellow and black label as the last, which reads *Datura* and *Coup De Poudre*. Which, if my French serves me rightly, means 'Powder Blow'. It's bizarre, and I hope all this means something to you, as it means absolutely nothing to me.'

Opening the vanity case last exposed anything but personal items. Instead, the shaped foam safely secured an item within. An old urn made of terracotta. Jonny took out the piece and inspected it. The shape reminded Dirk of a canopic jar from Egypt, something he'd once stolen for a client, but instead of an animal, it was adorned with Chinese script and sealed with what looked like wax. Jonny then spoke. 'Cremation urn, maybe? Has some age to it, but I won't be opening it.'

Jonny closed the case before putting them all back, exactly as he found them, and moved towards the drawers and wardrobes, where clothing and air tickets were found. He picked up a notebook and started quickly going through the pages. 'Looking at this shows a list of car and truck rental services.'

He moved on to the beds: these were already made, so it was assumed that the housekeeper had already been. But he found something under the bed. It was another case, coated in brown leather and showing a great deal of wear, unlike the others, and when opened, produced what looked like a toolkit of some kind. Jonny showed the camera a rag with lines of grime running across it and occasionally cut marks.

He sniffed it, adding, 'Smells oily to me.'

The rest of the contents showed tools of various

descriptions and a hand-sized stone worn over a long period. 'I think this is a whetstone and care kit for the dagger.'

Dirk interrupted the footage. 'No, that's for something else. The dagger was brand new and has never been used.'

'Agreed,' replied Garrick.

The briefcase was put back, again carefully as it was found. Jonny's phone then began to ring. 'Excuse me.' He turned off the camera.

It restarted with, 'That was you calling. As I said on the phone, I think I've finished here. Drop off and payment will be as we previously discussed. I hope what I found helped.' The film ended.

'Well, what did you think?' Garrick asked.

'Well, he's thorough. I'll give him that. But it's given me more questions than answers. Like, what's their plan regarding all the stuff in the cases? It's all very ritualistic, but for what? There's no guide to how Kirby's dealing with their heist. The only clear lead we've got keeps coming back to Mbundu.'

'So, where do you go from here?' asked Garrick.

Dirk soberly replied, 'As much as it pains me to say it, I think I need to meet up with Mbundu.'

'OK, I'll see what I can do,' Garrick answered.

Chapter 20

Sharyn had spent most of the next day on the computer, chasing her ideas on the tracking device, but her investigation had hit a dead end. So, deciding to take a break from her laptop, she went on a run, giving her body a chance to awaken after the constant sitting.

She was coming up to the local hospital when she noticed a large crowd had gathered outside its main entrance. News vans were parked everywhere, filming protestors with placards. Sharyn hadn't seen any news because of her investigation, so curious, she decided to see what was happening.

As she approached, she could now clearly read the placards, which declared *Mother & Baby Killers*, *Shame on You*, and many others. The associated chanting was just a din of obscenities towards the hospital and its staff.

Sharyn moved closer to a journalist who had just started filming his report.

'You join me here today, where angry crowds gather outside the hospital after their statement this morning. You will recall, the problems started over a week ago when it was reported there was a delay when the hospital generator failed to start during the storm and subsequent power cut.

'Several days later, the hospital issued its first statement about the death of the first infant and mother, which at the time was believed to be caused by the power failure and complications during the birth. But after a second infant and mother death was reported yesterday, the hospital's statement this morning specified that it now believed the deaths were attributed to a rare wasting disease. They continued to say that as a precaution, they have placed the maternity ward under quarantine and diverted any new patients to the surrounding hospitals in the Chicago area.

'The hospital is now liaising with the Department of Health to try to understand the cause of the disease and prevent the possible spread of the contagion.

'A spokesperson for the hospital has informed us that they're doing everything in their power to support the bereaved families and staff affected by the trauma. And they have asked the public to remain calm during this difficult time.

'The police set up a cordon around the main entrance this morning, shortly after the crowd began to gather, and have also been escorting staff members while undertaking security checks on anybody visiting the hospital. The public's mood is intimidating and unpredictable at times, but the police officers have done an outstanding job keeping the tension in check.

'A police spokesperson has requested that anybody with an appointment at the hospital bring their appointment details to prevent possible delays.

'It's been claimed that two women were cautioned

by the police this morning after they were found in the building spreading pineapple leaves around the hospital's windows. Though the police have refused to confirm or deny this story, it is unknown whether this issue had any bearing on this morning's statement.

'This is Simon Fletcher for Chicago News.'

Sharyn's heart sank when she'd finished listening to the journalist's account. Having no children of her own, she could only imagine what the families were going through, which gave her a deep knotting sensation in her stomach as she started her sombre walk home.

From the side of the mob, surveying the people around him, Semyon Pavlovsky took a large bite out of his burger. It was cold, but he gulped it down anyway before wiping some of the fat from his chin with a napkin. Then, taking the last mouthful of lukewarm coffee and wiping his mouth one final time, he disposed of his rubbish into a nearby bin before moving away, melting into the throng of people continuing to arrive.

Chapter 21

It was late the same day, and Dirk was about to go to bed when his phone rang. It was Garrick. 'I've arranged a meeting as requested, but they want to do it tonight at 1am in Calumet. They've said you'll need to drive to the end of East 87th Street, where a large flat wasteland is on either side of the road. Someone will meet you there, but they stressed you must be alone. There's no way I can protect you, so watch your back.'

'Thanks, and I will. I'll let you know when I'm done,' responded Dirk. They hung up.

Calumet, thought Dirk. It would take around forty minutes at that time of night, and it was under two hours to the meet, so he pulled up an aerial view on his phone to understand what Garrick had said. It seemed easy enough, so he poured himself a strong coffee and began making notes of what he wanted to ask.

When he was ready, he grabbed his keys, left the apartment, and got into his car, giving himself an hour for the journey. The drive itself was simple, with quiet roads and no problems. He wasn't in any rush to get there, trying to keep as level-headed as possible for the meet.

As Dirk drove off the Chicago Skyway, heading into

Calumet, he noticed wisps of mist creeping over the road in front of him. It swirled and caressed his car as he entered the low-lying haze that was coming from the direction of Lake Michigan.

When he reached East 87th Street, he was suddenly enveloped by a churning mass of dense grey fog cascading over the hood and windscreen like a shroud, causing him to brake abruptly.

Dirk opened his window and leant out, instantly feeling his face struck by the chilling, moist air of the thick fog he'd entered. He could barely see past the bumper while his ears picked out the sound of foghorns from the nearby port. He leant back into his seat and took in several deep breaths of sharp, cold air, his heart pounding from the sudden onset of the fog. He took a moment to compose himself, then went into his glove box, pulling out a hand towel before slowly wiping his face, and subsequently jumped when the sound of a bolt primed for a firearm could be heard. Dirk looked to see two figures approaching out of the fog, aiming their weapons in his direction. Knowing there was nothing he could do, Dirk raised his hands slowly.

One of them then spoke in a heavy Jamaican accent. 'What ya want?'

'I'm here for a meeting with Algernon Mbundu. He's expecting me.' Dirk tried to keep as calm as possible, but he could hear his heart beating like an express train in his ears.

'Turn off ya engine an get out di car. Real slow,' came the response.

Dirk turned off the engine as instructed, then slowly

moved his hand towards the handle outside the car to open his door to keep them in view. The figures positioned their firearms, ready to react. The door opened, and Dirk slowly got out. One of the figures rested his firearm by its shoulder strap, leaving it hanging by his hip, and with purpose, walked over and forcibly spun Dirk around to face his car, making him place his hands on the roof to steady himself. The figure then kicked at Dirk's ankles in a gesture to spread his legs. Dirk complied before being thoroughly and roughly handled while being searched. They did the same to his car when they'd finished.

After several minutes, the figure stated, 'He's clean, na weapons, ar wires.'

'Good, ya can go.' Both figures relaxed their postures. 'Get into ya car. Di boss will see ya now.'

Dirk got into his car and was about to question the men on their sanity of driving in the thick fog when one of the Jamaicans tossed something small through his window. 'Loa will guide ya.' And before he could respond, Dirk's car roared to life and lurched forward on its own accord, leaving the two Jamaicans standing there laughing as they were quickly left behind.

Dirk panicked and instinctively reached to open his door, but the lock bolted before the doors could be touched. He then looked at the door's open window, but that too had already begun to shut before attempting it, literally closing the only window of opportunity to escape the vehicle. He watched wide-eyed as the gear lever, clutch and accelerator operated independently, working up through the gears as the car accelerated along the unseen road, the throttle pedal seemingly welded to the floor. He stamped on the brake pedal repeatedly, even bracing himself, pushing with extreme effort with both feet, but it refused to move an inch. Finally, when the gear lever moved again, he tried forcing it to stay in neutral, even tried to twist and take out the key, but no amount of strength could prevent any course of action. The car began to steadily turn to the right. He grabbed the wheel with both hands, knuckles turning white under strain, trying vainly to change the course of wherever he was going. Dirk looked around in blind desperation, but the car was now bouncing across uneven ground, making it difficult to stay in his seat. Now, all he could do was cover his head with his arms to prevent injuring himself and pray that this would soon end.

When the car finally slowed, Dirk looked outwardly from his moving prison. Appearing out of the gloom ahead, Dirk could see a hazy ring of red hand flares burning on the ground. As he approached, two previously unseen vehicles on the other side of the circle turned on their headlights with full beams, blinding Dirk as they did so. Squinting and holding one hand up to shield his eyes, the car came to a standstill at the circle's edge, the engine turned off and the doors unlocked. It took Dirk several seconds to become accustomed to the light, and at that point, with a pounding heart, he slowly exited his car, trying not to make any sudden moves.

Before him, the two cars were at slight angles, their

hoods meeting at the corners, the headlights dipping in unison, their projecting beams crossing each other through the persisting haze. The burning flares were doing an excellent job keeping the fog at bay, thinning the vapour enough that they could all see each other.

Three Jamaican men, dressed in denim and T-shirts and holding submachine guns, standing behind the two vehicles, pointed casually in Dirk's direction. At the same time, he could barely see the drivers' silhouettes within the cars. Finally, a Jamaican dressed in a stylish plum-coloured suit, was using both car hoods as support; Dirk presumed that this was Mbundu. He looked younger than Dirk imagined, and as they walked towards each other, Dirk could see Mbundu had some form of tribal scarring on his cheeks, while a neatly trimmed beard was framed by dreadlocked hair draping across his shoulders. Dirk offered his hand, trying to hide any trace of his distress and anger from what had just happened. 'Mr Mbundu?'

Mbundu accepted and answered, 'Yes. And you are Bruce, or should I say Dirk?' His Jamaican accent was evident, but his English was much better than his brethren Dirk had just met.

'Dirk will suffice,' he replied sternly. 'Bruce wasn't my idea and not as secure as I thought, it seems.'

'Ah, yes. I must admit, it appears that you are... were Garrick's best-kept secret. He prizes you more than any other of his teams, even changing his choice of restaurant in a bid to confuse me, making it extremely hard to track you down.' Mbundu gestured self-assuredly towards the surrounding fog. 'Nothing escapes me or the spirits from perpetuity, even now. They help me by shrouding our meeting, even chauffeuring you to me.'

Dirk didn't respond. He didn't believe what Mbundu was saying and wasn't going to debate the matter either. However, Dirk knew that all this theatre was being used against him and he was mentally kicking himself for not expecting it while trying hard not to show that, in some form, this was affecting him.

Mbundu's voice was calm and composed. 'So, what can I do for you? I presume that this is not a social visit.'

'It's regarding a man called Kirby. I believe you sent him in my direction.'

'Ah yes, the young man from Hong Kong. As I understand it, you turned him down and did a good job of making him believe that you were not Bruce.' Mbundu then inclined his head slightly to one side, his eyes narrowing, before asking his own question. 'But why ask about a client you've turned away?' Mbundu's eyes widened slightly and continued. 'Unless somebody else beat him to the request... Interesting.' He brushed off Dirk's limp protests of the accusation with a simple gesture with his hand. 'So, what do you want to know?'

Of course, Mbundu was right about his employment, but he didn't want to give too much away. Dirk composed himself before responding, 'What's your connection with Kirby or his associates, and what are the ingredients and other items you supplied him in the briefcases?'

Mbundu looked impressed with what Dirk knew. 'And

127

what is this information worth? What are you willing to give me in return?' countered Mbundu.

Dirk had thought about this on the way here. But couldn't come up with anything other than the obvious. 'What did you have in mind? Money?'

Mbundu slowly stroked his beard, seemingly deep in thought, but Dirk felt he already knew what he wanted. 'No,' he replied.

'OK,' replied Dirk, giving away uncertainty in his voice.

Mbundu grinned before stating, 'What I want is the statues.'

'Not going to happen,' snapped Dirk quickly, unable to hide the anger in his tone.

Mbundu's men raised their weapons and levelled them directly at Dirk, poised to pull their triggers with a simple command. Mbundu just chuckled, then signalled his men to stand down. He then gestured with his hands while responding to Dirk's comment. 'I thought you would say that. Just look at you, such a slave to your morals. Remember this, Mr Davis, we are all slaves in one way or another, whether through need, addiction, or the heart. We are never totally free.' Mbundu stood with an air of superiority in his posture, before slowly pacing and thinking aloud. 'Let me see. I don't think you can tell me information about my competitors. No matter how good you think you are. You're just a footpad, a tool for extra pocket money for their cause. Plus, I think you're too loyal to those around you to give me the information I need. From what I understand, you're not the type of man to run drugs or weapons for me either. Besides, I have loyal men for that.' Mbundu then looked at Dirk intently. 'The bones have told me that you'll need all the help you can get in the chaos heading your way. And it appears now, Mr Davis, we are at a juncture. I have the vital information you require to understand and move on with your mission, and the only thing you will have that I want is the statues.'

Mbundu pondered before showing the signs of enlightenment of an idea. 'I tell you what. I'm feeling in a generous mood. You steal the statues and deliver as planned but tell me the drop-off point. I presume you get paid upon delivery, and I'll take it from there.'

'But I don't know the drop-off point until I've taken the statues.'

'Do you know Gary well, Mr Davis?' stated Mbundu. Gary was almost classed as an outer suburb of Chicago, across the state line in Indiana. A run-down place, trying hard to improve its infrastructure from its overbearing city neighbour.

'I know it well enough,' replied Dirk.

'Near the Indiana Harbour, next to the canal system, is a Jamaican bar. Once you know your extraction date, go there, and ask for Tristan. You won't get a warm welcome, but he'll help. Just make sure you select J13 on the jukebox in the corner first, and you won't be harmed. I think a man of your talents will find it easily enough. Tell Tristan the date, and he'll give you a mobile phone, for you to contact me on the night. How do you feel about that?'

While he'd listened to what Mbundu had suggested,

Dirk knew that only Mbundu could answer the questions continually pinballing around inside his mind about Kirby. Of course, Dirk didn't like it, but he believed he had no choice.

Mbundu continued. 'Of course, any reprisals from you and your associates, and you'll find those nearest and dearest to you will be ritually slain, and their innards fed to the local carrion. Do you understand?

Dirk nodded in response and hesitantly offered a hand before saying reluctantly, 'OK. We have a deal.'

Mbundu laughed as he shook Dirk's hand of defeat. 'Now, down to business.' And with that, he told his men to leave and guard the perimeter before sitting on one of the car hoods while gesturing to Dirk to sit on the other, which Dirk reluctantly accepted as he prepared to listen to what Mbundu had to say.

'In my circles, they're rumoured to be keys to the underworld. A link between the path of the living and the path of the dead. And there are two other groups after them.'

'Kirby and his associates and my employer,' Dirk stated.

'No,' replied Mbundu. 'With your employer, that now makes three.' He made his point by holding up three fingers.

'And what makes these pieces so special? Why not just take them from the other exhibition?'

Mbundu's response was impassioned. 'Because only the perfect ones can open the gate between worlds.'

'I see,' replied Dirk. But he still didn't wholeheartedly

believe the story. 'So, why not take them yourself?' countered Dirk.

'I was planning to do the heist with my men, then during the storm, the bones warned me that there would be too much competition. Kirby showed up looking for me two days later, and I spoke to his 'Master'—'

'You spoke to Quillon?' interrupted a surprised Dirk.

'Yes. But only by phone. He wanted me to help Kirby with his requests and pay handsomely for my efforts. After the call, I mentioned you, but after you turned him down, other avenues were blocked by your 'associates'. He found it difficult to go forward and couldn't find anybody else to accept the job. When I spoke to Quillon for a second time, he was in no mood to make an alliance. He just placed the order for the contents in the briefcases but told me not to tell Kirby what was in them, just to keep helping him with his requests on his behalf.'

'OK.' Dirk pondered before adding, 'But what did he want them for, and why come to you first and not my associates?' Dirk was finding himself becoming eager to learn more.

'Your associates would not have taken him seriously enough, while we are like-minded when it comes to the spirits. He claims to know the ritual of using the statues. The dagger and some of the ingredients are apparently for that. The rest, I believe, are for other rituals and safeguards to aid the heist.'

Dirk's eyes narrowed. 'That suggests that he's coming here.'

'He arrived yesterday,' countered Mbundu.

So that's where Anita was going yesterday, thought Dirk. 'What type of safeguards are they using?' And interrupting the start of Mbundu's response, 'Oh, yes. And what's TTX and the dried flowers for? I presume they're poisonous?'

Looking at Mbundu's facial expression, it occurred to Dirk that Mbundu wasn't used to interruptions, and he quickly backed down, raising his hand in a lame way of an apology.

Mbundu composed himself after the interruption before speaking. 'It appears that Quillon believes he's a shaman or priest to his cult, who knows different types of rituals 'borrowed' from other beliefs. So, I don't know what most of his ingredients are for. But the poisons you found, in his eyes, are to create zombies.'

'In his eyes?' Dirk was struggling to not sound like he was ridiculing Mbundu's statement.

'I'm a Houngan of Vodoun, Mr Davis. I've no need for parlour tricks to create my zombies. What Quillon is planning is dangerous, complicated, and unproven.'

'How so?'

'His victim needs to believe that they're dead, which needs an exact amount of poison added to a wound and a lot of trickery to make them believe they have risen as the walking dead. A large and repeated steroid injection or similar, while unconscious, is also used to boost their strength, which helps support the trickery.'

'I see. And your zombies?' Dirk was cynical in response.

'I ask Loa to help me to create them, and we ask spirits to animate the body of the dead, though I find them too problematic for my needs.'

'Problematic?' queried Dirk.

'They're strong, they never tire and have no need for sleep, so they make great guards, but are too slow, and you have to wire their mouths shut to prevent them from eating.'

'Brains…' Dirk found it hard to keep a straight face.

However, Mbundu was in no mood to jest. 'This is not Hollywood, with their Romero zombies, Mr Davis, nor is it *World War Z*. True zombies do not pass on a virus that creates more zombies, they've no need to eat, but they do indeed crave human flesh, though if they're able to eat it, they will die and rapidly rot.'

'So, you wire their mouths shut to prevent it?' Dirk asked.

'Correct,' confirmed Mbundu.

'And what will Quillon use them for?'

'Either as bodyguards or to carry the statues is my guess.'

'They're that strong?' stated Dirk with disbelief.

'Oh yes… Well… Mine would be, so don't let them hit you.'

'And how do you stop them?'

'You should be able to stop Quillon's like a normal person, though their pain levels will be greatly reduced, depending on the drugs he's administered. While a true zombie doesn't feel pain, and decapitation is the only thing that will kill them, breaking their limbs will only slow them down.'

'OK. What about the urn?'

'I don't know anything about an urn.'

Dirk looked puzzled before responding with a simple, 'OK.' Then took a minute to digest what Mbundu had said before questioning him further. He couldn't believe he was asking these questions, as his thought process was still finding it hard to believe this nonsense. So, Dirk decided to change the topic. 'What about this second team?'

'I know they're also from Asia, highly backed with links to the Triads. I heard through my contacts that they were smuggled into the country and are apparently after the statues for the same reasons as Quillon but know nothing more. What about your employer?'

'I've never met him. But according to my fence, he's requested jobs like this before. Why do you ask? Do you think he is part of this Asian team you mentioned?'

'Just curious, Mr Davis. As I said before, your employer is the third team I'm aware of.'

Dirk felt the cold air around him suddenly grip his body, and he believed that Mbundu's spirits had firmly rooted him to the spot before realising he'd just been flustered by his own thoughts. Dirk steeled himself before responding, 'Just checking,' though he sensed that Mbundu was holding something back. Raising his eyebrows, he had to admit that this job was different, but with zombies, spirits, and not forgetting Willkie's wendigo, it was becoming a step too far for him.

Mbundu spoke again as if reading Dirk's thoughts. 'I can only advise a non-believer such as yourself to start looking at everything with an open mind.'

'Then what advice would you give me?' replied Dirk, trying not to sound sarcastic. 'I'm still trying to understand when you had the time to take my car and fix the autopilot system. And if you truly have this power,' he gestured to the fog, 'why haven't you taken over Chicago already?'

Mbundu chuckled. 'If I were you, Mr Davis, I would start believing in the supernatural. Otherwise, you'll find yourself on the mortician's slab, or worse.' Mbundu's hand gestures were still helping him exaggerate his every word. 'As for Chicago, Mr Davis. Don't be a fool to think I'm the only one here with supernatural powers. Older, much stronger influences are at work that prohibit me from taking over. So, I must bide my time, like the spider does to catch the fly.' Mbundu then leisurely pointed towards Dirk's car. 'And if you can only trust me with one thing, then trust me that you'll find nothing wrong with your car.'

Dirk then decided that he'd heard enough and prepared to leave. 'Thanks for your time. You've been… helpful.'

Mbundu grinned, and the two men shook hands before Dirk got into his car and opened his window to speak to Mbundu again. 'Is my chauffeur ready to leave?'

'I can do better than that,' replied Mbundu, and he closed his eyes, turned his head skywards, and slowly raised his arms while doing some incomprehensible chant. Then, without warning, he exhaled a large breath and clapped his hands loudly once, making the transfixed Dirk jump slightly. Mbundu slowly opened his eyes and looked directly at Dirk.

'Remember, open your mind, Mr Davis.' He grinned, and it was broad and malicious. Dirk then noticed the fog beginning to lift rapidly. He looked around at the dissipating vapour before looking back at Mbundu, who was just looking at him with that mocking grin. Dirk became unnerved by what had just happened, promptly started the engine and proceeded to leave immediately. He never looked back, and all the way home, he tried to rationalise what he'd just witnessed, like trying to prove how a magician had accomplished his trick, but he was failing abysmally.

Chapter 22

D irk didn't sleep much that night and had spent most of the next day going over his car, trying to find how Mbundu had controlled it, but he only discovered a French centime in the footwell. On top of this, the team wasn't impressed with what he'd found out during his meeting. Cody scoffed at the information, voicing his opinions loud and clear, but after a heated debate, in the end, they carried on with the plan the best they knew how.

Over a week, Dirk and his team ramped up their information gathering. In addition, they held weekly meetings on Dirk's boat for updates and problem-solving.

Cody was practising almost daily with the hire truck, picking up deliveries and even using a cheap garden sculpture in a crate to simulate a warrior, making sure there wasn't any extra damage at the end of each trip, though this was proving difficult.

After sorting out the relatively easy job of the type of transport to be used, Willkie took up some of the slack in the repair shop in Cody's absence and, when time allowed, joined him to take notes on the possible routes through the city.

Sharyn was the busiest: multi-tasking between her

demanding day job and the team's requirements. The first part of her investigation was to look at all the information she'd collected regarding the extensive tunnel network under the city, built over a hundred years ago by the Chicago Tunnel Company. But the idea was shelved after lengthy discussions and inspections of the Near South Side area by Dirk and Willkie. While the tunnels were abandoned, they were also prone to flooding and in various states of disrepair. And since a terrorist scare several years ago, most entrances in the area had been filled with concrete or were too small for their needs. So, with all other avenues closed to them, it was decided that the only way in was through the museum itself.

Evidently, they couldn't just rock up to the museum with a truck, walk in and take the statues. Using Ms Jenson's haulier company, Sharyn proposed creating a false email account within the company, which would be deleted when the job was complete. Dirk was hesitant when Sharyn suggested it but relinquished when she put her case forward that the museum already trusted the haulier. Sharyn laid down an email trail and planned to create a phoney delivery of an artefact to the museum. This took a lot of ingenuity that came naturally to Sharyn, looking at the up-and-coming events the museum was planning, and with details of an imaginary item linked to one of these events, cajoling the museum into taking the delivery.

While arranging the delivery, the museum made a mistake, stating that they couldn't take delivery on July twenty-fourth due to an outage but could accept it the following day. Sharyn knew this was the date the system changeover would occur and quickly arranged to speak to the guys about it. 'I'm not suggesting going on that night, or the night after—'

'And this has nothing to do with the bonus?' interrupted Dirk.

'Come on, Dirk.' Willkie stepped in to support Sharyn. 'Even you've got to admit it looks promising. Hear her out before shooting her down.'

Dirk folded his arms defensively. His eyes narrowed shrewdly while deliberating on what was being said. He trusted his team, but the niggles of the past goaded his paranoia feeding endless visions of past mistakes. He wanted no errors.

Sharyn smiled at Willkie as a thank you before continuing. 'Yes, it still falls within the bonus window. But there'll be more people onsite than normal during the implementation because that's what I'd do if I were hired to bed in a new system. If we target a couple of days after the insertion, then, we not only have the benefit of the glitches but also the relaxed police response as well. The later we leave it after this date, the glitches will be fixed, and the police response will be back to normal.'

'Even you can't ignore that reasoning, Dirk,' chirped in an upbeat Cody.

Dirk looked at him, took a deep breath, and looked at an empty space on the cabin wall for several moments to gather his thoughts. The rest of the team looked at each other silently, waiting with apprehension, anticipating Dirk's response.

'OK, book the slot,' stated Dirk finally, ending his ruminations and releasing the built-up tension in the room with only a sigh of relief.

'Do we know anything more about the other teams?' Cody asked.

'Yes,' Sharyn replied, still buoyant from Dirk's decision. 'Quillon is staying at the Hilton alongside Kirby and their PA. He has his own room. But unfortunately, there's no evidence of what they're up to.' Her speech tailed off, realising she hadn't added much.

'Our fence has been helping out with this situation as well,' Dirk added, carrying on where Sharyn had left off. 'Quillon's been looking at transport like we have, but his mission's been made more difficult. He still can't gain much in the way of assistance from the city's criminal element, thanks in some part to our fence, but it also appears that with Interpol hanging around, it means his movements are being monitored. I'm hoping that this will deter him, or at least give us enough time to beat him to the target. We've heard nothing regarding the third team, so I'm hoping Mbundu got it wrong.'

'And what about Mbundu?' stated Cody.

'Still working on that,' replied a deflated Dirk. 'But on a positive note,' he tried to quickly change the subject, 'I've another meeting with Lin this weekend. So, hopefully, we'll get more information about the museum and maybe the statues.'

'A meeting…' smirked Cody. 'I see.' And he winked with a chuckle. Dirk felt the heat rise with a light blush to the skin while Sharyn looked at Cody, disgusted with his attitude.

Chapter 23

On Saturday, Dirk had freshened up with a change of clothes before arriving at the museum at 11:00, then waited patiently outside the main entrance for Lin to appear. And he didn't have to wait long; she exited the building dressed in a smart-casual jean and blouse outfit. They smiled when they met, and Dirk offered his arm, which Lin accepted.

They caught the next bus downtown, and as promised, Dirk took her to see the sights of Chicago, including those not frequented much by the tourists, spending a lot of time walking and chatting, getting to know each other. Late in the evening, they went to a restaurant to eat.

'So, how did you get into museum work?' inquired Dirk.

'I love history, and the older I got, the more I wanted to learn about other countries. But it's the Terracotta Warriors that have always plucked at my heartstrings. How about you? You've not told me what you do.'

Dirk chuckled before he responded. 'Not as intellectual as your profession. I'm a repair shop manager, a mechanic.'

'That surprises me.' Lin raised an eyebrow. 'I had you down as an art dealer.'

Dirk replied, laughing. 'An art dealer? Why did you think that?'

Lin smiled. 'Your appreciation of things. Plus, you're exceptionally clean for a grease monkey.' They both started to chuckle.

'Does that disappoint you?' enquired Dirk jokingly.

'Not in the slightest. My father was a village blacksmith.'

'That's very admirable,' replied Dirk in awe. 'It seems the world is losing the knowledge of manual skills nowadays, relying too much on tech. Even my profession has changed over the years, with the addition of management systems, it seems more electrical nowadays.'

'I think so too. Both my parents did everything to make sure I had a good education. So how did you get to own your repair shop?'

Dirk chuckled before answering. 'Let's just say I was a naughty boy when I was young and needed to do something to keep my hands busy. Found out I was good with engines and slowly built myself up to the handsome man you see today.'

Lin's curiosity had been piqued. 'A bad boy? Sounds exciting. Tell me more.'

'Not as exciting as you think,' started Dirk, still smiling. 'I was young, needed money, and I stole. Then I stole from the wrong person. And for a while, I was trapped. But someone looked after me and gave me a way out.'

'As long as you're not stealing our statues, Mr Davis,' Lin asserted mockingly.

Dirk laughed, trying to hide his nervousness. 'Rest

assured your statues are safe.' He took a mouthful of coffee to wet his rapidly drying mouth. He wasn't lying; it was just too close to the knuckle for his liking.

'And what do you do when you're not repairing cars and visiting museums?' asked Lin cheekily.

'Fishing mainly.' It was a snap response, knowing full well that he couldn't state he was an antique thief. 'Though the bookkeeping of the shop keeps me tied up a lot. How about you?'

'Reading mostly when time allows. I miss the nature of my homeland, so I sit in parks to read. But here, I've been using the Shedd Aquarium on my lunch break instead. We've been given free passes while we've been here and made the most of it.' Lin was hesitant before asking the next question. 'Is there a woman in your life?'

'Not in a long while.' Dirk looked down at his coffee briefly and gave a wry smile.

'Sorry. Am I making you feel uncomfortable?' asked Lin, her tone showing concern.

Dirk looked at her and chuckled while shaking his head slowly. 'No, no, not at all.' He sighed before he continued. 'No. Guess I'm just out of practice with talking to women. It feels strange,' he quickly countered, feeling his words may have offended. 'But in a good way, if you know what I mean.'

'I think I do,' said Lin, smiling knowingly. And she rested her hands upon Dirk's.

Dirk was more surprised at how relaxed and open he'd been around Lin; perhaps Sharyn was right, it felt good to talk. And for a moment, there was a mild awkwardness between them; they looked at each other before Dirk asked, 'Where do you want to go now, madame?'

'Actually, I'm getting tired from all the walking. My apartment happens to be around the corner; can you walk me home?' Lin shuffled her feet under the table. Dirk stood, placed his money on the table, and with his warming smile, offered his hand to Lin.

'Your wish is my command.' Lin appreciated his actions as she accepted his hand and stood to join him.

The walk to her apartment was almost in silence. They periodically looked at each other as if one of them were about to speak, but instead, they could only smirk, embarrassed by what they might say next, trying not to spoil their perfect day.

When they reached the foot of the steps to the main door of her apartment block, Lin stopped. 'This is me. This is where I'm staying,' she stated, tucking her hair behind her right ear while looking at Dirk.

'I see,' said Dirk, disappointed that their walk had ended.

Lin took hold of both of Dirk's hands. 'It's been a great day. Thank you for being my guide.'

'You're welcome. I'm glad you enjoyed it,' before adding, 'at least I know what job I can do if I get bored with mechanics.' Lin giggled.

Dirk was about to start saying his goodbyes, but it was Lin who began first, her voice tinged with nervousness. 'It would be a shame to finish the day so abruptly. Would you like a drink before you go home?'

'I'd better go. You're tired—'

'No,' interrupted Lin. 'I insist. I just want to thank you for all your effort.'

Dirk exhaled. 'Only if you're sure?'

Lin smiled back before adding, 'Of course, I'm…' but her voice abruptly tailed off.

'What's wrong, are you OK?' asked Dirk, now looking concerned.

'I… I… I just remembered,' stuttered Lin.

'What is it?' He gently rested his hand on her shoulder as if to somehow reassure her.

'I just remembered. I had an accident last night.' Her eyes were now wide open with the mortification of what she was about to reveal.

Dirk was now bemused. 'What accident? Are you sure you're OK?'

'I was making kimchi last night—'

'Kimchi?' interrupted Dirk, his tone quizzical.

'It's pickled cabbage. I was making a fresh batch last night, when… when… I… I…' The panic in her voice was becoming more evident, and she looked away in embarrassment.

'Relax, whatever it is, it can't be that bad,' said Dirk, trying to reassure her.

Lin looked back at Dirk, clearly mortified at his statement. 'But… but… I dropped an entire jar of vinegar, and the apartment now reeks of it.'

Dirk began to laugh. 'Is that all?' He looked down and shook his head slowly in disbelief.

'What?' It was now Lin's turn to look bemused.

'Do you think that bothers me? I thought it was something bad.'

'But it is. You haven't smelt it,' countered Lin, but Dirk was still chuckling. She sulked briefly but slowly realised how silly she must seem, and they were laughing together before long. When they finally stopped, they looked at each other, still trying hard to not start laughing again, and they both headed up the steps to the main door before climbing several flights of stairs to the top-floor apartment.

They got to the front door, and when the door was opened, the waft of vinegar filled Dirk's nostrils, and he briefly choked. 'God, you weren't kidding.' He laughed.

'I'm so sorry,' said Lin embarrassedly before rushing into the apartment to open the windows. She then turned on several lamps before lighting several incense sticks, attempting to mask the smell of the pungent vinegar. Dirk entered and closed the door behind him; it was evident that she'd not been expecting visitors, as Lin was now hastily tidying up some of her belongings scattered around the apartment.

It was a tiny place, basically decorated. It had a kitchenette with a small dining table with two chairs to the left, while to the right was a leather two-seater couch and TV. Several home mementoes adorned various shelving units to make it feel like home during her stay in Chicago. Three doors exited the room on the right, and as Dirk lived in an apartment also, he recognised by the style that one was the bedroom, one a bathroom and, finally, the last one was a storage cupboard.

'Sorry about that,' said Lin. 'Take a seat.' She gestured

to the couch while opening a kitchen cupboard. 'Do you want a drink? I have wine or bourbon, if you prefer.'

'Wine will be fine,' Dirk replied while sitting down, leaving Lin to take two high ball glasses out of another cupboard, filling them with a decent amount each. The acrid smell of the vinegar began to disperse through the open windows, and the soothing scent of the incense sticks was now enveloping the room.

'There you go.' Lin gave a glass to Dirk. 'I hope you like red. It's all I had,' Lin stated as she sat down, kicking off her shoes before curling up with her feet on the couch, positioning herself to look at Dirk.

'Red's fine.' Dirk grinned before he took a mouthful. 'It's been a fun day.'

'Yes,' replied Lin, and they both chuckled again.

Dirk closed his eyes for several moments, still smiling, taking in the perfume of the incense and the gentle waft of the warm air from the open windows. He savoured another mouthful of wine, appreciating its deep, full-bodied flavour before swallowing it, feeling contented.

Dirk then felt something warm and soft touch his lips, making him jump, sending the remaining contents of his glass upwards. With eyes now wide open, he quickly looked around to see that Lin had moved closer to him, but her clothes were now covered in the wine that had just been expelled from his glass. 'I'm so, so sorry,' blurted out Dirk, startled at what had just happened.

'No, no, it was my fault. I shouldn't have made you jump,' Lin stated apologetically, looking stunned at her now red-stained clothes. Dirk quickly went to the kitchen to grab a cloth before hurrying back to hand it to Lin. She mopped herself up the best she could before standing up and wiping the couch, giggling.

'I'm so sorry, Lin,' repeated Dirk, feeling embarrassed about what had happened.

'Dirk. There's no harm done. Get yourself another drink while I clean myself up.' As Dirk did what he was asked, Lin walked into her bedroom and closed the door.

Dirk sat quietly, fidgeting with the refilled glass in his hands, now feeling that he'd outstayed his welcome. It was several minutes later when the bedroom door opened.

Dirk was about to make excuses to leave, but what he saw prevented any words from escaping his mouth, which was now wide open. Lin stood there, but the only thing she was wearing was a clean white blouse. There was now a silence between them, their eyes locked, as if exploring each other's souls. Dirk had frozen in his appreciation of Lin's appearance, but then found his eyes slowly wandering, studying every curve presented to him, which was silhouetted through the sheer blouse by the brighter bedroom lamp behind her. Lin's right foot gently caressed the back of her bare left leg, her left arm hanging loosely by her side, while her right hand toyed with her raven-black hair.

Since entering the room, Lin's confidence was buoyed by Dirk's stunned reaction, and once it had reached its pinnacle, she began to slowly walk towards his still frozen form. Dirk's eyes returned to meet Lin's, her body tantalisingly close to his. She gently rested her left knee on the couch before straddling Dirk's body. He stayed motionless, like a jackrabbit caught in a set of headlights, allowing Lin to cup her hands around his jawline, breathing heavily. Lin paused briefly, her lips excitingly close to his before they closed their eyes and began to kiss passionately. The night was now theirs, and theirs alone.

Chapter 24

D irk awoke the following day, finding himself alone in bed. As he became accustomed to his surroundings, the smell of freshly ground coffee permeated the air, doing its best to mask the odour of the vinegar, which was still giving him a tang at the back of his throat. He stretched, letting out a low groan as he did so, feeling content.

Several moments later, Lin walked into the room wearing a satin dressing gown while carrying a tray with two mugs of coffee and some food on a plate, their aroma banishing the vinegar remnants from the next room. 'Good morning,' she said.

'That smells great. What is it?' asked Dirk as he sat up.

'Egg pancakes with coriander, green onion and spices. It's a traditional dish from where I come from,' replied Lin, placing the tray on the bedside table before kneeling next to Dirk. She leant forward and placed her lips tenderly on Dirk's own before asking, 'How did you sleep?'

'Like a log, the best night's sleep in a long time,' said Dirk.

'Good.' Lin proceeded to take a piece of pancake with a pair of chopsticks and feed it teasingly to Dirk. Both smiled as they looked at each other.

'Tastes great,' replied Dirk, the satisfaction etched across his face.

'I'm glad you approve.' Lin fed herself a piece of the pancake.

'Service with a smile, breakfast in bed. I feel like a condemned man being given his last meal.' Dirk laughed.

'Funny you should say that,' answered Lin awkwardly while feeding Dirk another piece of pancake; her face became serious, with Dirk's becoming curious by contrast as he accepted the serving of food.

'Sounds serious,' he replied but still managed a wry smile after swallowing his food.

'I've enjoyed our time together…' started Lin but became hesitant to continue.

'But?' enquired Dirk, his tone giving away what he was expecting to come next.

'Now, don't take this the wrong way,' she replied, looking extremely uncomfortable. 'As I've said before, I normally don't have time to go around the cities we visit, let alone date anyone. You've been kind and thoughtful in the short time we've had together, and it has been wonderful—'

'But it's not me, it's you,' interrupted Dirk jokingly.

'No, stop,' responded Lin, while she slapped Dirk playfully on his leg. 'You're making this difficult for me.' Her voice was edged with the unfairness of being teased.

'Sorry,' said Dirk, though his wry smile was still present.

'Look…' Lin rested her hand on Dirk's leg to somehow prepare him for what she was about to say. 'My work at the museum has finished. They now want me to move on to prepare the next museum in January.'

'OK, I see.' Dirk's face became slightly wrinkled as he took the information in.

'You know that this wasn't long-term, don't you? It wouldn't have worked out with my job and travelling worldwide.'

Dirk looked serious for a moment. Leading up to this moment, he thought Lin might be the person to settle down with. But now, faced with Lin's sentiments, he was surprised at himself for not feeling upset. He thought that what she'd said was making sense, and they had only spent one day together.

Lin then sounded concerned. 'Are you OK?'

Dirk looked at her and smiled warmly. 'Where're they sending you?'

'It's not been decided yet. I'll find out later today. There're four sites we are working in conjunction with. New York, Seattle, Taipei and Kaohsiung. But I won't be given a choice.' Lin steeled herself before giving Dirk what she thought was the final blow. 'The chances are, I'll be moving to the new site in several days' time to help it prepare for their arrival.'

Dirk looked mildly surprised. 'That soon?'

'Yes. Remember what I said about London.'

There was an expression of recollection on Dirk's face before he responded calmly. 'So, in a polite way, what you're saying is that this could be our last day together.'

Lin's shoulders drooped in response before she

153

mumbled, 'Yes... Sorry.' She looked away, unable to make eye contact with Dirk. He caressed her cheek before gently persuading her to look at him, and as her face presented him with doe eyes, a single tear ran down her cheek.

He spoke to her in a soothing voice. 'Hey. I'm not angry. Surprised that it was that soon, yes, but never angry. I would've liked to have taken it further to see where it took us. You've also shown me a wonderful time, and I've enjoyed your company.' He smiled at her, still tenderly caressing her cheek with his fingertips. Lin closed her eyes and smiled slightly in reciprocation to his touch. It was several moments of quiet before she opened them again to see Dirk's comforting smile, and he spoke again. 'Now, shall we make the most of this last day together? Before this lovely breakfast gets too cold.' And as they drew closer to each other, they both smiled before they kissed.

Chapter 25

On Tuesday, the repair shop had a surprise visitor, Semyon Pavlovsky. Dirk noticed him as he appeared through the main door heading towards Cody, who was finishing a phone order with a supplier by the counter. Dirk saw Semyon talk and flash his identification, which he could instantly see made Cody uncomfortable. Cody then pointed a finger towards Dirk's office, and he quickly made himself look busy as if he hadn't noticed. There was a delay before a gentle rap on the door came, and Dirk looked up, acting mildly surprised. 'Hello,' responded Dirk cheerily.

'Are you the owner, Dirk Davis?' asserted Semyon, his Russian accent evident. He was still wearing an ill-fitting suit with several grease stains on his lapel.

'I am.' Dirk stood up, offering his hand, which Semyon walked forward and took with a firm and solid grip. Dirk gestured him to an empty seat with his other hand, and as Semyon sat down, Dirk noted how his broad frame seemed to dwarf the chair he'd sat upon. 'What can I do for you?'

'My name is Semyon Pavlovsky,' he stated while showing his identification again.

'Interpol?' exclaimed Dirk, feigning shock. 'Have we done something wrong?'

Semyon looked stern as he answered. 'Not that I'm aware of. I just want to ask some questions.'

'Oh, OK.' Dirk poured himself a coffee. 'Do you want some before we start?'

'No. I've not long had one. But thanks.'

'OK.' Dirk sat down, making himself comfortable. 'Let's see if I can help.'

'I can tell from your accent that you're not from around here,' started Semyon.

'New Jersey originally. Came here twenty-odd years ago. Fancied a change of scenery. Your accent's familiar too,' said Dirk. 'Russian?'

'Yes, Mr Davis.'

'Please, call me Dirk. Everyone else does.'

'OK,' replied Semyon. He looked through the office windows at his surroundings before adding, 'Looks like a busy place. Been here long?'

'Over fifteen years. Built up a good reputation in the area, and we've lasted the course.'

Semyon slightly repositioned himself in his chair and asked another question, making Dirk sit up and think. 'Sounds good. You hear of too many businesses that don't make the cut these days. If business is good and keeps you in a comfortable lifestyle, you wouldn't complain.'

Dirk hesitated briefly before answering. 'I just put it down to doing an honest job.'

'No such thing in my line of work,' stated Semyon.

'Excuse me?' replied Dirk sharply, unhappy with the remark.

Semyon interrupted, appearing apologetic. 'My apologies, just thinking out loud. In my line of work, honesty is a rare thing.' But he then added with a cynical smile, 'Your colleague back there seemed a little jumpy.'

Dirk chuckled, trying not to make it sound false. 'That'll be Cody. He gets a little nervous around the authorities. Tough upbringing when he was a kid if you know what I mean.'

'And you've put him on the straight 'n' narrow, I presume?' Semyon looked serious again.

Dirk responded, though he felt Semyon was trying to get the measure of him. 'I saw something that others couldn't. He just needed direction and a way out. I gave him both, that's all. He's done the rest.'

'I see.' Semyon nodded and produced a photo from his jacket's inner pocket before handing it to Dirk. 'Have you seen this man, Mr Davis?' It was a picture of Kirby.

Dirk looked like he was studying it for a moment, but instead, his mind was setting out multiple avenues of responses before answering. 'Yes, he came in about two weeks ago, early on a Saturday morning, was looking for someone called Bruce, and thought this guy was me.' Dirk then gave the photo back to Semyon. 'Should we be concerned?'

'Unfortunately, he was found dead yesterday afternoon. We found your business card in his pocket and just trying to trace his movements before his death.'

Dirk was shocked. 'Christ! What happened? It must be bad if Interpol's involved?'

'Regrettably, I cannot say, Mr Davis. And it's nothing too serious. He wasn't dangerous, just a person of interest to us. Like your colleague, got in with the wrong crowd, that's all.

'Did he say why he thought this Bruce was you, or why he wanted to meet him?'

'Apparently, he was given the description and area by somebody he talked to. When he saw me walking to work, he thought I was the man he was after and followed me here. He seemed disappointed when I told him he'd got the wrong guy, but said something like 'his master wouldn't be happy', which I thought was strange. He didn't tell me why he was looking for him.' Dirk looked sad. 'Shame really, he seemed nice enough, though he stuck out like a sore thumb.'

'Is that dangerous here?' quizzed Semyon.

'Probably not. But every neighbourhood has its thugs. They probably thought he was Mafioso or something, too scared to touch him.'

'I see. Is there anything else that you can remember?'

'Not really, he didn't stay long, but he did come across as a little anxious.'

'OK, thank you,' replied Semyon.

'Oh, is that it? Sorry, I don't feel like I've helped much.'

Semyon stood up. 'Actually, you have. Thank you for your time, Mr Davis, and if you remember anything more or find out who this Bruce is, please don't hesitate to contact me.' He produced a business card and handed it to Dirk, who stood up and accepted it. They shook hands, and Semyon added, 'And if I've any more questions, I'll call you.'

'Yeah, sure, of course,' replied Dirk.

'I'll see myself out, Mr Davis.' Semyon turned and left the office, thanking Cody as he went.

Dirk sat and looked at the card Semyon had given him, tapped it several times on his desk before tossing it into his drawer, somewhat relieved. Several moments later, an exasperated Cody stormed into the office and started to ask questions in quick succession. 'What's going on? Why was Interpol here? Have we been rumbled? What are we going to do now? Are we walking away from the job?'

A calm Willkie followed Cody and responded while putting a hand on his shoulder. 'Give him a chance to breathe, Cody.'

'Cody,' began Dirk, as he stood up slowly. 'Everything's fine. He's just chasing up leads on Kirby. He knew he'd been here, that's all. There's no need to be alarmed. Just relax. Remember, we fobbed Kirby off. Besides, it now seems he's been found dead.'

'*What?*' exploded Cody. Both he and Willkie looked stunned before Cody spoke again. 'What happened, and how?'

'The detective wouldn't say,' stated Dirk.

There was a look of disbelief on Cody's face before he started spluttering an answer.

'How can you be this calm?'

159

'We've dealt with the cops be—'

'*This isn't just the cops, though, is it?*' Cody shouted, his voice edged with panic. An uneasy pause filled the room before Cody sighed as he looked up at the ceiling, before proceeding in a quieter but still anxious tone towards Dirk. 'This was Interpol. If they're interested, I bet the Feds are too. And I bet his death wasn't an accident either. What if we're next?'

'Cody,' Dirk began, trying to be reassuring in his tone. 'If they've got something on us, do you think we'd still be standing here? No. On this job, our activities have only been legit so far. Unless you know something that I don't?' Dirk paused to give Cody a chance to reply, but he kept quiet. 'I didn't think so. And regarding Kirby's death, I don't think it was an accident either. Otherwise, this guy wouldn't have turned up.'

Dirk sat on his desk. 'Look, Cody, tell me. What's the problem? You've never been this jumpy before.'

'Don't know, boss,' mumbled Cody. 'Just not sitting right. Seems we're getting in over our heads.'

'How so?'

'Interpol, for one thing,' Cody stated uneasily.

'OK.' Dirk's tone was still compassionate, but he pressed home with the positive while accentuating his remarks with a gesture of bouncing his right hand slightly with the tips of his thumb and index finger touching as he did so. 'You're right. It's different. Different objectives, challenges and diverse ways to come up with the goods, so each job has been unique.' He then rested his hand back on the desk. 'Try to look at it afresh, with no similarities to our previous jobs. As for other teams, we've never knowingly encountered any before, but it doesn't mean they weren't there. So, take it as we were good enough to get there first. And cops... Yes, we've luckily only dealt with the cops on a handful of occasions, through slight errors we made, but we got away with it. This guy was from Interpol. Just an upmarket cop, as far as I'm concerned. He won't find anything on us, and as I said before, he's investigating Kirby, not us.' Dirk crossed his arms as he prepared himself to now confront Cody. 'I have to say that I'm concerned, but I think I understand. I need you at your best, Cody. If you're unhappy, the question is, do you want to continue with the job? Don't answer me now. Just go have a think and let me know.'

Cody looked awkwardly towards Dirk, nodded, and walked out of the office, closely followed by Willkie, who gave Dirk a knowing wink and nod before closing the door behind him.

It was near closing time when Cody re-entered the office. He'd been quiet all day, obviously deep in his thoughts. 'Are you OK?' Dirk asked sympathetically.

Cody was hesitant before responding, 'Just want to say sorry for earlier.'

'There's no need to apologise, Cody. You know I'd rather have you all speak your minds. You wanna talk?' Cody nodded. 'Close the door, sit down. What's on your mind?'

As Cody took a seat, he began. 'Just struggling to come to terms with what's been happening to us, that's all. We've never been threatened at gunpoint, our cars tracked, and this superstitious mumbo jumbo frustrates me. It's been getting on top of me.' Cody sounded like he was embarrassed by his statement.

'You wouldn't be human if you didn't have your concerns. And truthfully, it worried me—'

'It did?!' interrupted Cody, sounding amazed.

'Come on, Cody. I plan every job in detail to ensure we're ahead of the curve. Of course, I don't like surprises. I'm going to get edgy when strange stuff happens. But I'm getting used to it. I'm preparing myself for each challenge, just one step at a time. That way, I can overcome each new obstacle and plan around it.'

'Oh, OK.' Cody seemed to be buoyed slightly by Dirk's response.

'Good. But please do me a favour.'

'What's that?'

'Talk to us. Discussing and sharing your worries is not a weakness, neither does it make you less manly. I'll never think less of you because you have concerns, Cody. We can get through this, but we must work together.'

'OK, boss.' Cody stood up and was about to walk out of the office when he spoke again. 'I still want in, boss. If that's all right?'

'Of course. I'd rather have no one else. Not only are you my best driver, you're my friend.'

Cody smiled as he left the office, and no matter how

slight it looked, it was warming to Dirk. But a few minutes later, he began to feel the pangs of guilt. Dirk hardly discussed his problems and telling Cody to share his concerns made him a hypocrite. He'd also been struggling mentally with everything that had been going on. Dirk just had a lot of practice of masking his thoughts and feelings. Deep down, he believed the same as Cody, but he didn't want to tell him that. If they were going through with the job, he needed him at the top of his game.

Chapter 26

With the twenty-sixth decided, following Sharyn's advice, on July twentieth, Dirk got his team together to finalise their plan to target the museum.

He started the meeting. 'Willkie, have you decided where we're getting the truck?'

'Yes, I've decided to steal the truck we've been using for the practice. With what I've seen, the security to the rental yard is pretty poor.' Willkie looked at Sharyn. 'Sharyn, if I give you the rental company, can you double-check and make sure they're not having a security upgrade within the next week?'

'Shouldn't be an issue. I'll do it after this. But I've never understood why you don't hire one under a fake ID or steal one and swap plates,' replied Sharyn.

It was Dirk who responded. 'On jobs like this, Sharyn, whatever we use, we must have minimal contact with the vehicle. As you probably know, most of all commercial vehicles now have trackers, which are situated on the OBD2 port under the steering wheel. Being linked to the city's wi-fi network, recording in real time, our movements can be linked to traffic cameras.

'Keeping the tracker running gives the authorities

insight into our movements before the heist, and disabling it too early lets the owner know something's wrong and they'll alert the authorities, making our job that bit harder. Now I know you're great at what you can do, but to me it's unnecessary work, when we need you focused in other areas. So, we take, we use, and then dispose of it as quick as possible.'

Willkie continued, 'Hiring means we need to hide it somewhere leading up to the heist. We can't use the repair shop for obvious reasons, and we don't have access to any other premises within the city.

'When we take the vehicle, we'll swap the plates as you said, but as I see it, Cody is now familiar with the vehicle. Choosing an unfamiliar vehicle now, even if it's sound, and as good as Cody is, runs the extra risk of damaging the pieces. Plus, if we do have to rush to dispose of it, our DNA can be masked with us hiring it.

'Ah, I see now,' Sharyn replied.

'Excellent,' Dirk said. 'We'll aim to take the vehicle by 22:15 at the latest. According to Sharyn, there're no other deliveries, and we're expected at the museum at 23:30. They've given us an hour's leeway on each side of the booking time. We'll be refused entry if we arrive too early or too late.

'Cody, after we've taken the truck and climbed in the back, you'll drive to the museum and present the guards with the documentation Sharyn's created for the fake delivery. We'll only expect the one guard on the door on the shift, so when they open the vehicle on the bay, Willkie and

I will surprise them with the stun batons. We'll move on to the security hub and do the same to the remaining guards, where we'll tie and gag them as usual. And Cody…' Dirk couldn't help but give a mischievous grin. 'Remember to tap your foot when the rear door is being opened. We don't want a repeat of Montreal, do we?'

'Will do, boss,' responded Cody, smirking back, shaking his head, embarrassed.

Dirk turned to Sharyn. 'You'll deal with the tech in the hub, deleting the security footage, disabling their cameras and alarms, etc.' Sharyn nodded as Dirk looked back towards Willkie and Codie. 'The rest of us will lure any remaining guards if they're still on their rounds and stun them before placing them with the other two. We must secure the hub before moving on, understood?' The two men responded with a nod.

Dirk continued. 'Once secured, we'll proceed to the equipment stores along the corridor and take the items Lin mentioned for moving the statues. We'll use the elevator to move the equipment to the hall where the statues will be waiting for us, then package them the best we can before carefully sending them down one at a time in the lift to our awaiting vehicle, where they'll be secured before we leave. I'll then make the call to our employer on this phone.' Dirk held up the phone Garrick had given him. 'And once we've been given the drop-off point, I'll call Mbundu on the phone he's giving me and let him know. We'll then proceed to the meet, where I guess they'll inspect the statues before we get paid and are allowed to leave. I also think they'll requisition the truck to save handling and damaging the statues. Remember, always wear your masks and gloves.

'I expect all hell will break loose when Mbundu turns up. I'm hoping he'll honour our agreement and wait until we're paid before he kicks off, but I'm anticipating he won't be asking nicely, so be prepared to run at the drop of a hat. We'll split up and meet at our rendezvous. Is that understood?'

They all answered 'yes'.

'We'll follow the normal procedure for lying low for a couple of months and then decide what we do after. Any questions?' They all responded with shakes of their heads, but Dirk noticed that Cody was holding something back. Their eyes made contact, but Cody quickly turned away. Dirk left it alone, not wanting to place undue pressure on him.

He continued, 'I'll make my way to Mbundu's bar tomorrow night to pick up the phone. We'll have one more team brief here on Friday and relax for the weekend. Stay focused, and above all, stay alert. OK?' They all nodded, then settled down for the evening.

Chapter 27

irk had been mulling over the information Mbundu had given him since the meeting, so it was with trepidation that he'd travelled to the Jamaican bar the following evening.

The parking lot was small and unkempt, and the cars all looked like they'd seen better days, as did the bar. The shiplap boards and surrounding vegetation gave it a rickety appearance. At the same time, wisps of mist, extending from the nearby canal, hovered gently, hugging the base of the building and creeping across the parking lot. The backdrop of the nighttime sky and the looming warehouse development around it made it look as if it had been plucked out of a horror movie.

Dirk noted two men on the balcony of the two-storey bar, and upon noticing him, one flicked away his cigarette and went into an adjacent room on the upper level. The other remained, staring at Dirk as he walked towards the bar.

Hearing the activity from within, he became hesitant before entering, drawing in a deep breath before opening the door, trying to act relaxed. He was greeted by a haze of tobacco smoke hovering around each group of people within. All were of Caribbean descent. Those men around Dirk's age or older played dominoes on tables made from wooden barrels, while the younger generation gathered around the pool tables or stood at the bar talking. The internal décor was much more maintained and cleaner than the outside, with wooden cladding on the walls and furnishings that would make the inhabitants feel at home.

The door groaned loudly as it closed behind him, and immediately all activity within the bar ceased. All eyes were now looking in Dirk's direction, scrutinising the newcomer with probing gazes. He saw the man from the balcony outside, now on the landing overlooking the bar, leaning on the handrails. Dirk felt awkward, imagining Mbundu laughing and stating how a spirit caused the door to creak as an alarm, but he closed his eyes, took in another sharp intake of breath, and banished this notion. He looked around, found the ageing jukebox Mbundu had mentioned, and walked towards it. He used a finger to guide through the list of songs while his other hand pulled out a coin.

He found J13; the song listed was Peter Tosh, 'Vampire'. He placed the coin into the machine and selected the 'J', '1' and '3' buttons, then turned to wait with bated breath for the clientele's reaction. He could hear the jukebox select the chosen record, and the tension in the room was becoming heavy with anticipation. The connecting sound of the needle to vinyl could be heard, piercing the silence, and the tune began with a baying hound and the rattling of chains before erupting into song.

Dirk didn't know what the tune was a signal for, but it seemed to have the desired effect as they reverted to their previous actions. Only the man overlooking the bar continued to hold eye contact with him before Dirk realised the barman was also trying to get his attention, so he walked over to speak to him.

'I presume you're Tristan. Your boss told me that you'd have something for me.'

'Aye, I av. Drink?'

'I'm fine, thanks. I won't stay long. I can see you're busy.'

Tristan shrugged, nonplussed by the response, before speaking again. 'Do ya av a date?'

'Yes, this coming Tuesday night.'

Tristan nodded, then looked to his left. The man from upstairs had just finished positioning himself at the end of the bar, nodded at Tristan, before looking at Dirk. Tristan reached under the counter and pulled out a dated smartphone. 'Boss said to call him when ya av di items. E'll be ready.'

'Thanks,' replied Dirk, looking at the phone before making an acknowledgement towards Tristan and placing it into his jacket pocket. Dirk turned around and walked towards the exit, noting that some younger men watched him leave. However, he stayed focused, not looking back, giving no reason to provoke the lions as he departed their den.

Dirk took several deep breaths in the cooler, cleaner air while walking toward his vehicle. He'd only been inside a matter of minutes, but he could smell the tobacco smoke that clung to his clothes lifting into the air.

He sighed with relief when he got into his car before speaking to himself. 'Well, that was easier than I thought.' He looked around before driving off, seeing that two men were still looking at him from the main entrance. Dirk raised his hand in acknowledgement before he drove away.

On the way home, he constantly checked his rearview mirror for tails, and took a couple of impromptu turns to ensure he wasn't being followed; once satisfied, he headed for the nearest gas station to meet his team as planned.

The team worked like a well-oiled machine. While Dirk filled up, Sharyn jumped into the passenger seat and began looking at the phone he'd collected, while Willkie went over the vehicle looking for any trackers. Cody was in his car in an eatery opposite, keeping an eye out for tails while he sat eating a burger.

Willkie found a tracker at the rear, and he showed it to Dirk, who gave it the once over before nodding, giving the signal for him to dispose of it onto another vehicle. Willkie chose a taxi that had parked up nearby, and while the driver was paying for his gas, he slipped it onto it before heading into the building himself to pay for Dirk's gas.

Sharyn finished working on the phone when Dirk got into the car.

'Found anything?' he asked.

'Just a couple of things,' she said. 'I've disabled the location service for starters and found a tracking app, which I've uninstalled. I presume you've not been given a charger, so I've also turned the phone off. We don't want a flat battery, do we? But other than that, the phone's clean.' Sharyn handed it back to Dirk before asking, 'Did Willkie find any trackers?'

'Yes. He's dealt with it. It's a different model to what we found before, so I'm guessing it wasn't Mbundu last time.'

Two minutes later, Willkie got into the back of the car.

Dirk signalled to Cody and started the engine before leaving. Willkie asked how the meet went, and he responded while looking at Willkie in the rearview mirror. 'I went in, gave them the date, and got given a phone. That's it.' Dirk glanced at Sharyn, who was looking concerned. 'Don't worry, nothing else happened.' He smiled before adding, 'Just currently suffering from information overload, that's all.' Sharyn smiled back warmly, her support giving Dirk some welcome reassurance.

Chapter 28

O n Friday twenty-second, the crew were having their final team brief on Dirk's boat, going through the plans, and ensuring that everyone remembered their part in precise detail. Afterwards, they reviewed Dirk's meeting with Mbundu two weeks earlier, and Cody was still sceptical. Dirk reminded him that no matter what they thought, the beliefs had to be accounted for, for that was the driving goal of the other two teams. It was Willkie who backed Dirk up, reminding Cody of his own Amerindian beliefs. 'Yeah, but zombies? Come on. It's just voodoo mumbo jumbo,' Cody snapped. 'It's a tool for delivering fear, trying to scare us off the job.'

'I agree with you, Cody,' replied Dirk. 'But you can say that about any other religion. And you're missing the point. Don't get hung up over believing it or not. What I'm trying to say, and rather badly, is that if, and I stress the *if*, we meet one of these other teams on the night, they may throw strange stuff at us, so be prepared. And as far as scaring us off the job, I don't believe that for a moment. For whatever reason, Mbundu doesn't want to risk getting the statues himself. He wants someone else to do the dirty work.'

'And what do we do if he tries to take them before?' enquired Sharyn.

'Especially when they're going to have guns, and we won't,' Cody retorted.

Dirk sighed before answering. 'I've given it some thought, and I must admit, my mind's been in overdrive with no decisive answers. At the moment, much of it relies on luck, which I'm not used to. The options I see are these. We walk away now and treat it as a failure… and while our fence will understand, I think Mbundu will want some form of compensation. I thought we could get the cops involved, but that also runs the risk of getting caught. We could ask our fence for help, to somehow take him out of the equation, but I believe his cut will be substantially bigger, or worse, we'll owe them a debt of gratitude. Now, we've spent a lot of time trying to be as independent as possible, and I don't want to start doing jobs for free—'

'Makes you think whether this meeting with Mbundu was worth it,' vented Cody sarcastically; his attitude was like that of a grouchy teenager.

Dirk stopped, lost for words. His decision of authority and logic was questioned and not debated for the first time. He began to feel nauseous as his heart and breathing increased rapidly, the onset of panic setting in. Self-doubt washed over him like a tsunami, and he now found himself frozen, not knowing what to say or do next. Cody was relentless with his words, but it had just become a torrent of noise to Dirk, whose eyes started to flit around the room. He searched for a focal point that would help him regain his composure from the now self-judgemental mind, his own worst critique. He found it when he heard Sharyn's voice.

'Cody.' Her tone was that of anger. Cody averted his gaze, his arms and legs now firmly crossed, knowing full well that he'd stepped out of line.

Dirk rested against the table behind him. 'No, no, Sharyn. He's right,' responded Dirk solemnly.

Sharyn looked at Dirk. 'No. I'm not having him talk to you like that.'

'But we deserve an explanation,' replied Willkie, his tone measured, holding the air of mutual respect. Sharyn turned quickly to verbally round on Willkie as well, but seeing Willkie's sincerity in his expression, she quickly understood that he was right, and her shoulders slumped in defeat.

'Yes. You're right, Willkie.' Dirk, dejected, stood up to face his critics. 'Yes, I must confess, I expected a lot more information from my meeting with Mbundu, but while it gave me some answers, it's mainly given me more questions.

'And to answer your question, Cody, no, it wasn't worth it. I handled the meeting naively. I wanted answers to understand what we're up against, to eliminate any chance of surprise that we might encounter. I went in expecting hard facts but came out with ghost stories. I arrived predicting a request, a small favour in return, information on his competitors, or money. I didn't anticipate the demand for the statues. All I can say is

I'm sorry. I made an error. One that's put your lives at risk, and I don't know how to avoid it.' Dirk looked at the floor despondently, his mind racing ahead, relentless, uncontrollable, rapidly flitting between different scenarios, trying to get out of the mess he'd put them in. Finally, he closed his eyes and tried to focus again on one thought, a lifeline to prevent the overwhelming clouding of his mind that was mentally drowning him.

Tension now descended on the room. Cody's body language was still defensive, but he could not look Dirk in the eye, emotionally guilty for what he was putting his mentor through. Sharyn was looking and feeling sorry for Dirk, longing to put an arm around him, comfort him, tell him not to worry, but feared it would make him feel ridiculed or in some way less manly.

It was Willkie who broke the tension, his voice calming to those around him. 'I don't need an apology, boss, and I've always known that you've had nothing but our welfare at heart. What's done is done. We can't rewind the clock and undo the situation we find ourselves in, but the question is, where do we go from here? I've known you long enough to know that you sometimes struggle with piecing the mental puzzle together, and I can see that in your eyes now. But what you think is your greatest weakness is also your greatest strength. Yes, this is our most challenging job yet. We're facing challenges that we've never faced before. But we can't know everything, boss. And yes, this is probably the biggest mess we've been in. But we've always looked to you to come up with the ideas, and we've succeeded. So, let that strength come to the fore now, Dirk, like it's done on so many occasions before. You can do this.' Willkie looked at all of them in turn. '*We* can do this.'

Dirk looked at Willkie and blinked several times, beginning to control his thoughts.

Cody momentarily looked towards Dirk. 'Sorry, Dirk,' he said solemnly. Dirk just responded by closing his eyes, gently shaking his head, and lifting his right hand in acknowledgement. Sharyn was still fighting the urge to hug Dirk and was now sitting on her hands.

Willkie kept a watchful eye on Dirk to let his mind settle before asking him, 'Let's forget about Mbundu for the moment. Dirk, what do we need to do to get the job done?'

'Well…' Dirk took a sharp intake of breath. 'We must go into the museum, get past the security, steal two heavy statues…' he began to tail off as he said the next word, 'undamaged.' They could see Dirk's eyes narrow slightly, ignoring everyone else in the room before he started again. 'That's it. Undamaged.' And he looked at Willkie. 'Thanks.' Willkie just smiled politely and shrugged.

With renewed vigour, Dirk started to express his thoughts. 'If we consider what Mbundu says as accurate, then all the teams are after these statues because they're some sort of keys to the underworld, and they're only of any use if they're not damaged. If that's the case, we may have the upper hand.' The team had had their curiosity piqued. 'As long as we're first to the statues, we can threaten to damage the pieces or use them as a defensive 'wall', so to

177

speak. They won't want to risk damaging them,' declared Dirk.

'Or they could just shoot us,' stated Cody. His negativity hadn't improved, and it wasn't helping the situation either.

'But it's a lifeline,' stated Willkie firmly, staring hard at Cody. Then looking kindly back at Dirk, said, 'What about the fence option you mentioned? If we don't ask, we won't know for sure.'

Dirk pondered before responding, rubbing his chin with his left hand in the process. Willkie had a point. 'OK. I'll ask, and I'll let you know.' The room briefly went silent again, and it seemed an age before Willkie spoke, this time taking charge of the meeting in a sympathetic tone.

'Before you call this meeting closed. I just want to say some things. With all this tension, we've forgotten some of Dirk's rules.' Dirk and Willkie looked at each other, with Dirk giving a curious expression, wondering what Willkie was going to say. 'We've let the money rule our train of thought. If we can't do this, we walk away now. If we damage the pieces, you call 'walk away', and if we get held at gunpoint, we let them have the statues and walk away. Yes, our rep may take a knock, but we'll bounce back. We won't get paid, but I'd rather be alive than dead. And I'd rather be sitting here, calling you friends than leaving loathing each other, all because we couldn't get the extra buck. If the statues are that important to someone else, they're welcome to them.'

Dirk managed a smile before Willkie continued. 'Now I think we should stop for the night. We have the plan nailed, so let's open some chilled beers from the fridge and relax for a bit.'

Dirk began to feel at ease with himself once more. Willkie's pep talk had helped put his mind into a better place.

Chapter 29

On the evening of the twenty-sixth, Dirk was suiting up for the heist, his coveralls fresh out of their packet. The TV was on, playing the cult film *Highlander*. He'd seen it countless times before, but this time it was just background noise while he sipped water frequently. A rucksack was by the door, holding equipment and new clothes for when the job was completed. Work had carried on as normal, but he couldn't help feeling a little tension in the air when they spoke because of the events of Friday's meeting.

He felt the butterflies in the pit of his stomach, more noticeable than usual, but he took this as a good sign. It meant he wasn't being complacent. And so started his ritual of preparing for a job, triple-checking everything needed while drinking more water, with periods of relaxation exercises. When it was time, he turned off the TV before heading out of the door.

At this late hour, the air outside was still and warm. Dirk leisurely looked around as he got into his car to see if anyone else was about, but he was the sole person on the street. He drove to the rendezvous.

He spent most of the journey ruminating, reliving

what happened at Friday's meeting, continually over-thinking how he could've done things differently before self-doubt started to creep in; would anybody be there at the rendezvous? When he arrived, he was relieved to find they'd all turned up, suited in coveralls and already wearing vinyl gloves.

Dirk nodded appreciatively as he approached them. And upon reaching them, he began to speak. 'Thank you for turning up. Before we go, are there any final questions?' He listened to their replies of 'No,' sensing a touch of uneasiness in the air while noticing Cody couldn't look him in the eye. He also surmised from Willkie's eye-line, looking directly at Cody, that words had been said prior to his arrival. Dirk carefully put his rucksack down before speaking to them again.

'I've made a decision. Whatever happens tonight, this will be my last job.' He had to quickly put up his hand to prevent Willkie interrupting. 'Look, I know after Friday's meeting that your confidence in me has been knocked.' The others conveyed a look of unease towards each other, but Dirk carried on regardless. 'We'll go ahead tonight and do what we've always done. We'll take each step as it comes, and if it gets too hot, we'll walk away and come home safe. Is everyone OK with that?' The atmosphere seemed to relax a little as they all nodded silently.

'Now then,' continued Dirk. 'If we're all ready, can you remember the plan?'

'Yes,' came the response, their tones a little more eager than before.

'Good. Let's do this.' And they headed to the rental yard.

Chapter 30

illkie had chosen his vehicle rental well. It was as if they wanted to be broken into. The cameras were easily disabled before entering the premises. It took them less than five minutes to steal their new mode of transport, and replace the plates as planned.

Dirk, Willkie and Sharyn stood in the back, keeping a wide stance, steadying themselves as it gently swayed. When they arrived, they felt the vehicle slow before there was a slight jolt as the brakes were applied, making them lose their balance momentarily. 'That was unexpected,' said Willkie quietly to Dirk.

'I expect Cody's tense,' replied Dirk reassuringly.

After hearing the cab door slam, several nervous minutes went by, with only the rumble of the engine ticking over keeping them company before Willkie spoke quietly to Dirk. 'I didn't want to say anything in front of Cody earlier, but did you speak to our fence about helping us?'

'Yes,' Dirk whispered. 'He said we're on our own.'

The vehicle wobbled slightly, and they heard the door slam again as someone got back into the cab, leaving all in the back hopeful it was still Cody. Then, listening to the distinctive bleeping as the vehicle was reversed, they steadied themselves as they moved backwards.

The bleeping began to echo, and Dirk knew they were close to the bay doors of the museum. The vehicle then shuddered as it stopped before the engine was turned off. Shortly afterwards, they heard the cab door shut again.

The three of them tensed, with Dirk and Willkie creeping to the rear, stun batons at the ready, waiting for the door to open. It was a couple of minutes before they heard movement on the other side as the bay door was opened, followed by the tail lift of their vehicle being lowered.

As the roller door slowly began to lift, a beam of light appeared across the base of the door, cutting the darkness within their confined space. But instead of the four shafts of shadow they expected from two pairs of legs, there were only two. Dirk and Willkie quickly glanced at each other, and Dirk instinctively squatted to get a better look as the door was still being opened. He saw Cody's boot tapping away, the signal that it was him, but at the other end of the room, he noticed what looked like a guard slumped against the wall. Dirk then stood up and put his baton away. Willkie, looking at Dirk, followed in response as Cody's torso and then his head came into view.

'What happened?' Dirk asked Cody.

'Beats me. I found him already like it. The other two guards are dead in the security room as well. The door over there was also open wide.' Cody pointed to the personnel door next to the roller shutter doors before anxiously adding, 'Do we walk away?'

'Not yet. Let's investigate first,' replied Dirk, then looking at Willkie and Sharyn, he asked them, 'You two go to the security room, check it out and see if the alarm has been triggered.' He looked back at Cody. 'You and I will check this guard before looking for the equipment we need to move the statues.'

Willkie and Sharyn did as they were asked, while Dirk bent down to look at the guard in front of him, feeling his neck for a pulse through gloved hands, and was relieved to find one. But he also noticed blood trickling from the guard's mouth and nose, and the tell-tale signs of bruising had begun to appear around the jawline, which Dirk could now make out was broken.

'What do we do, boss?' a still anxious Cody asked as he noticed a spider run along the wall, presumedly disturbed when Dirk touched the guard.

Willkie came back. 'The alarm hasn't been triggered. But we need to show you something.'

Dirk silently nodded, took the security guard's comms unit and security card before standing up and heading towards the security room with Willkie and Cody.

Chapter 31

hen Dirk walked into the security area, there were three doors on the left-hand side of the room and the expected bank of flat-screen monitors to the right, only half working. The two-man security system was in the centre, looking towards the screens. He could also see on the wall opposite an electronic floor plan with the various floors of the museum; each room and hall named and numbered.

Within the room, two lifeless guards lay on the floor. No examination of the bodies was necessary; it was easy to see they were both dead. One at Sharyn's feet beside the chair he must have been sitting on, his neck snapped, leaving the head at a sickening angle, his eyes staring vacantly towards the wall. The other was by the door where Dirk stood, and it looked like she'd been trying to flee. Her left arm was broken, but the back of her head was irreparably damaged; a bloody pool had gathered on the floor around her and was now dark and coagulating.

Dirk bent down to each body and gently closed their eyes, took their comms units as his plan dictated, just not from unconscious guards as intended. He handed a set to Willkie and Cody each while keeping the last one for himself.

Dirk stood next to Sharyn, who looked uncomfortable standing beside the guard's body. 'What've we got? Willkie said the alarm's not been triggered.'

Sharyn took in a deep breath for composure before answering. 'Correct. Any alarm triggered would have lit up on the electronic map over there. Whoever was here has disabled the security leading to and including the exhibit hall where the statues are housed, even wiping the camera footage, so I'm somewhat redundant. The question now is, who are we up against, and how far ahead are they?'

'And how many are there?' Dirk added. 'Can it be fixed?'

'It would take too long,' replied Sharyn.

Cody repeated his question from a few moments ago. 'What do we do, boss?' He was visibly agitated by what he was seeing.

'We continue as planned,' replied Dirk.

Cody snapped back a response. 'Really? After seeing all this?'

'For the time being, yes,' said Dirk.

Willkie, who'd been checking out the three rooms, interrupted them. 'Looking at the armoury, all weapons are accounted for, so none have been taken.'

'Thanks,' responded Dirk before turning back to Cody to continue their conversation. 'Look at it this way. Whoever this is, they're not using guns, plus they don't know we're here, so I want to continue. But if the rest of you want out, just say now.'

Dirk looked at each friend in turn. Willkie responded

with 'I'm in.' Sharyn nodded confidently. Cody shook his head in disbelief before responding in exasperation. 'OK, OK. Let's get on with it.'

Dirk firmly placed his hand on Cody's shoulder to give him some form of reassurance before adding, 'Right then. There's nothing else we can do here. The equipment should be in the storage room down the corridor. Let's collect it, move on to the elevator and above all else, stay alert.'

Chapter 32

he elevator came to a measured stop, and the doors slid open, revealing the deserted main hall. Dirk and Sharyn leant out of the confines of the elevator, checking to see if the area was clear before leaving the safety it provided. The dim security lighting added to the shaded, unnerving quietness of the hall; even Sue the T-Rex had an eerie if not menacing look about her.

Once they were both satisfied the coast was clear, they signalled to Cody and Willkie, who moved the equipment out into the open, the rumbling of the wheels reverberating around the once noiseless hall. They paused as the doors of the elevator closed behind them before nodding and prepared to move to the room housing the statues.

'*Freeze!*'

Dirk spun round to see police officers, FBI agents and Semyon Pavlovsky appearing from behind the exhibits in the hall, handguns held towards them. Flashlights from the officers flickered between the team, momentarily blinding him.

It was like watching roaches coming out of the woodwork. A cacophony of shouts and orders quickly ensued, blending with the radio chatter as the bright torches danced around the hall. Dirk looked up and saw armed officers leaning over the rail of the upper level, aiming weapons in their direction. The officers were closing in and surrounded them.

Dirk looked down at his feet and accepted defeat. He looked up towards one of his captors and raised his hands. To his immediate right, Cody did the same.

There was shouting behind them, Dirk looked around to see Willkie resisting arrest and being assaulted by two cops. Obscenities were being thrown between the three men, and after a scuffle, Willkie was put flat on his back, though he kept the men at arm's length with pure strength, his mask hiding gritted teeth.

Dirk was about to bark a command for Willkie to cease but was stopped dead in his tracks when he heard Sharyn's bloodcurdling scream. He whirled around to see her writhing on the floor, trying to defend herself against the onslaught of kicks and baton hits from the officers surrounding her. With her headgear already removed, tears streamed down her face reflecting her terror. Another agent approached her, preparing to use the butt of his shotgun to knock her out and stop her frightened shrieking.

Witnessing Sharyn's trauma broke Dirk's resolve. He felt his rage boil over and he shouted, 'Leave her alone!' He leapt to her defence, running over to pull the officers off her. He didn't get far before he felt the dull pain from a baton connect with the back of his left leg. It was enough to drop him to his knees. The agent who was going to silence Sharyn now stood in front of Dirk and proceeded to press the shotgun's muzzle against his forehead. The firearm's metal was cold to the touch, and the agent applied further pressure with the weapon, pressing home his advantage before saying, 'Don't move, pal. Don't even breathe.'

Dirk looked up, staring at the agent intently, the anger in his eyes evident, and the agent used this to his advantage. 'What's the matter? Don't like us roughing up your girlfriend?' He began to laugh.

Semyon Pavlovsky stepped in. 'Enough, Garfield. Back off.'

Garfield's smile disappeared, and he glared at Semyon before stepping back as ordered, but not before giving one final nudge with the muzzle to remind Dirk who was in charge.

Semyon stepped forward. 'Now then, let's see who we have here. Take off your headgear… real slow now.'

Dirk and Sharyn's eyes met, and for that one brief moment, it was like they were the only ones present in the cavernous hall, both feeling helpless to aid the other. All around them, time seemed slow compared to their feelings and thoughts racing for each other. It was then Dirk watched Sharyn mime, 'I love you.' His heart sank, making his posture slump, and he had to steady himself on the floor with one hand. Had he really been so blind?

He was snapped back to his reality when Semyon reminded him again to take off his headgear, but the tone was now more threatening. He looked at Semyon, tears now welling up in his eyes, and he solemnly nodded. He raised his hands slowly as ordered but looked again at

Sharyn. Her eyes were wide in dread, and she slowly shook her head, miming the words, 'No, no, no.' Dirk looked down to escape her gaze and closed his eyes.

He took off his headgear piece by piece. The din of the agents, alongside the added distress of Sharyn and Willkie, was unbearable for Dirk to hear. And even with his eyes now tightly shut, he still felt Sharyn's eyes tugging at his soul. It was all becoming too much for him to bear. He finally started to remove the hood over his head, expecting an onslaught of officers to force him to the ground and rough him up at any moment.

When the hood slipped from Dirk's crown, a yell from Cody and a scream from Sharyn were made in unison. '*Nooo.*' Then… silence.

Chapter 33

irk opened his eyes; the agents and officers had vanished. He looked around in disbelief while wiping away the tears, trying to ascertain what had just happened. Looking towards Sharyn, she was exactly where he last saw her, lying on the floor, sobbing uncontrollably, her eyes tightly shut. He softly called to her. 'Sharyn… Are you OK?'

She opened her eyes wide and stared at Dirk, not expecting him to be there. Then she slipped and staggered towards him and fell into his arms, bowling him over onto his back.

'I thought you were dead.' She planted a kiss on his lips before hugging and squeezing him tightly.

'What do you mean dead?! I wasn't the one being beaten by cops.'

Sharyn released her constricting hold on him and leant back, staring at him again but with a confused look. 'Cops?! What cops?! The room was infested with spiders. Mbundu was here with his goons. He stood behind you and placed a black widow into a sack before putting it over your head. He was going to kill you.'

'Spiders?' Cody asked before Dirk could respond. 'Dirk

was about to get his head blown away by the Mafia!'

Dirk became confused and turned to look at Willkie, who was sitting on the floor, looking down, hands together, his arms resting on his knees. 'What did you see?' enquired Dirk.

'I fought the wendigo,' he replied, though he had some uncertainty in his voice as he continued, 'it felt so real. And exactly as the legends I was told.' They became quiet while they struggled to comprehend what had just happened.

A loud, methodical clapping broke the silence and echoed around the hall. They looked around, startled, to see a figure slowly stepping out of the shadows. Unsure if this was real, they looked at each other for support. With only their survival instincts guiding them, they got up. They began to move closer together, like an exhausted herd of bison, defending themselves against a pack of hungry wolves.

'Bravo, bravo.' The figure's tone was condescending by design as he stopped clapping and stood still, now bathed in the soft glow of one of the security lights in the hall. He removed a walking cane from under his right armpit with black-gloved hands and its tip created a sharp 'tap' that resonated as it connected with the marble floor. Resting both hands upon its silver orbed handle, six other figures slowly stepped out of the gloom and stood on either side of him.

Dirk looked across the figures first. Five were dressed in drab hooded cloaks, their physical appearance masked from view. The sixth was a female, and with what Dirk could see, she was Asian and short in stature, dressed in a predominantly black sari with black trousers. A thin veil covered part of her face from her nose down, and with her brown skin, the whites of her eyes were framed, presenting her piercing gaze. Dirk could also see on her clothing some form of thin, intricate, swirling gold design that reflected partially in the lighting. Her hands were each hidden up the opposing arm's sleeve, which, unlike the rest of the sari, were loose-fitting and led to extra-wide cuffs.

Dirk finally cast his eyes over the leading member of their group. A tall, slender male dressed in a smart suit, his posture was that of superiority. His hair was silver, and he had narrow facial features leading to a pointed chin. The eyes gave away a dangerous intellect that dissected all information they perceived. Dirk recognised him as Quillon, so he deduced the female was Anita.

There was a brief standoff between the two groups, all weighing their options. It was Dirk who spoke first.

'I take it we've you to thank for that charade back there. And for the guards being out of commission?'

'Guards, yes, but the *charade* as you called it,' replied Quillon, shaking his head before giving a malevolent chuckle. He continued, 'That? No, that was a spell trap, housing what looked like a fear incantation linked to this hall. Ingenious by design, even by my standards. I was looking at a way to circumvent it, but hearing you arrive by the lift, we held back, and I watched you walk straight into it, triggering it for me. Luckily for me, we had to use the stairs.' He gestured to his entourage with his cane. 'So, to you, I give my thanks.' Quillon mocked them by giving a little bow with a flurry of his wrist.

Cody, frustrated, tried to put scorn to Quillon's reply. 'Spell. What do you mean spell…' Dirk quieted him with a firm hand on his shoulder. They looked at each other, and Dirk shook his head slowly. It was enough to halt Cody's rant before it went any further, but Quillon quickly countered with his riposte.

'Oh, Mr Davis. Don't stop him on my account. I'd love to hear what the young man has to offer to counter my claim.' Dirk looked straight at Quillon. 'Yes, Mr Davis, I know who you are. 'Now, I admit, you covered your tracks exceptionally well, and Anita here found extraordinarily little about you. But it was not until you took off your headgear and I saw your face that I recognised it from a photo that Anita took of you. Mbundu was indeed correct. You are the talented Bruce the antiquity thief.' He gave an annoying, all-knowing smile.

Dirk smiled back and replied, 'Well done, Quillon.'

'Ah, touché,' he replied, his smile fading into nonexistence. But regaining some composure, he double tapped his cane on the ground in the way of appreciation before changing the subject. 'Before we go any further, I will first answer your colleagues' questions.'

Quillon turned his focus back to Cody. 'As I was going to say before your outburst. 'I knew an incantation was attached to this hall by the various markers situated around this entrance.' He started to wave the tip of his cane in the general direction of the doorway. 'Unfortunately, I cannot

196

show you from here due to the poor lighting, but trust me, they are there.

'Now, from my extensive knowledge of the occult, I knew its parameters were for one use, and that it had only been placed here recently. But could not discern the type of spell being used until you haplessly walked into it, where I deduced it was a fear spell, which uses its own fiendish nature by your own invention, and to great effect. Though I am unsure why it didn't last longer. These types of spells only normally end when death has been reached.

'You see, your own terrors are shown in such reality that whatever you, and more importantly, what those around you do, is so believable you will eventually suffer heart failure. That is why the squirm of the lady's fear was deemed to be something else by Mr Davis.'

Dirk tried to interrupt, but Quillon was having none of it and stopped him by raising his hand and giving a steely glare. It was like watching a mother scolding her child.

'As I'd just said to your boss here, he has done a grand job of covering his, and consequently, your tracks on who you all are. But I could surmise by watching what unfolded before my eyes and listening to you all in the aftermath, the young lady has an immobilising fear of spiders and losing Mr Davis.' Quillon briefly placed a finger to his lips and pointed at Cody. 'I presume you have a fear of the Mafioso via a double-cross.' He looked at Dirk. 'Now your boss here has a fear of getting caught, which is natural in your line of work, but it also appears he has a weakness for the young lady.' Cody looked at Sharyn and Dirk, arching his eyebrows in surprise. Sharyn averted her eyes down to the floor while Dirk stared at Quillon. 'Don't be surprised, young man. I don't think even Mr Davis knew by his body language until the fear spell was triggered. But the main prize goes to your Native American friend over there. He mentioned the word wendigo. Which is fascinating. The wendigo, you see, is a cannibalistic beast with a tall, lean, almost skeletal physique. Dark, mottled grey skin, with snow-white hair and ice-blue eyes. The beast is always hungry, looking to hunt those rapacious in nature...' Quillon paused as he noticed the confused look on Cody's face, and he rolled his eyes upwards in despair before shaking his head. 'Rapacious implies greedy, you understand now, young man? Anyway, that leads me to believe that your Native American colleague feels guilty over his illegal activities and fears that the wendigo will someday come for him. Am I right?' He looked at Willkie, waiting for a response. Willkie responded with a nod and a grunt. Satisfied, Quillon grinned with a smugness that deserved to be punched.

Dirk looked at Willkie and quietly asked curiously, 'Blue eyes? Not green?'

Again, Willkie just grunted while staring at Quillon.

'OK then,' said Dirk quietly before turning his attention back to Quillon. 'OK, enough monologuing. What do you want? There must be a reason why you're stalling. I presume it was you who had Kirby killed.'

Quillon just laughed. 'Oh, I'm not stalling. And Kirby is here, Mr Davis. Look, I'll show you.' He walked over to one of the cloaked figures and removed the hood, revealing Kirby. The look on Dirk's company was horror-struck. Kirby's mouth had been wired shut with thick metal wire crisscrossing and drilled through his jawbones. His skin was ashen, while his eyes looked hollow, unblinking, and void of all life.

Dirk remembered what Mbundu had told him, making his anger rise. '*You*—'

'Silence, Mr Davis!' interrupted Quillon abruptly. 'Such obscenities are beneath you. Unfortunately, after one too many mistakes, I'm afraid Kirby had outlived his usefulness and is now a zombie, with his fellow cohorts.' He gestured towards the other cloaked figures.

'But the police had his body.' exclaimed Dirk.

'And to which I am the guardian. So very easy to get back after it was deemed he'd died of natural causes.'

Maybe it was his professionalism or simply fear that Dirk resisted the urge to run over to Quillon and start laying into him. But he still managed to answer back furiously. 'Zombies? You and I both know that's a lie. They're drugged, and you've made them believe they're the walking dead. So, I'll ask again, what do you want?'

Quillon placed his left arm around Kirby's shoulders, looked at him, and then turned to look at Dirk with a smile. 'Oh, that's easy. I'll give you two options. First,' he said, pointing his cane towards them, 'is for you to help us take the statues.'

'And the second?' seethed Dirk.

'That's even easier. Just walk away… Though you could

also take a third option and be killed. But that's entirely up to you, isn't it?'

'I'll give you a fourth option, Quillon. You walk away, then leave us alone,' replied Dirk, who was now beginning to tightly grip the hilt of his stun baton.

Shaking his head while shrugging, Quillon answered, 'I cannot allow that, Mr Davis. And I think you know that all too well. But if that's the way you want it…' Quillon tapped his cane firmly three times, pointed at Dirk, and commanded, 'Kill them.' Quillon stepped back while the five cloaked figures shambled slowly forward, leaving Anita to stand her ground, surveying the area intently through narrowing but watchful eyes.

Chapter 34

Dirk signalled his team to move backwards, giving them more time to prepare. All four readied their stun batons, and Dirk softly spoke to his team. 'Right. *If* these are zombies, then remember what we've been told. They may be slow, but they pack a wallop, though I don't want to test the theory. Stick together, side by side and take on one at a time.

'Sharyn, I want you to stay behind us and back us up with sneaky hits. Remember, try to target the neck or chest, holding the baton there for a couple of seconds should drop anyone. Now on my mark, we'll all move round to our left to flank them. Hopefully, that means they'll arrive one at a time. OK, are we ready?'

The three of them agreed and prepared. Dirk called out. 'Now!' And they moved into their formation, starting the manoeuvre he'd planned. The first zombie arrived a few moments after they reached their intended position. Cody hit first, targeting the chest. There was a blue flash as the current of the batons struck their target. The zombie stopped and shuddered as over a million volts surged through its body. Cody gave a triumphant, 'Yeah!' as it shook but became distraught when it started to move again.

Willkie and then Sharyn struck the same zombie, holding it there for several seconds, thinking it would be the end, but became speechless when it did the same thing.

As the second zombie came alongside the first, an air of panic ascended between them. They became unsure of how to proceed, and their plan began to flounder.

'Quick, move right.' The third zombie tried to muscle its way into the action on his left.

Moving right gave them enough freedom to regroup, but not for long. Dirk's team now lashed out with their batons, using both shocks and as a club, attempting to stop the relentless attack. It was just enough to avoid being hit by the zombies, but they soon found that they were beginning to get hemmed into a corner by the zombies each time they moved.

Cody's voice was strained as he connected another blow. 'This is senseless. What are they on? Crystal meth? We'll run out of charge if we don't think of something.'

'I'm working on it. Any input would be welcome,' replied Dirk, but he had to take avoiding action from a swinging fist, becoming separated from his team in the process. He found himself with two zombies upon him: one of them, Kirby. Dirk looked at Kirby's expressionless visage and was overcome by pity and remorse, feeling partly to blame for his condition. But this momentary lapse of concentration was all his other adversary needed to connect a grasping hand.

The pain was excruciating, as he felt his right shoulder being crushed by a vice-like grip, and no amount of yelling relieved it. Dirk began with haste flitting his eyes from one part of the cadaver to another, trying to find some means of weakness to escape the attack. He dropped to the ground, attempting to shake the clutches of his assailant, but he only succeeded in dragging the zombie on top of him.

The creature's other hand then latched on and gripped Dirk's clothes tightly, lurching its head to bite unprotected skin. Thankfully, the wire did its job, preventing its mouth from opening and taking a mass out of his throat. Its face pushed as hard as it could, grunting and snorting, as it tried in vain to taste Dirk's flesh; its stench was unbearable. Finally, using his hands and a lot of effort, Dirk pried the being's face away, so he could breathe easier.

Then, in between groaning, a crumpling thud was heard, and his team yelled a triumph. They had dropped one of the zombies. 'Zap the wire on the jaw. Zap the wire on the jaw,' shouted a lively Sharyn repeatedly.

'Would if I could,' said Dirk through clenched teeth. 'I could do with some help,' he added, looking out of the corner of his eye. Kirby was now looming over him, raising his fists.

Now that they knew how to deal with their attackers, Willkie and Cody quickly dealt with the two zombies in front of them while Sharyn ran over and struck Kirby's wire with her baton just before he laid in his hammering blow. Kirby's body shook, his eyes rolling backwards before collapsing into a heap on the floor, periodically twitching.

Sharyn looked at Dirk, still struggling with his cloaked figure. 'This may hurt a little.'

'Just... get... it... off,' said Dirk, whose voice was fraught while he struggled to keep his attacker at bay.

'OK, honey, here it comes.' Sharyn struck the zombie in the shoulder. Both Dirk and the zombie shuddered as the current ran through their bodies, Dirk's face grimacing with pain. But it was enough for Sharyn to see the wire she wanted to hit, and, with cat-like reflexes, she lashed out again, striking her intended target and holding it for several seconds.

The zombie slumped motionlessly on top of Dirk, who heaved the now lifeless form off himself, and then wearily looked around to see Willkie and Cody's assailants lying flat on the floor. With the aid of Sharyn, Dirk struggled to his feet while holding his shoulder, obviously in a lot of pain.

He glanced towards Quillon, whose face showed sheer disbelief. Dirk couldn't help but give a wry smile. However, Quillon's face turned to anger, and he looked at Anita and barked an order. 'Deal with them.'

Upon hearing the command, Anita began to take her hands out of her sleeves. Dirk's team heard blades being slowly drawn from their sheaths as she did so. They observed her holding a hilt in each hand attached to long ribbons of steel, three on each. The blades appeared out of the sleeves, like watching a continuous string of silk scarves revealed in a magic show. She gave a final flourish with her wrists, and the remaining part of the blades fell to the floor. Each ribbon was around six feet in length, and they coiled and twisted onto the marble, like snakes being released from a basket, while the sound they made reminded Dirk of metal banding cut from around a wooden crate.

'How did she hide them?' Asked a surprised Cody.

'Them…' Quillon snorted, his rage evident. 'They are urumi, or to simplify it for you, Indian whip swords, of which Anita is a master, as you will soon discover.'

Quillon's statement spurred Anita into a physical response, starting to whirl her arms, causing the metal ribbons to flail, hitting the floor around her. Her fluid, continuous movements sent the blades over and around her head while her body danced across the floor. It was mesmerising to observe, like watching a mongoose tackling a cobra.

Dirk shouted, 'Fan out and keep your distance. Don't engage.' Which his team immediately did, without hesitation. He looked around to see what he could do to limit injury. Closing within weapon length would need to be timed to perfection as Anita was a whirlwind with the weapons. He shouted for Cody to come to his side, and when he did, he whispered something into his ear. Cody then ran off in a wide arc to Willkie and quickly spoke to him before separating again.

Anita was confident with her urumi, singling out Dirk, beginning to corral her prey into a corner for an easier target while simultaneously keeping the others at a distance. Her plan was to kill the snake's head, making the rest of the body useless.

Dirk prepared his baton and took a stance to prepare for an attack. Anita spotted this and swung the sword in her left hand, bringing it down onto its intended target, the sharp blades connecting with significant effect. The first bladed ribbon struck the baton, while the second slashed his lower right arm, cutting through his coveralls, just grazing the flesh. The final blade struck his right hand near the base of his thumb, nicking the principal artery. The sharp pain caused Dirk to drop the baton, and he clutched his hand as a tiny, steady, pulsing stream of blood began to appear from the wound. Dirk dropped to one knee, trying to make himself a smaller target, but Anita soon followed up with the sword in her right hand.

Dirk shouted. 'Now!' And he averted his head, letting the three ribbons of steel hit, with their momentum dragging across his back. Again, they cut through the coveralls, scoring into his flesh. Dirk arched his back, his face twisting with the pain.

Anita spun around and whirled her blades, expecting one or more counterattacks from Dirk's team, but was caught off guard, when she saw Cody and Willkie had run over to the packing crates. They took the loose lids off before spreading out. They held the lids like shields, so Anita reasserted her resolve.

She began weighing up her options and manoeuvred herself into a better position to defend and refresh her attack. She saw Sharyn hanging around the side, looking concerned at Dirk. Her analysis concluded that the guys were a distraction while Sharyn was going to rescue Dirk, or they were going to shield rush her at any moment. She formulated a plan and rooted herself to her position while continuing to whip the blades round in a frenzy, within easy reach to hit Sharyn if she made a move towards Dirk. If the guys were going to shield rush her, she would easily whip their legs from underneath them before they reached her. Anita then decided to press home her advantage and tried to force a mistake from one or all of them by preying on their patience, frequently lashing out at Dirk, injuring him with each stroke.

Quillon watched with a menacing grin that slowly widened across his face, beginning to sense that victory was near, gripping his cane tighter and tighter in excitement and anticipation.

Cody and Willkie looked at each other and nodded. With ease, they quickly changed their grip on the lids. It took several moments before Anita's eyes were struck with a look of shock as the comprehension of their strategy sunk in. Cody and Willkie now threw the lids towards her. A plan she knew she had no defence against, as her blades were too flexible to stop the now incoming missiles.

Anita did her best and dodged the first spinning frisbee. But the timing of the two men was perfect, and with their physical strength behind them, the second connected with Anita, sending her and her weapons sprawling across the floor. Her now unconscious body lying motionless. Sharyn hastily ran over to Dirk to attend to his wounds.

Comprehension had also hit Quillon, and for the second time that night, his smile quickly vanished from his face. Knowing that his plan was in disarray and with Dirk's team's attention focused elsewhere, he took several slow steps backwards before pivoting on his heel and withdrawing into the shadows while attempting to leave. His last thoughts were of formulating a new plan, but his mind went blank before finishing it, as he was forced to close his eyes after receiving a heavy blow to the head. His unseen assailant caught him before hitting the floor and he was quietly carried away.

Chapter 35

D irk was breathing heavily from the stinging wounds across his back. Sharyn looked at the lacerations and looked at Cody. 'Get me a first aid kit. There should be one under the information desk over there.' Cody quickly did as he was instructed.

Dirk looked around slowly, trying to see if Quillon was still around and was relieved when there was no sign of him. Willkie bent down next to Dirk to assist Sharyn. 'It's OK, boss. We'll return to the vehicle and leave before anybody else realises we're here.'

'The hell we are,' retorted Dirk.

'But you're wounded,' said a concerned Sharyn. 'You'll need treatment.'

'And remember what you've taught us about making rash decisions,' added Willkie.

Dirk took slow, deep breaths, attempting to block out the pain, but he found his mind was now pushing him, and he gave his reply. 'Quillon's gone. We're not going to get a second chance.'

Cody returned with the first aid kit and spoke. 'He's right. He's nowhere to be seen.'

Sharyn shot Cody a look as if to say, 'You're not helping,'

before turning her attention back to Dirk. She opened the first aid kit and started to attend to his wounds. 'You're bleeding, Dirk. Any spillage will be picked up by the police, so there's a chance they'll capture you. If we clean up and escape now, the less likely we'll be caught.'

Dirk's eyes were now closed, he was still trying to block out the pain, and after several minutes, he started to speak, sometimes through gritted teeth, as Sharyn cleaned and bandaged the wounds the best she could. 'Look. It's not about the money or my retirement. It's about your safety. If I fail, I don't know what Mbundu will do. I can take it if he just wants me, but I sensed that he's not the type of person to kill just me for compensation. He won't be happy until we're all dead. To make an example of us. So, forgive me if I'm not bothered by a little spillage of blood on the floor. But look around you. If the police turn up, they'll have someone to blame and will be less likely to chase anyone else. The guards are either dead or unconscious, and the cameras are out of action, so no one has seen us. Besides…' Dirk opened his eyes and looked at Sharyn while he lifted his left arm and lightly caressed her cheek with his fingers before continuing. 'I know of a great woman who can hack anything and help remove incriminating reports.'

Sharyn's eyes were closed as she reciprocated Dirk's touch, then opened them and turned to Cody and Willkie. 'What do you guys think?'

Cody was the first to respond. 'I'm with Dirk. No question.'

Willkie responded, his tone measured with caution, 'We'll see if it can be done, then move accordingly.' Dirk couldn't help but give a wry smile at this comment. 'Are the wounds life-threatening, Sharyn?' continued Willkie.

'I'm no nurse,' she answered as she pinned the bandage into position. 'They're not deep, though I think some parts may need stitches, which I can't do. He won't be able to use his right arm, as you can see, as I've heavily strapped it and put it in a sling to reduce the bleeding near his thumb. Both that and the bandages on his arm and back will hold for a couple of hours, but they'll need changing regularly. I've just used the last of them, but if he keeps bleeding...' She looked at Willkie and Cody. 'We'll need more supplies, so keep your eyes open for any more first aid kits.' Sharyn looked back towards Dirk. 'As for the crushed shoulder, it may be fractured, or it may be just bruised. Only a doctor will know. But the sling should help keep that in position. So, no sudden movements, OK?'

Dirk nodded, though with some reluctance.

Willkie spoke to Dirk. 'What about the pain? And I want no bull. Be honest.'

'The good news is the pain in my shoulder has lessened, my back stings like hell, but it's bearable. If I don't do any running, I'll be fine.'

'You may have to,' replied Willkie. 'But let's help you up and see if you can walk first.'

Cody and Willkie helped Dirk to his feet; he was uncomfortable and looked slightly stiff as he moved towards the Levin Hall.

'I'll carry him if needs be,' stated Cody. 'If we get to that point, the statues will need to be left anyway.'

'OK. It's settled. Let's do this.' Willkie passed Dirk, marched to the equipment with Cody, and they all headed to tackle the statues.

Entering Levin Hall, they stopped and surveyed the room before moving towards the statues and placing the equipment nearby. Looking around again, Dirk sensed something was amiss, but because of his wounds couldn't quite put his finger on it.

'How do you want us to do this, Dirk?' asked Cody, interrupting Dirk's jumbled thoughts.

He pulled his thoughts together through the constant throbbing on his back and began to speak. 'Well, according to the expert, they place one sling under the arms and around the chest, another goes around the waist, as they're the strongest points. While on the hoist, the staff help steady the statue, wearing gloves, which we have more of in Sharyn's rucksack. They normally wrap them in a special fabric, but we haven't got time for that now. Instead, we'll use the packaging we found in the crates to help prevent damage while in transit.'

The next ten minutes were spent placing the hoist and crates into position. Then, with a new set of gloves, they were poised to put the slings around the first statue before becoming aware they were being watched.

Leaning against the entrance to the main hall was Semyon, arms folded and with his shirt still hanging out of his ill-fitting suit. 'Oh, don't mind us,' he proclaimed as he stood upright, and another figure joined him from the main hall. 'But I wouldn't do that if I were you.'

'Because you're going to arrest us?' retorted Dirk as he eyed up the other figure, an East-Asian man, and if Dirk didn't know better, he would have said he looked like a Shaolin monk. Strapped to the man's back by a cord was a long piece of rolled fabric, while a knapsack adorned his hip.

'No, Mr Davis. But I would reconsider touching the statue,' asserted Semyon, as he stepped forward along with the figure for a couple of paces.

'Let me guess,' responded Dirk, his tone almost sarcastic. 'You and your friend want the statues too. We've already dispatched one team, and I'm not in the mood to give in now. I take it your cover allows you access to help your illicit means.'

Semyon just stood there, lips pursed in indignation and his fists clenched. It was apparent to Dirk that he'd struck a nerve with the agent. The other figure gently placed his hand on Semyon's forearm, which seemed to relax him slightly, before answering calmly, 'OK. As you wish.'

Sharyn positioned herself behind Dirk, who watched Semyon and his friend like a hawk, before nodding to Willkie and Cody to proceed. As the guys placed the first sling around the statue, they heard cracking sounds, like rock hitting rock. It was followed by the recognisable deep growl of a large dog. Surprised, Dirk whipped round to see that the mastiff statue had come to life and had knocked Willkie to the floor. Within an instant, the hound jumped, placing its forelimbs and full weight upon Willkie's chest and locked eye to eye with him, snarling with its drool-less mouth. Not even Willkie's strength, with both hands pushing against the solid mass around its throat, could keep it in check as its snarling teeth bared down on him. The rest of the team was stunned, not knowing whether they could trust what they saw.

It was Cody who acted first. He moved forward and was preparing to grapple the beast, thinking that his and Willkie's strength behind it could somehow defeat it, but as soon as he got near, the mastiff looked at him and barked loudly. It was a stark warning that stopped Cody in his tracks. The hound drew back its head and slowly, purposely, reconnected the eye contact with its intended victim, and the stone golem was now set to deal the killing blow. But as it lurched forward, intent on ripping out Willkie's throat, there was a roar, and a blur of orange, black and white wrenched the stone animal off Willkie's torso.

The team were still motionless, their eyes wide open, transfixed, as a fight began to ensue. The hall flooded with deep, muffled growls and loud rabid barks, blow after forceful blow trading between the two individuals. Each hit from the adversaries was premeditated, but the stone mastiff never stood a chance. It was rapidly overcome and pinned to one spot, not allowed to gain the upper hand. In moments, the contest had finished, with the jaws of the golem being wrenched from its head. The beautifully sculptured figure of the hound was now destroyed, raked with deep-running claw marks and now nothing more than several lumps of lifeless stone.

Crouching over the rubble was the victor. It stared at Willkie with eyes that briefly reflected green in the room's lighting before it decided to delicately lick a small wound on its upper left arm. At the sight of what crouched before him, Willkie scrambled backwards across the floor, slipping and sliding in distress, as it struck him that he'd seen these eyes before.

As it sat on its haunches, it was over six feet at the shoulder, so standing, it probably reached nine, maybe even taller. It surveyed the room, looking content with what it had just accomplished. Its head looked feline as it opened its maw in a full yawn, revealing a set of sharp teeth, with two canines that looked like they could carve through anything they'd clamp on to. The creature's fur was like a tiger's, with its striped pattern and white chest, except the body was more humanoid, with the frame buoyed by a large amount of athletic muscle, which spontaneously made parts of the fur twitch briefly. Its arms were long compared to the body and connected to hands the size of dinner plates, with each digit supporting a giant retractable claw. The legs were more like a cat's, with the beast resting on its large, clawed toes, ankles stretching backwards away from the floor before shaping forwards and upwards to the knee, while its feline tail flickered gently.

Dirk and his team were struck with a mixture of fear and awe just staring at the creature, and it was several moments before Dirk noticed that Semyon was no longer in the room. He glanced around and stopped when he saw what had been bugging him more than ten minutes earlier.

The imp mounted on the wall was missing from its plinth, revealing a hole. Dirk became lost in thought, wondering what all this meant. He shook his head, trying to clear his rapidly fogging thoughts, decided to refocus his eyes on a spot on the floor and began taking slow, deep breaths to avoid being overwhelmed.

As his mind calmed, he saw ripped clothes strewn across the ground. To be precise, the remains of Semyon's suit. Dirk looked up and shot a glance at the man-tiger, still squatting over the debris of the mastiff. *Could it be… Really?* thought Dirk, and all other thoughts disappeared.

'Yes. It's Semyon Pavlovsky,' declared the Asian figure, looking at and walking straight towards Dirk, speaking excellent English with a slight East-Asian tone. 'Mr Davis… Do not be alarmed. We will not harm you. I am Ru Mang, and Semyon, whom you've already met, is an Ambanai. Your culture may refer to him as a were-tiger, though I would not call him that directly. May I have a look at your wounds?' Dirk nodded once but couldn't take his eyes off Semyon, who looked majestic while defending the area. Sharyn joined Dirk by his side while Cody helped Willkie up to his feet, both staring at Semyon's prowess.

Ru Mang examined Dirk's injuries for several minutes, especially around the shoulder, making Dirk wince as he was firmly inspected. He then spoke again, looking at Sharyn. 'Did you do this, Miss?'

Sharyn nodded, though a fear struck her. *Is Dirk going to be OK?*

Ru Mang continued. 'You have done a good job.

216

There will be no need to change the bandages yet but add more bandages on top when the blood seeps through too much. If the blood seeps through to the second set, you must change them. I take it the shoulder was done by the zombies in the great hall?'

'Yes,' replied Sharyn quickly, happy that Dirk would be OK. 'One grabbed him with his hand.'

Ru Mang nodded and responded, 'You were lucky they weren't carrying weapons. Otherwise, it may have been a different story. The bones are not broken, but there is a danger of blood clots from the crushing.' He took something from a small knapsack, then snapped a piece off and placed it into Dirk's hand. 'Eat. I cannot do anything else for the moment.'

Dirk looked at it and answered while moving his gaze back to Semyon. 'What's this, miracle cure?' It was evident Dirk hadn't been listening to the discussion.

Ru Mang smiled as he answered. 'No. I'm not that good, Mr Davis. It's just a piece of dark chocolate: it will give you some energy.'

Dirk looked back to Ru Mang. 'OK. You've got my attention. What do you want?' Ru Mang was about to answer but was interrupted by a deep, rolling growl from Semyon that reverberated in all their bones.

'The same thing as you and me, Dirk.' A familiar voice sounded from the other entrance to the hall. It was Lin entering with two men. 'Good evening, Mang, am I fashionably late?' Her smile matched the mischievousness in her tone. Dirk was speechless.

Chapter 36

There was now a standoff: Ru Mang joined Semyon's side while Cody and Willkie stood in front of Sharyn and Dirk to defend their colleagues. Lin and her team, in comparison, just stood there, looking pleased with themselves for catching everyone off guard.

Lin was wearing an emerald-coloured cloak that touched the floor, wrapping her entire body and emblazoned with a shimmering golden Chinese dragon. To her right was a stocky East-Asian gentleman, wearing grubby jeans, a T-shirt and sporting long dishevelled hair. His dirty bare feet flexed their toes, anticipating the inevitable trouble. He ignored Dirk and his team but showed nothing but contempt towards Ru Mang and Semyon.

To her left was a lean East-Asian man wearing a stylish, shiny, electric blue suit, looking at all parties involved. Upon seeing him, Willkie and Cody made eye contact, and in surprising excitement, Cody quickly looked back towards Dirk and whispered, 'It's him, the guy who attacked us in the car.'

'You sure?' Sharyn asked.

'You're joking, right?' snapped Cody angrily, barely

managing to keep his voice a whisper. 'He had a fucking gun to my face.'

Sharyn looked away, avoiding eye contact, not knowing whether to apologise or not.

Dirk slowly nodded and then spoke, his voice edged with restraint. 'Keep calm, eyes front and stay alert.'

Lin surveyed the scene, her smile showing confidence that unsettled most in the room, before turning her full attention towards Dirk, her voice becoming almost angelic. 'Don't look so worried, Dirk. Aren't you happy to see me?' This began to play instantly on Dirk's emotions, his mind going into overdrive.

Why is she here? She told me she was leaving. What's going on? Have I been played?'

Almost relentlessly, the same questions repeated themselves, and he tried just as hard to answer them before he realised that he was breathing rapidly. Dirk felt a hand softly rest on his left shoulder, and without turning around, he knew it was Sharyn. He closed his eyes and took several deep breaths, instantly feeling most of his anxiety lift, though his mouth felt dry as he responded, 'Just surprised to see you. You said you were leaving.'

Lin ignored the response, glaring at Sharyn before turning her full attention to Ru Mang and speaking Chinese. Dirk couldn't understand what was being said, but the tone of Lin's voice seemed to express sarcasm. Ru Mang, however, was unflustered by her manner. The mocking from Lin continued. Even her subordinates joined in, laughing along at several of her comments.

Dirk stood there, listening to what he felt was nothing more than a rant, but as it continued, he began to zone out, with Lin becoming nothing more than an unfocused blur, leaving other questions to creep to the forefront of his mind.

Was this the same person he'd met weeks before? The woman he fell for? Realising what he was doing, Dirk closed his eyes for about a minute, inhaling and exhaling deeply, trying to remove his distracting thoughts. When he reopened them, Dirk decided to focus on Ru Mang.

In comparison to Lin, Ru Mang stood motionless, expressionless, taking in every word Lin uttered as if waiting patiently for his turn. Semyon, on the other hand, was a different matter. He was fidgety; the knuckles on his paws were in slow spasms of contraction, making his claws jerk in tiny movements as they scraped across the floor.

Dirk sensed the tense atmosphere and that he and his team were in the middle of it. In silent commands, using his hands, he signalled to the others to step back slowly. They complied, but the man in the blue suit noticed and grunted to Lin.

'Where do you think you're going?' She asked, returning to her practically perfect English. 'I was just telling Mang here how you told me how you were taking the statues.'

Dirk snapped as his team looked at him in surprise. 'Like hell I did!'

'Oh, you did, Dirk, oh, but you did. Truthfully, I knew who you were all along. I was just tapping you for information.'

Bewilderment struck Dirk and he stammered. 'But…
but how?'

'You men are all pathetic and so easily swayed,' retorted
Lin with a sneer. 'One of my many talents is that I can
control minds. We travel alongside the Terracotta Army
exhibition, controlling their staff, allowing me to gather
information about possible leads to other artefacts for our
cause.

'When we heard about these two statues here, we
decided to manipulate the local Mafia to help us take them.
So, imagine our surprise when we discovered someone else
wanted to steal them. I spoke to your fence and garnered
all the information we wanted. Which is where I found
out about you. I then had Tung with his militia of friends,'
she looked at the portly man to her right, 'gather as much
information about you as possible. Next, I asked Feng,' she
looked to her left, 'to threaten your team to stay away. That,
as predicted, did not work, though it was interesting to see
how you adapted.

'Once I realised you didn't know who you were working
for, and that it wasn't Quillon, I took your plan and wiped
your mind, just like I did with your fence. Though with
you, I gave you the memory of a romantic and passionate
evening.

'When I saw Mang here with you, I should've known
that he was behind your hiring. Clearly, trying to keep me
on my toes. And all credit to him, it worked. I can only
presume that his pet was there to keep tabs on you and feed
him information on your progress.'

Lin laughed as she saw the perplexed look on Dirk's face. 'Oh dear, poor Dirk. Look at him. How he believes he had feelings for me. But in truth, his feelings run deeper than even he realised… to his colleague next to him. I stand by my earlier comment that men are pathetic.'

Dirk had indeed become baffled, though it wasn't the mention of being mind-controlled by Lin, but by what Lin had said about Garrick. Garrick had met the employer several times; he'd said so at the meeting for this job. Had his friend lied to him, and if not, why was Lin saying differently? That's if Lin could indeed manipulate minds, as she stated. Or had this Ru Mang done something similar to Garrick?

His confused thoughts were then broken by Lin's next words. 'I've had enough of this posturing. Leave now. You're no match for us and you know it, Mang.'

Ru Mang stared at her, poker-faced as before. The following silence instantly raised the tension further.

'So be it,' replied Lin, her tone showing that she'd become bored.

A squawk echoed within the room, and something putrid green in colour darted out from underneath Lin's cloak; it looked something like a small muscular toddler with tiny claws on fidgety fingers. Its cloudy eyes darted about as it sniffed and snarled, showing its sharp, needle-like teeth through a broad, lipless mouth. As it darted off, Semyon growled, lurching at it with his claws but he missed before it went out of view.

There was a hint of panic in Cody's voice as he announced, 'What now, boss?'

'Back off, and we defend ourselves with the batons. Lin's right. We cannot fight against this. If an avenue of escape presents itself, we go for it. Agreed?'

'Agreed,' replied his team, as they huddled for support, protecting each other's backs while still feeling helpless, observing what was happening around them.

Semyon had crouched defensively, growling, preparing for battle. Ru Mang was backing away, using Semyon as a shield, while he searched his knapsack for something as the explosion of action began.

Tung began to contort as his back swelled. The T-shirt ripped apart, and several spiders of various sizes fell to the floor and ran in different directions. His broad, hairy, rounded back revealed pustule blisters that enlarged either side of his spine and burst. Four sets of large, hairy spider legs were expelled from the wounds. Three pairs arced towards the ground and lifted him off the floor, while the fourth and top pair positioned themselves defensively. His eyes became ruby red and began to glow while his bottom jaw distended, and a set of thick black fangs protruded. His hands moved so they were interlacing.

Sharyn gripped Dirk in fear, causing him to wince at the stinging pain her hands caused to surge through his wounds.

Feng clapped once before pushing them downwards forcibly, generating a loud, guttural grunt as he did so, adopting a fighting stance.

Lin leant forward and hissed loudly, her mouth baring a set of long, sharp canine teeth, and she floated above the floor. A long tongue slowly protruded from her mouth, flickering the air like a snake.

Tung launched webbing from his hands towards Semyon; the lattice of sticky threads hit their target and entangled his forelimbs with little effort.

Ru Mang had produced a parchment and brush from his satchel and was chanting while slowly painting something. His eyes flickered between the parchment and the beings in the room, trying to keep track of what was happening around him.

Feng was now hopping from one foot to another, unable to decide on his first target. But after several seconds of dithering, his motions became a blur of blue as he launched himself unnaturally fast at Ru Mang. Ru Mang saw the incoming attack, pivoted neatly on his right heel, and ducked as Feng's fists missed him. He completed his spin and pressed home his advantage, connecting his right palm with Feng's forehead. The unravelled parchment somehow held firm against Feng's skin, freezing him solid, the facial features held in exertion while his body was caught in the mid-motion of his intended next move.

Semyon ripped out of his bindings with a deafening roar of rage, cowering Dirk's team, who were now paralysed in fear. Then, with arms now free, Semyon lashed out towards Lin with his splayed claws. The first claw missed, but the second snagged her cloak and wrenched it from her body.

What it revealed produced a mixture of revulsion and fear from Dirk's team. Lin was still hovering in the air, but below her head, instead of the delicate curves Dirk thought he'd caressed, hung her internal organs in all their unsightly and veined glory. Her engorged lungs and intestines glistened with a wetness that made them sparkle in the room's lighting. And now that her true nature was on show, the intestines began to unravel as she launched her attack at Semyon.

Tung launched another web at Semyon, only managing to capture one hand, before running towards Ru Mang. The rhythmic patter of his legs carrying his bloated body made Sharyn's skin crawl in horror. Ru Mang tried desperately to defend himself, but with the onslaught of legs, he couldn't stop his opponent. Tung was snapping with his jaw, which was now showing signs of venom oozing from the fangs, and it was only a matter of time before Ru Mang would lose his battle.

The putrid green toddler crawled around the walls on all fours, using its claws to grip. But it looked confused, quickly darting its head from one place to another, sniffing incessantly, ignoring everything around it.

Meanwhile, with Semyon's right hand glued to the floor, Lin had wrapped her viscous intestines around his upper body and free arm. Semyon repeatedly snapped his jaws, trying in vain to fight her. She looked at Dirk and grinned maliciously.

'You're next,' she said before fixing her gaze back to Semyon. She began to draw breath, and Dirk's team saw a white, misty substance slowly escaping from Semyon's now open mouth. Her eyes had almost entirely rolled back into her head, like a shark that had breached the water, devouring its proposed victim. Semyon's hapless gaze was staring towards the ceiling, leaving Lin's tongue to feverishly lap up this substance with eagerness and apparent rapture. Open sores began to appear over Semyon's skin, and his body seemed to be slowly wasting away. Rotting.

Dirk's team looked at each other, and, without speaking a word, they knew it was time to leave. They tried to sneak towards the exit where Lin had entered, but all jumped when the little putrid green monster appeared from nowhere. It snarled at them while brandishing its claws, but it looked through them with its milky eyes before barging past them. Dirk, Sharyn and Cody moved forward but soon halted when they realised that Willkie wasn't moving. He was looking back at the battle.

'Come on,' stated Cody, his voice filled with frantic urgency.

Semyon's arm became sluggish as the fight began to leave him. And likewise, a restricted Ru Mang was also struggling as Tung weaved more silk to bind him further. It looked grim for the pair of them.

Willkie looked towards Cody. 'That man saved my life, and they now need our help. But all we want to do is run away. What type of man does that make me, or any of us?'

Willkie didn't wait for a response; he just turned and ran towards Semyon, his stun baton extended backwards, poised to strike as soon as he was in reach. Dirk and Cody looked at each other, resigned to what Willkie said was right. They then nodded and ran to join Willkie, leaving Sharyn wondering what the hell was going on.

Lin was so consumed in her own ecstasy while having her 'meal' that when the electrical charge hit her intestinal tract, it wasn't the pain that made her uncoil from her victim but the mere surprise that someone had the audacity to spoil her pleasure. Her euphoric high was soon replaced with rage through hissing teeth. Her eyes rolled back to the fore, focusing on the person who had disturbed her... Willkie.

Cody joined his side, and the last intestinal coil left Semyon, leaving him to slump lifelessly onto the floor. Lin hissed at them as she hovered and looked down at them, her bowels now writhing in agitation while she decided her next course of action.

On the other hand, Dirk had decided, through his hurting wounds, to help Ru Mang instead, who was still doing his best to keep the bloated Tung at bay. Even though his left leg was pinned to the floor by the man's webbing, Ru Mang was using his martial arts to escape and deflect the mass of legs that were trying urgently to pin him down. With Tung concentrating his efforts on Ru Mang, Dirk struck one of the rearmost legs with his stun baton. The leg crumpled under the shock and Tung stumbled towards a surer footing before wheeling round to face his new foe. Tung's jaw was now distended, showing fangs slowly secreting oily venom.

Dirk became overwhelmed by the task he'd just taken on. His confidence left him, and he took several steps back, holding his baton in front of him. It was soon swiped from his hand. He could see Ru Mang looking at him while struggling frantically to free himself from the bindings, desperately trying to come to Dirk's aid.

Dirk halted; pain shot through his wounds as his back found the wall he'd just reversed into. With Tung now confronting him, looking like he was trying to grin, Dirk conceded that this was it. Tung placed his forelegs gently on the wall, either side of Dirk, preventing him from escaping, before withdrawing his bulk slightly. Dirk felt everything slow as Tung prepared to take the final strike with his fangs.

His maw opened wider, but as he started to lurch forward to finish Dirk, he stopped, his eyes widened before rearing, screaming in an unearthly fashion, his legs and arms now whirling while stumbling backwards. It was only when the bloated man had staggered back enough and turned that Dirk realised what had happened. Embedded in Tung's back was the katana from the exhibition, and Sharyn stepping back, avoiding the death throes of her victim, her face streaked with tears, showing resolve. The bloated form was now thrashing wildly, trying to remove the sword from its own back.

The thrashing soon ceased. The legs twitched feverishly as they began to curl inwards and under his body, as Tung's life force ebbed away.

There was a squawk, followed by a clatter, and Dirk and Sharyn whipped round to see an air vent cover bouncing on the floor. A snarling noise made them look at the ceiling to see the little monster hanging from the opening. It tried to escape but struggled to climb into the hole above it.

Ru Mang released himself from his sticky bindings

using a sharp knife from his knapsack. Looking up at the creature with intent, he stood and, with great accuracy, threw the blade at the prone monster, buried up to its hilt. The creature squealed in agony as it let go of the edge of the vent and fell towards the floor, but before it reached the impending surface, it exploded in a wet, sickening way, like a cyst that had reached its limit between the pressure of two fingers. Green and blue sinew covered all those nearby, and the stench was almost intolerable.

While all this was happening, Cody and Willkie had managed to keep Lin at arm's length as they tried to work together on different flanks. But her supernatural abilities of second-guessing their attacks, coupled with the writhing mass of offal, made it difficult to gain any advantage. Several times, one of them found themselves face down, flat on the floor, after being tripped up by a length of intestine, to only be saved by their friend before Lin could finish them.

Sharyn ran to Dirk to assist him. He'd eased himself down to the floor, wincing in pain. Away from the battle with Lin, she immediately started to wipe bits of green flesh and blue blood off his face and re-dressed his wounds with the equipment Ru Mang had given her. But it was evident to Sharyn that all this was taking its toll on Dirk.

Ru Mang had now joined Willkie and Cody to aid them and shouted, 'Aim for the heart. It's the seat of her power.'

Lin withdrew her writhing mass upwards, her eyes darting around the room to evaluate the situation: she had been told to retrieve the pieces at all costs by her master, but it wasn't going as planned. Willkie, Cody and Ru Mang

229

were preparing to refresh their attack as soon as she came within arm's reach. Lin surveyed her companions, hopeful for one of them to come to her aid. Tung dead, the scattered body parts of her imp, and the undignified statuesque form of Feng, held in mid-attack. Then, out of the corner of her eye, she saw Semyon begin to stir, and she knew that all was lost. Her self-preservation came to the forefront of her plans.

With her new strategy in mind, Lin rushed over the heads of her attackers towards Feng as they lunged at her in desperation, trying to prevent her escape, while Semyon was beginning to get to his knees, looking somewhat unsteady. As Lin flew over Feng's head, she knocked the parchment away from his forehead before fleeing towards the door.

Feng rushed forward, finishing the move he had started several minutes before. When he saw Lin floating out of the exhibition, he turned around to see Ru Mang, Cody and Willkie running towards him, brandishing their weapons with determined faces. Feng vowed not to fall for the same trick again and prepared to take on the inferior beings, grunting with his all-knowing superiority. He was about to start a flurry of punches and kicks to slay these infidels. But the last thing he saw was the open jaws of a half-rotten and macerated humanoid tiger, leaping over those he was trying to eliminate. His head was cleaved from his body, his stubborn supremacy coming to an end. What remained of his body fell to the floor and crumbled into blackened ash, leaving his pristine electric blue suit and shoes lying crumpled on the floor. Lin's plan had worked; releasing Feng aided her escape by using him as a distraction, allowing her to vanish into the night.

Chapter 37

Dirk knelt, staring at the floor, while Sharyn checked his wounds. When he glanced up and saw Semyon, he scoffed, 'You've gotta be kidding me!' shaking his head in disbelief and exasperation. All but Ru Mang gazed upon Semyon, witnessing his wounds healing.

As he got to his feet, Dirk spoke gingerly. 'I wish I could do that.'

Ru Mang responded in kind, 'And we thank you all for saving us. The one thing we're not immune to is death.' He smiled at Dirk warmly before walking over to his countryman lying on the floor. Several exhibits were strewn around Tung's body, his legs periodically twitching, the katana still entrenched in his back. Ru Mang placed his hand over the eyes of the inert figure to close them.

Once healed, Semyon collapsed onto his knees, the orange, black and white mass fading as he reverted to his naked human form. Without embarrassment, he stood up, walked to Ru Mang's satchel, pulled out a pair of green slacks, and put them on.

There was a tinge of sarcasm in Dirk's voice that he couldn't entirely hide. 'Now I understand why you have ill-fitting suits. It must cost a bit every time you do a Hulk.'

'You've no idea,' said Semyon calmly, ignoring Dirk's mood, before starting to help Ru Mang with clearing the area. Dirk realised how thankless he must have sounded and looked at the floor awkwardly.

'What now, boss?' asked Cody, looking at Dirk with concern in his voice.

But it was Ru Mang who answered before Dirk had a chance.

'You do nothing for the time being. Rest, you've earned it. Help us prepare if you must, but we do not have much time. Luckily, the statues were not damaged during our struggle, and we don't know if Lin will return with reinforcements.'

'I think you owe us an explanation,' replied Dirk.

Cody was nodding, backing up Dirk's words as he squared himself up towards Semyon before remembering his form from several minutes earlier, and he quickly backed down. There was a quick chuckle from everyone in the room as they realised how futile the posturing was.

Semyon and Ru Mang looked at each other, and Ru Mang nodded as if confirming his thinking. Semyon walked over to Dirk and sat down next to him. Under Ru Mang's direction, Willkie helped him clear the area around the statues, though he kept his ears open, along with Sharyn and Cody, who also stood close to Dirk, eager to hear what was about to be said.

'We're here to retrieve the statues…' started Semyon.

Sharyn and Cody protested immediately, but it didn't take Dirk long to stop them, though he couldn't help but add his own passing comment. 'This better be good.'

Semyon chose his words carefully. 'OK, my apologies. Let me start again.' Semyon took a deep breath. 'Everyone thinks they know the story about the Terracotta Army. That the first emperor of China created an entire city of statues to accompany him during the afterlife—'

'Pretty hard to go against the history stated in the next room,' interrupted Dirk.

'True,' replied Semyon. 'But is it hard to believe that history and science can get it wrong? Just because they can't comprehend the existence of the paranormal. Yes, sometimes intentionally, the waters of history are mired by those who only believe in their greater good. For example, history books made us believe that Vikings wore horned helmets for hundreds of years. All because learned men, monks, depicted them as silhouetted men with horns amongst burning buildings. Probably linking in their mind's eye, they were heathens in league with the devil. Not surprising, really, when many monks were slaughtered during the Viking raids, but it was only recently we discovered that they didn't wear such horns, and their society was complex, orderly and more travelled than we knew before.'

'You're contradicting yourself there,' stated Dirk. 'You stated science can get it wrong, but science gets it right in your example.'

'Forgive Semyon, Mr Davis.' This time, Ru Mang spoke, and everyone turned to look at him as he walked over to the group, now finished with what he'd set out to do. He placed a hand on Semyon's shoulder with a smile. 'He's passionate about our work, but it leads him to say a hundred words when only one is necessary.'

Semyon felt a little hurt by the comment, though he knew it to be true. But it took a firm squeeze on the shoulder from Ru Mang and a reassuring smile to know that no harm was done.

'Is this where you tell us about the warriors being keys, a portal to the afterlife?' asked Dirk.

'No, Mr Davis, not keys.' Ru Mang restarted the story. 'Two thousand two hundred years ago, the first emperor of China created a moulded civilisation to protect and entertain him in the afterlife. What we refer to today as the Terracotta Warriors. But what was lost to history is that a spirit was bound to each piece.

'The ritual of creating each piece was complex and lengthy. But we have learned that the first emperor's sorcerers took samples of hair from loyal subjects, pressed them into the clay as each terracotta piece was made, somehow creating a link between the person and the statue. When the ritual was completed, the figure took on its owner's image for perpetuity. And when the subject died, their soul was trapped inside their piece until called upon by the first emperor.

'There's a myth that a favoured general of the first emperor was ritually slain, so he could welcome the other souls into the afterlife to prepare and maintain the emperor's discipline. We guess hundreds of loyal subjects were killed to bolster the ranks in the underworld before the emperor arrived.

'However, in the netherworld live the Juniten. Twelve divine spirits who preside over their separate courts. They war continuously, with each other and mortals alike. They'd heard what the emperor was doing and became curious.

'One of these spirits, named Emma-ō, sent his spectres to spy on the proceedings. But the emperor's sorcerers were prepared for this, and any shades caught were press-ganged into the emperor's service and ritually tied to Terracotta pieces, increasing the power of his army.

'At first, the emperor's council was more than willing to help fulfil his wishes. They knew the power of the Juniten was great, and they thought this would help the newly formed China. The army would also interact with the living world if China was ever invaded by foreign lands.

'However, the council became paranoid when the emperor became ill and deluded by the mercury coursing through his veins. The same mercury given by his physicians to supposedly lengthen his life. They feared when the emperor died, he would unleash his army on them.

'The council knew that the statues had to be undamaged to be of any use to the emperor. So, a few men loyal to the council began slowly damaging each piece, releasing the spirit trapped inside. It worked, but the side effect meant that the souls had nowhere to go so began haunting those who damaged their vessels of slumber. It quickly stopped the council's plan, especially when it gave away who had committed the crime. These men were executed alongside other criminals and then used as foundations for the surrounding roads and fortified walls, leaving the council fearing for their lives.

'When the emperor finally died, he was placed in his acropolis to meet his eternal afterlife, and his remaining loyal subjects were buried alive alongside him. The council, in their fear, seized the moment and began to destroy the pieces in earnest, no matter the consequences. But their worst fears were a reality. With the emperor now dead, he had complete control of his pieces.

'When the council's men attacked, the Terracotta Army sprang into service and defended their emperor's land. The council's men were defeated and pushed back, and even setting fire to the area didn't halt the army. After the battle was deemed to have been won, the army resumed its positions in the complex.

'What remained of the council began to act smartly, finding what you would call a loophole, by ordering the entire site to be covered in earth, preventing the army from getting out again. As this was not a direct attack on the guardians, they never awoke to defend themselves.'

Sharyn then spoke. 'So really, through the council's own fear, they created their own backlash? If they'd just let the emperor's reign play out normally, they would've been sitting pretty, with a vast army protecting them. Now they had nothing?'

'Correct,' Ru Mang replied. 'The human mind is a wonderous thing, yet a danger unto itself.'

'But now they were trapped. How could they protect the emperor and China?' asked Cody.

Ru Mang continued, 'Yes, they could no longer protect the physical plane on earth. But the realm in which the spirits and the emperor resided was like a mirror image to this one, though more vibrant. They could travel as far as they were ordered. Well, until 1291 AD, anyway.'

'What do you mean until 1291 AD?' replied Dirk confused.

'Well, humans had already forgotten them, but the Juniten finally defeated the emperor's realm. With the emperor gone, the surviving terracotta pieces became dormant. When they were rediscovered in 1974, virtually all the pieces were broken. Though science found evidence of the fire, they misinterpreted the data, mainly because science denounces the existence of spirits. When summoned into the physical realm, the pieces are practically immune to damage, so they would have been untouched by fire. But for those pieces that were blackened,' Ru Mang pointed to the soot-covered warrior, 'that is the only visual evidence that shows a spectre is bound to it. And they're the most dangerous.

'Some spirits would have perished during battles with the Juniten, which would've shattered the corresponding statue. But no doubt, the weight of the earth pushing down upon them, seismic activity in the area, or even sheer age would have broken most of them.

'And once broken naturally, the restless spirits would have roamed the underworld to await their fate. For those fully intact, the souls wait to do the bidding of whoever calls their name.

238

'It's believed that only one piece was ever found fully intact, and as you no doubt found out, the Chinese government vehemently denies that any more exist. But in truth, the site was pillaged by robbers before it was made secure. Any perfect pieces would have been sold secretly to private collectors. But there may be more, lying undisturbed, still to be unearthed.'

'You can see why so many people want them,' said Willkie, who was still in the background, examining the stone dog's remnants.

'The dog that attacked you was not the same thing. That was a stone golem, an earth spirit, animating the statue. In this case, as a protector. Many have tried to harness the power of the first emperor's sorcerers over the years. But they were buried alive in the mausoleum, and the knowledge was lost.

'After the discovery in 1974, the news caught the interest of two factions. They both knew of the spirit-bound soldiers' legend but had never found them. The first belongs to the Juniten, Emma-ō, who wants to harness the army for its own power. And that's who Lin works for. The other faction, where we belong, wants to stop Emma-ō and its plans by cleansing the pieces and sending the spirits to their rightful home, making the statues inert.'

Then Cody spoke up. 'So, when Semyon said you wanted the statues, he meant, what's inside them?'

'Yes.' Semyon smiled.

'So why hire us if you only wanted what was within?' Cody asked.

'We didn't hire you,' stated Ru Mang. 'That was the only thing that Lin got wrong.'

'Let me get this straight, there are – were – four groups after these two statues?' Dirk said.

'It appears so,' answered Semyon. 'We knew about Lin, obviously, and Quillon, but your hirer is new to us, and we've been trying to find out who they are.'

Dirk looked perturbed. 'Lin detailed how she found and followed us, but how did you?'

'Unfortunately, Lin was correct with her analysis. We are no match for her and her team. We must rely more on technology than our supernatural crafts, as their magical prowess is a lot more powerful than ours.

'When we knew that Quillon would be involved through Semyon's contacts at Interpol – and as you may have gathered, he is not subtle in his approach – we decided to place electronic trackers on all those Kirby encountered. You found yours. We noted it was destroyed, after—'

'Hold on,' interrupted Dirk. 'If you planted the trackers on Cody's car, how did Lin's team follow us?'

Semyon pointed to the lifeless body of Tung. 'Tung was a rare form of Jorogumo, a spider demon. They're normally female. He controlled spiders with an empathic link and used them as spies or assassins. I was following Feng.' He pointed to the dusty blue suit lying on the floor. 'I saw him attack Cody and Willkie.' Semyon looked at Cody. 'Did you feel a shiver down your spine when Feng's gun touched your head?'

Cody looked puzzled while answering, 'Yes.'

'Well, that wasn't nerves. I saw a spider crawl from your neck and onto the gun barrel.' Semyon looked at Dirk, leaving Cody shuddering at the thought of it.

'We have always believed that Lin's team had some form of empathic link with each other, but that night confirmed it, as it did your involvement with the statues. Though we originally thought you were with Quillon until we found them doing their own legwork.'

'So, it was you who Willkie saw?' quizzed Dirk.

'Yes,' said Semyon, looking at Willkie. 'I was going to capture Feng to try and find answers, but when Willkie and Cody arrived, I thought it best to stay in the shadows. Humans don't cope so well when they see something they don't believe exists. They try and rationalise it with something similar, but they're often placed into asylums when they can't. I don't like hurting the innocent. It was only after the event that I pieced everything together fully. My bestial side is more often instinctive than rational, you see.'

'We had to find another way to keep tabs on you,' Ru Mang said.

It then hit Dirk like an express train. He rubbed the back of his neck before saying, 'For crying out loud. The guy fishing in the harbour.'

'Yes,' replied Semyon with a wry grin. 'He's a water deity who occasionally helps us. Supernaturals are habitually paranoid by nature, so they often don't work together. But we made a trade, and thanks to the tracker he put in your arm, we found out where Lin is living. Tonight, she'll head to her apartment and find the rest of her body missing. She would have been storing it in a large vat of vinegar.'

Dirk sighed, emptying all other thoughts before looking down, shaking his head in disbelief. 'Lin told me she'd spilt vinegar while making pickled cabbage.'

'That was unusual and her biggest mistake,' responded Ru Mang. 'I can only presume she was truly taken with you, as it may have given her a way out of her curse. But as you heard, with her abilities to retrieve information, once Lin found your feelings for Sharyn, she knew there was no salvation for her this time.'

'A curse? What is she, a vampire or something?' asked Sharyn.

'Close,' stated Ru Mang, 'but not of the western myths, like Bram Stoker's *Dracula*, and Lin's not undead either. She's a penanggalan. She was once a woman like you, but Lin has made a pact with a demon, wanting to become more beautiful. This demon would've told her to not eat meat for forty days. However, not all demons state this fact when they enact the ritual, or Lin couldn't complete the fasting. Either way, when Lin failed, she became an immortal penanggalan; a beautiful woman by day and a floating head with trailing internal organs by night. She must feed upon the life force of others to survive. Sadly, penanggalan's find feeding on infants and their mothers tempting.'

'It was her who killed the newborns and their mothers at the hospital after the storm.' Sharyn sounded both disgusted and shocked.

'Regrettably, yes,' said Ru Mang sullenly. 'When we

heard the news, we knew she was here. 'We tried to find her, but until we could verify her address, the only thing we could do was send ladies who believed into the hospital with pineapple leaves.'

'Pineapple leaves?' retorted a sceptical Cody.

'Yes, I heard that from a reporter on the scene. But why?' questioned Sharyn.

'The leaves are spiky and a form of deterrent against the soft tissue of her kind. But it's not foolproof,' replied Ru Mang.

'What about the storm? What did that signify?' asked Dirk.

'Nothing,' stated Ru Mang shrugging. 'As far as I'm aware, it was just a storm. But no doubt, some people will see a hidden meaning behind it, as others will see global warming.'

'What now then? And how are we going to carry the statues? I see that one piece of equipment has been damaged,' Dirk said.

'Now we call the spirits, and we and the statues will walk out of here. I presume that you have brought a vehicle?' asked Ru Mang.

Dirk nodded, but he also had the look of sheer disbelief at Ru Mang's statement.

His team then stood, keeping alert while watching and listening to Ru Mang speaking to the statues in Chinese. Semyon translated what was said.

After several minutes of chanting to the first statue, a ghostly apparition appeared, glowing iridescently pale green, nestling neatly over the cold stone form of the warrior. Ru Mang started to converse with the spirit, and according to Semyon, it was stubborn and wanted proof of the emperor's demise. But after several minutes of cajoling, the spirit's name was obtained.

The second, soot-covered statue was a different matter. After Ru Mang completed the chant this time, the room darkened, and when the blackened apparition appeared, its eyes glowed a fiery red; it glared with anger at Ru Mang.

Even without the translation, Dirk could tell it spoke with malice, but unlike the coaxing of information from the first statue, Ru Mang was demanding the name, treating the malevolent spirit the same as it was treating him, threat against threat. It soon became a war of words. They argued for several minutes, seemingly not getting any advantage over the other. In the end, Ru Mang relented and told the spectre that he would release it from its prison once the task had been completed.

Once they were ready to leave, Ru Mang ordered the statues to move, and with glowing, unblinking eyes, they all eerily moved out of the exhibition hall. It seemed surreal to Dirk that he planned to carry these statues out of the museum all this time, yet here they were, walking out next to him.

Chapter 38

Cody and Willkie got into the vehicle's cab and prepared to drive away while everyone else entered the truck's rear; Dirk partially shut the roller door. The statues took in their strange surroundings, and it didn't pass Dirk's attention that the spectre was more vigilant, both wary and attentive of everyone and everything around it. When it noticed Dirk, the shade grinned back, the unblinking of its fiery eyes unsettling Dirk, as if the devil was judging him, welcoming him personally to hell. Dirk looked away and banged the wall directly behind the cab, signalling Cody that they were ready to leave. The spectre malevolently chuckled to itself.

As the truck began to rumble forward from the bay, Dirk took the phone he was given from his first meeting out of his pocket and dialled the only number on it. It rang for a moment before a male voice answered. 'Hello.'

'We've got the two items you requested,' Dirk said.

'Very good. Meet us at the Soldier Field parking lot. A helicopter will be there in five minutes.'

'Soldier Field?' exclaimed Dirk.

The voice responded, almost threatening in nature. 'Is there a problem?!'

'No… No, of course not. Just concerned how open it is,' said Dirk, trying to sound professional.

'Let us worry about that. I just hope for your sake they are still in one piece.'

The phone call abruptly ended.

Dirk pursed his lips and then put the phone in his pocket before taking out the phone Tristan had given him. He dialled the number and Mbundu answered.

'Ah, Mr Davis. I presume that you are en route with the statues.'

'Yes. However, the client wants us to meet at Soldier Field in several minutes. Can you be there in time?'

'Don't worry yourself. We're close by.' Again, the call ended abruptly, and Dirk didn't like the tone in Mbundu's voice. He jumped when banging came from the cab, and Dirk felt the truck begin to slow.

'We've got company. The road's blocked,' Willkie stated over the comms unit.

Dirk knew precisely who it was. 'Mbundu.' Moving to the back of the truck, he opened the roller door and stuck his head out over the tail lift, looking down the side of the vehicle. As Willkie had stated, two cars blocked the road ahead of them, and as their truck came to a halt, Dirk saw men holding automatic weapons. Amongst them, he could see Mbundu.

Dirk pulled his head back into the truck. Sharyn asked, 'What are we going to do?'

'I think we stretch our warriors' legs,' responded Ru Mang, looking out the other side of the truck, and Dirk sensed relish in his voice as he continued, 'Semyon, the weapons.'

Semyon unrolled the fabric they had been carrying to reveal two new swords.

Ru Mang began to converse with the statues, and after they accepted their order, Semyon handed them the weapons. They both looked pleased with themselves, testing the weapons for balance.

They heard Mbundu's shouts. 'Hand them over, Mr Davis. We know you're not armed.'

Dirk looked at Ru Mang. 'What if they're damaged? Why not send Semyon instead?'

Semyon looked at Dirk with a raised eyebrow; he didn't look impressed.

'Sorry. No offence,' pleaded Dirk. 'But you can heal rather rapidly.'

Semyon replied sharply, 'My healing powers are not infinite, and I'm not immune to pain either. It takes a lot of effort to heal.'

'Trust me, Mr Davis, they'll not be damaged in their current state,' Ru Mang said.

Dirk couldn't look them in the eye, admitting to himself he was becoming selfish; he ached all over and was longing to lie down and rest. His shoulders sank as he half-heartedly nodded to Ru Mang, who barked orders at the statues. They both bowed in acknowledgement before vaulting over the tail lift to the ground below.

After several moments of shouting, gunfire ensued. Everybody in the back flung themselves to the floor as a spray of bullets hit the side of their vehicle. The wheels began to spin and squeal as Cody gunned the truck in reverse; engine fumes and the stench of rubber filled their nostrils. Cody was looking out of the side window, trying to look where he was going, leaving Willkie transfixed by the statues in front of him. When Cody reached what he thought was a safe distance, he slammed on the brakes, sending those in the back sliding across the floor, their muffled complaints coming from within.

The statues relished their task, using centuries of pent-up aggression to significant effect, connecting with the flesh of any who opposed them with prowess. They worked as one, using a mixture of martial arts and the weapons Ru Mang had given them, not even troubled by the bullets hitting their bodies. At one point, in unison, they kicked one of the cars effortlessly into several posse members, like a lawnmower taking care of the grass.

The Jamaicans became hesitant, and Mbundu, now distressed, shouted at his men, issuing orders while gesticulating frantically with pointed fingers from behind a wall of his brethren. But within a few moments, seeing the shock of their opponents' power, three of his followers began to run, only to be shot in the back by one of Mbundu's lieutenants. Mbundu stood, acting defiantly, before even he pulled a handgun and joined the affray, making his last stand. In the end, it was the spectre who cleared a pathway straight to a terrified Mbundu and lifted him by the neck into the air using its stony fist. Its face began to crack and radiate with heat, and after a short intake of breath, it belched forth a river of black and orange flame that enveloped the protesting Mbundu like lava. The screams of the Jamaican leader were short, and his shaking body soon went limp. When his body had become unrecognisable, the warrior dropped the scorched cadaver like litter, leaving the charred remains to hit the floor in a crumpled heap.

The spectre looked to the starry heavens, then shouted with an unearthly bellow of triumph, its body tensed, like a wrestler spurred on by an unseen baying crowd. The other warrior watched in disgust.

Willkie, staring at the scene before him, opened the comms. 'It's over. Mbundu's... gone.'

'Yeah, we know,' came the sombre response from Dirk.

Cody looked out of his driver's window and saw his passengers congregated at the side of the vehicle. There was a stunned silence between them, with a mixture of awe and revulsion etched on their faces.

The statues walked back towards the truck. The Jamaican posse lay ahead of Dirk and his team, dead and twisted on the floor. The fight had only lasted a couple of minutes, but they could not put into words the carnage they saw in front of them.

The spectre's face was still gloating with victory, and as they came closer, Dirk and his crew could see the small amount of damage that had been sustained being 'healed' as glowing cracks of fire appeared on both warriors, making them as new.

Dirk looked at Ru Mang and said, 'Now I understand.'

Ru Mang didn't say a word. Instead, he placed a soft

hand on Dirk's shoulder and nodded in sympathy before heading into the vehicle's rear. The warriors jumped into the back also, assuming their original positions, while the mortals adopted theirs, keeping their thoughts to themselves.

Cody threaded the truck carefully through the miniature battleground and looked down at those who lay around him, hoping there would be someone he could stop and help, but nothing except lifeless eyes stared back at him. Save from the rumbling sound of tyres upon tarmac, what remained of the short journey was silent until the air began to fill with the sound of a helicopter as they approached Soldier Field.

Ru Mang then nodded to Semyon, and they sprang into action, catching everyone else off guard. From behind the spectre, Semyon transformed into his humanoid tiger form and grappled it with force. A struggle ensued. While protecting Sharyn, Dirk quickly moved to the back of the now confined space. 'What the hell's going on?!' shouted Dirk.

'Our legacy!' came Ru Mang's hurried response before he started chanting angrily at the statue.

An unprepared Cody cursed under his breath as he began fighting with the wheel against an increase in weight and a now shifting load. Willkie tried to contact Dirk, whose only intent was to shield Sharyn and not answer his radio.

Cracks again began to appear across the surface of the spectre's torso, and Semyon felt and smelt his fur and flesh beginning to singe in the growing heat. Ru Mang's rantings became more forceful in tone as the spectre struggled against the strength of Semyon and the now swelling pain caused by Ru Mang's words.

Dirk, still shielding Sharyn, finally answered Willkie's call with, 'Just keep going.'

After the initial surprise, the remaining warrior steadied itself against the side of the vehicle, looking at the coupling of Semyon and its fellow statue with calculating menace. Semyon's eyes rolled to meet his, and upon seeing the warrior preparing to strike, he growled to Ru Mang as he struggled against the movement and increasing pain. 'Hu… rry… up… Ru.'

The spectre began to inhale, and the heat quickly became more intense. They all knew what was about to happen, and only the harsher tones of Ru Mang were stopping the inevitable eruption.

Semyon's eyes were still fixed upon the other warrior, and he could see the poised strike uncoiling towards him like a cobra. He closed his eyes momentarily, preparing for the attack, but when it connected, it was not the force, or target, that Semyon was expecting. The warrior's open-hand strike clasped firmly around the mouth of the spectral warrior, whose hatred against his former compatriot now showed in its eyes, burning as fiercely as the furnace building up within.

The spectre now struggled against its three adversaries, harried by the constricting hold of Semyon, while the other warrior's vice-like grip around its mouth prevented the expulsion of its hellfire. And with each passing moment, it felt a pounding pain, increasing in tempo, as Ru Mang's incantation was taking hold. Its body now glowed in a dark orange hue. The chest was almost white, the heat within nearly reaching its pinnacle. Even Dirk and Sharyn, at the furthest point from the battle, were wincing as they felt the overwhelming high temperature. Semyon was beginning to roar in anguish as the pain became unbearable, his flesh smoking as it seared and blistered in the intense heat.

Without warning, a loud *POP* was heard, followed by a bright blue flash. Ru Mang ceased his chanting.

The heat started to dissipate out of the back of the moving truck; the fresh air drawn in was a welcome relief. But, as Dirk watched, he saw the once invigorated spectre become motionless, just as it was when he'd first laid eyes on it, its heated glow quickly ebbing away, back to its original stone-coloured self. Semyon collapsed into a heap on the floor of the truck, his pain punctuated by a mixture of low growls and groans.

Ru Mang bowed in thanks to the remaining warrior, who reciprocated with a firm but clear nod before firming up his stance, waiting for a new order. While Ru Mang began to converse with the warrior, Dirk looked at Sharyn. 'Are you OK?' he asked as he squeezed her gently to reassure her. Sharyn looked into his eyes and just smiled while nodding. She rested her head on his chest as they sat in the corner of the vehicle, then began to hug him tight until he winced with the pain of his wounds.

Dirk smiled warmly and then looked back at Ru Mang,

holding a feather and a small phial of clear liquid. He pulled the stopper from the phial and dipped the tip of a feather into the fluid before proceeding to dust the warrior with simple sweeping actions, chanting in softer tones. It only took moments before an iridescent pale-green light formed around the living statue, which began to coalesce into a ghostly form and rise above the terracotta warrior. Before it dispersed into the ether, its last act was to bow deeply towards Ru Mang and Semyon. But what should have been a surreal moment of silence was ruined by the sound of the helicopter landing and the notification from Willkie that they'd arrived at the parking lot of Soldier Field. The statues rocked slightly as the truck came to a gentle halt.

Dirk and Sharyn exited the truck's rear, leaving Ru Mang to tend to Semyon's wounds, who had reverted to his human form. Willkie and Cody had climbed out of the cab to join them. Six men, wearing fatigues, masks, and holding handguns, had already positioned themselves around the helicopter, holding point, before two suited men exited and headed towards Dirk, each carrying a briefcase. Two men in fatigues joined them, one guarding either side.

'Do you have the consignments, and are they intact?' shouted one of the suited men above the din of the whirling rotor blades.

'Yes!' replied Dirk.

The man nodded to the other suited figure, who signalled to the two guards with them to follow him, and they moved to the back of the truck. Dirk signalled to

Cody to follow them. When they arrived, there was a series of sudden shouts, and the two guards stepped back and raised their handguns, aiming them into the back of the truck. They'd found Ru Mang and Semyon. Cody stood in front of the armed men, raising his arms and defusing the situation.

Ru Mang slowly came into view, helping a stooped Semyon, who looked dishevelled. His hair was unkempt while his midriff was wrapped in a blanket. The blistering he'd received from the heat had lessened, but was still largely visible and undoubtedly incredibly painful.

The two men in fatigues took several steps back, holding them at gunpoint. Willkie ran over to assist Cody.

'Friends of yours?' quizzed the suited man next to Dirk. 'I was told you were a team of four.'

Dirk's eyes narrowed before he bluntly responded. 'Yes, they're with me. and how I run my team is none of your business.'

'He seems to have taken a beating. As do you.'

'And your boss could've warned us that other parties were interested, going after the same pieces.'

The suited figure thought it prudent to say nothing more and responded with a wry smile while Dirk continued with his scowl.

Ru Mang and Willkie aided the wounded Semyon to one side while the nearby suited figure and an armed guard hopped into the back of the truck, overseen closely by Cody.

The suited figure prepared himself with latex gloves

and a head torch but commented to the guard about the unprofessionalism of how the statues were transported before inspecting them in detail, cross-referencing them against a computer in his briefcase.

Outside, Dirk was surveying the area, making mental notes of the armed men around him as he went. The suited man in front of him noticed his eyes darting from one point to another. 'Nervous, Bruce? You needn't worry about the hardware. It's predominately for defence… unless you are concerned that we might find something on them?' The smile that followed was sly, almost provocative.

Dirk just calmly and nonchalantly shouted back, 'Nah. I'm just wondering what's taking the police so long. They pride themselves on a five-minute response time. Now, I can understand the museum, but we just had to get through a gun battle to get here. And yet here you all are, calm and collected, standing in a prime secured lot next to Burnham Harbour. Both with cameras and no ominous sounds of sirens. Your hardware. That just enforces the fact that your boss knew other parties were involved.'

The man acknowledged Dirk's words by nodding. But after a few seconds, he felt the urge to respond, anyway. 'I wouldn't worry about the security cameras. They've been taken care of.' His smile returned, accompanied by smugness.

The expert in the truck took a step back and looked at Cody in disbelief before signalling to his compatriot outside via subvocal microphone. Cody grinned back and gave a wink.

The man next to Dirk had put a finger to his ear, listening intently before looking at Dirk and speaking; the surprise was evident in his voice. 'It appears that everything is in order. Here's your fee and the bonus, as agreed.' He handed the case he was holding to Dirk, who quickly passed it to Sharyn. She moved a safer distance from the helicopter's downdraft and opened the briefcase to check the money.

'I think you'll find it's all there,' said the man, his pompousness now returning to the fore. Dirk didn't reply. He just flicked his eyes between Sharyn, the man and his armed entourage. After checking the contents of the case, she looked at Dirk and nodded with a grin.

Dirk turned to the man. With everything that had gone on, he responded with frayed patience, purposely being confrontational. 'Thank you. If you could take them off the truck, it would be appreciated.'

'What?' asked the man, obviously shocked, not used to being spoken to by someone he considered below his station.

'We've done what we've been hired to do. Retrieve and deliver. Nothing about unloading. So, if your men can remove them from the truck, we'll be off.'

The man's face became red, staring speechless for several seconds, perhaps even wondering if Dirk was joking. But when he realised that he wasn't, he barked a command to several members of his team, who now moved towards the truck.

Dirk sensed that the man was now nervous with the task forced upon him.

While the statues were being moved, his commands were tinged with panic and edged with dread. Dirk watched, understanding fully why. His assignment was to make sure the statues were not damaged in any way. He'd been severely concerned about damaging the pieces on the way here. Dirk could only surmise that this man, unlike Dirk, knew who the owner was and was anxious over the consequences of any breakages after the handover. He was possibly even new to the role, as the money had exchanged hands, giving away the only leverage to have Dirk move the statues instead.

As soon as the statues cleared the truck, Dirk signalled to Cody to prepare to leave, which he did without hesitation. When the engine started, Willkie and Ru Mang helped Semyon into the back of the truck while Sharyn joined Cody in the cab. Dirk watched briefly as the guards delicately moved the statues towards the helicopter. He made eye contact with the man he'd been speaking to, who returned his gaze with an icy stare. Dirk continued looking while thinking, *Why didn't he just ask for the vehicle?* And he smiled to himself as he climbed into the cab and joined Cody and Sharyn. They drove away.

Minutes later, they heard the helicopter rotas increase pitch and then watched as it took off. 'What now?' asked Cody.

'Get rid of this truck first. We'll dump it by what's left of Mbundu, set fire to it, and then clean up. I'm not thinking about a beach until all the usual loose ends have been tied up.'

It was helpful that Ru Mang and Semyon had their vehicle nearby as they drove them away from the area. Nobody said a word after that, but Dirk's thoughts kept wandering. He briefly looked down at Sharyn between him and Cody, who'd snuggled up against him. He smiled warmly before turning around, looking out the side window again. Something was still niggling him, right at the back of his mind, but all the answers were out of reach.

Chapter 39

Ru Mang and Semyon stayed close by for the first week until Semyon's wounds were fully healed, though he now had some scarring. Before leaving, they came to say farewell at the repair shop. To each of them, Ru Mang bestowed upon them a gift. A necklace with a pendant, each uniquely crafted into the shape of an eye. Ru Mang explained in detail while handing them out individually how in many cultures, from the ancient Greeks and Egyptians to the more modern beliefs of today, the symbol of the eye is seen as a protector or a focus for clarity and truth. 'They will protect you from the unseen hand of the supernatural world,' he stated.

After the many thanks, handshakes and discussions, Semyon took Dirk to one side for a private word. 'How are you feeling? You look as if you've got other things on your mind.'

Dirk paused before considering his answer. 'I just want to say thank you and say sorry for what happened on that night. My attitude towards you was wrong.'

Semyon placed his right hand gently on Dirk's shoulder. 'That means a lot. And having time to reflect, I understand why you were like it. Cody and Willkie have spoken very highly of you over the past week, and I, too, am a passionate being. I also can get frustrated, especially in my other form. So, don't beat yourself up over it. You and your team did well and better than most in your situation. And you'll be pleased to know that no evidence was found that pointed towards your activities, even before I looked through the data.' Semyon patted Dirk on the back, which gave him cause to wince in pain discreetly as he did so.

Over the next two months, Dirk and his team stuck to their usual game plan after any job: to act normal, following the same routines as they'd always done for years. Dirk's wounds were almost fully healed, though there was still redness where scars began to form.

The only fundamental difference was that Sharyn and Dirk were officially a couple. Just two people who'd found each other and were finally free to express their feelings for one another. Many who knew them congratulated them both, telling Dirk it was about time he'd found someone to settle down with, while Sharyn was complimented on her happiness. It was true, Sharyn was more relaxed than she'd been for some time. But while both were enthralled with each other's company, Dirk was not comfortable enough to fully appreciate his feelings. When he was alone, doubts crept into his mind. Not over Sharyn, for he'd never been more certain over anything else before. But the night of the job just kept playing over and over in his mind, and the local news reports over the first two weeks, notably the lack of it, had only made it worse.

The papers mentioned a gunfight between two rival

gangs nearby. In Dirk's mind, it was an apparent reference to their altercation with Algernon Mbundu. But there was no mention of any attempt on the museum, nor the death of the guards they'd found. The guys put it down to Semyon. But had he been able to hush the theft completely? And what of the dead guards? What had their families been told? It just didn't sit right with him; something was missing, and he was beginning to have restless nights over it.

Sharyn had been an unseen rock for so long, and now their feelings towards each other were in the open, he felt more relaxed in her presence, his thoughts dissipating. But he didn't want to burden his reflections on her. Well, not yet, anyway. Dirk feared some form of ridicule, rejection, or overwhelming her too soon with his problems. So instead, he kept his ideas to himself, a dangerous game of balancing his mental health on a tightrope, where his thoughts were either going to be controlling or controlled.

By late autumn, he was beginning to learn to live with what happened in the end and began to appreciate his newfound freedom and relationship a little more every day. He began looking at selling his repair shop, going on more fishing trips, and most importantly, retiring and being happy.

That was until he had an unexpected visitor.

Chapter 40

Dirk was at the repair shop, locking up for the evening. Willkie and Cody had left five minutes earlier to head to the gym. The nights were drawing in now, and a brisk breeze made the fallen leaves dance around the floodlit car lot. He noticed a lean man wearing a suit and trench coat walking towards him as he headed to his car.

'Sorry, sir,' Dirk said, 'we're closed for the day. You can either call back tomorrow, or I'll happily contact you in the morning if you've got a business card.'

The man gave a cynical smile, and before speaking, he produced a business card from his wallet and gave it to Dirk. It read: Ernest and Son's – Elite Lawyers of Law – for all your business and personal requirements.

'Good evening, Mr Davis. I am Mr Rickman, James Rickman. I'm glad I caught you alone. I've been instructed by my client to give you this envelope personally.'

Dirk hesitantly took the packet and replied, 'OK, you have my attention. What's this about?' He opened the envelope. The lawyer said nothing but seemed to be waiting for a reaction from its contents.

Inside were several photos and another envelope, and after a brief fight against the evening's breeze, he focused on the images. Dirk froze, and as he swallowed, he felt his throat and mouth dry. He was looking at a photo of himself in the museum, taken on the night of the heist. He glanced at the lawyer, who just stood there, steadfast, expressionless, waiting for a response. Dirk looked at the following two photos in quick succession. They were close-ups, looking down at his face. There he was, no wishful blurred outlines to hide behind.

Dirk placed the photos back in their package and tucked them under his left arm before opening the remaining white envelope and reading the letter found within. He began to feel his fingers tremble, and his head flushed with heat as his anxiety kicked in.

The letter stated:

Mr Davis,

Your presence is demanded immediately.

Hopefully, the accompanying photographs are reason enough why. Please do not think that you or your friends can run from me.

If you refuse, I will have no alternative but to hand this information to the police.

Ms A Jenson

Dirk rolled his tongue around his mouth, attempting to regain his dispersed moisture and at least some composure before speaking. 'I presume I can't take a rain check on this?!'

'No, Mr Davis. Ms Jenson was most insistent.'

'I bet she was,' said Dirk, his mind's eye now looking for escape routes and places to hide.

'Your associates are also being collected as we speak, so they can join you,' Rickman added.

Dirk responded despondently, 'OK, lead on.' They headed to the lawyer's car, where his chauffeur and bodyguard stood waiting. The drive took an hour, and during the journey, no conversation was made; only the rumble of the tarmac under the tyres prevented total silence.

It was dark when they'd reached a gated driveway between high walls.

So, this is the Jenson mansion, thought Dirk.

A security guard looked out of the gatehouse as the driver opened his electric window. He nodded and could be seen pressing a switch to open the main gates. Dirk could see two armed guards as they drove through, one controlling a German shepherd barking towards the car. They continued along the gravel drive, and with the driver's window still open, Dirk could hear the crunching sound as the tyres traversed the loose stones. When the car stopped outside the mansion, a small entourage was ready to open the doors to let everyone out. The lawyer waited for Dirk to join him before walking up to the large front doors.

A servant offered to take Dirk's coat, but he politely refused. He was led through the mansion and finally into a room where he was left alone. The door was firmly shut behind him.

Chapter 41

Dirk was standing in a large, old-fashioned study, with most of the wall space lined with wooden cabinets filled with books. Main lights were evident but not in use. Instead, the lighting was being supplied by several table lamps dotted around the room. The overwhelming presence of dark lacquered wood, alongside the forest-green carpet and deep-red crushed velvet curtains gave the room a somewhat oppressive look, especially with the shadows created by the lamps and fire. The only everyday items he could see were the computer on a sizeable leather-topped desk and the sixty-inch flat-screen TV mounted on the wall.

While waiting for someone to appear, only the ticking of an antique clock and the crackling of embers in the log fire prevented complete silence. He looked calm, but his mind was beginning to sprint ahead, going over scenarios of what might be asked or how he'd counter the questioning he was expecting. Dirk was surprised at himself, as he didn't yet feel panicked.

After several minutes, he decided to check his mobile phone. First, to see if the time matched the antique clock, and second, to see if he had any missed calls, which he hadn't, before noticing he had no signal and put the phone back in his jacket. Another couple of minutes went by, and he decided to head to the door he'd come in when the other door in the room opened and a figure entered.

'Going somewhere, Mr Davis?' a stern female asked.

Dirk turned to see a woman dressed for business, and once she was in a better light, he could see it was Ms Amanda Jenson. 'I was just becoming bored. I don't like being kept waiting,' responded Dirk, keeping an air of composure. Ms Jenson just smiled before turning on the TV with the remote. His picture appeared; the same one he was shown earlier.

'You've been a busy man, haven't you?' Her tone was mocking as she spoke without even looking at the display.

'Wouldn't it be best to wait until my friends arrive?' countered Dirk. 'Save you going over things twice.'

'They're not coming. That was a deception to get you here and prevent you from calling them. And as you may have noticed, you have no phone signal in this room.' With that, she sat down at her desk.

Dirk had suspected as much when he checked his phone but didn't say anything. And the way Ms Jenson made her last remark made Dirk look around the room for cameras before taking off his jacket. He headed towards one of the high-backed chairs near the fireplace, facing the desk fifteen feet away. Dirk presumed the mirror had a camera hidden behind it. He was now beyond caring, he sat in the chair with his greasy overalls, and Ms Jenson didn't bat an eyelid.

'So, what am I here for? Do you need us to service your fleet of cars?' asked Dirk. He already knew the answer but wanted it to come from her lips instead.

'Such bravado, but we both already know the answer to that, don't we?'

'Excuse me?' Dirk replied, trying to act a little disgusted by the accusation. 'That might be me on the screen, but as you can see, I wear coveralls for my occupation. So, what are you trying to frame me for?' He was determined to stay level-headed, trying to keep his thoughts one step in front.

Ms Jenson selected the play switch on the remote, again only staring straight at Dirk.

The photo was just a film on pause, and now the recording began to pan outwards, wobbling slightly as it did so, to see Dirk and his team, clearly by the statues, not long after they'd dealt with Quillon, as he could now clearly see his bloodied overalls and the bandage on his hand. He sat in silence.

'What's the matter? Cat got your tongue?' The comment was laced with venom, knowing she'd caught him red-handed. 'You stole my statues, and I now want recompense for your actions.'

Dirk didn't reply; he was still watching the film and could see themselves talking to someone off-screen when the film was paused again. 'I think you've seen enough.' Her response had a hint of annoyance; it appeared she didn't like being ignored.

Dirk looked at her. 'What do you want from me? If it's justice, you would've turned me into the cops already.

And something tells me it's not about the money either. I believe you're too smart to not insure against such things.'

There was a smile of appreciation from her, but it quickly disappeared.

'As it seems, you have a penchant for obtaining objects not belonging to yourself. I think you can take something for me. It will go some way towards the compensation.'

'And if I don't accept your offer?' He knew it was a pointless question, but he wanted time to think.

She expected more from her quarry. 'Then a selection of photos will find their way into the hands of the Chicago police, and you and your team will be arrested. Even I thought you'd figure that out.'

'OK. What did you have in mind?'

'Good. I'm glad we understand each other.' And knowing her prey was cornered, she stood up, walked over, and opened a drinks cabinet. 'Drink?' she asked, while pouring herself a bourbon.

'No, thank you,' replied Dirk.

She poured him a glass anyway, and there was a warming smile. 'It's nice to see manners, though sadly they're quickly disappearing in this day and age.' She handed him the tumbler, not taking no for an answer.

Dirk took it begrudgingly.

'Did you really think you wouldn't get caught?' Ms Jenson said, sitting back down at her desk. 'Did you think I'd just give up looking for my possessions? I think you've severely underestimated me, and from what I've learned about you, I expected more, so forgive me if I sound a little disappointed.' And she took a mouthful of drink from her glass. Dirk didn't say anything. He seemed to be sulking. 'Come now, Mr Davis. It's no-good moping like a teenager. You're acting like my son before he goes back to boarding school. What choice do you have? It's my way or jail.'

'OK. Let's hear your terms,' responded Dirk.

Ms Jenson became businesslike again, pressing home her advantage, even leaning forward, relishing the moment. 'Have you heard of a place called Knossos?' She took another drink from her glass.

'No. Should I have?' Dirk replied, gently swirling the untouched liquid in his glass, staring at her directly. He was listening, but his mind was starting to ask unanswered questions like a devil sitting on his shoulder, goading him into asking her for the answers.

'The palace of Knossos is on the island of Crete, in the Mediterranean Sea. I need you to retrieve something from its ruins.'

'I'm not an archaeologist, nor am I Indiana Jones, Ms Jenson,' replied Dirk sarcastically.

She responded, her tone reprimanding. 'Correct. An archaeologist records information from excavation and analysis of human prehistory. But Indiana Jones was a thief, just like you. Not one bit of work he did in those films was archaeology. So, let's get your facts straight, shall we, no matter how fictional or pretentious they may be.' Dirk just stared at her, eyes narrowing, his disdain rising.

Ms Jenson recognised his contempt and stood up, placing both hands on her desk and leaning forward before continuing in her powerful, businesslike manner. 'Like it or loathe it, both you and your team *will* do this for me. You will be taking something I want. No pay. No deals. Do I make myself clear?' The cold, hard stare between them continued for several long seconds, neither giving way to blinking first.

Ms Jenson's face flushed with anger due to the lack of response, and she was about to let loose a torrent of verbal abuse when Dirk stood up, elevated himself to full height, and raised his voice, before she had the chance to start. This was the last straw for Dirk. The unanswered questions that had ebbed and flowed in his mind for months now came to the fore, falling forth like water from a burst dam.

'What I want to know is why was there a stone guard dog protecting the statues? Something tells me you know more than you're letting on. What did you know that we didn't? Why did you place them in the museum if you knew something would happen? Why not just keep them here where it was safer?'

It was clear from the brief look of shock on her face she wasn't used to such a riposte. She blinked a couple of times, and took a second or two to regain her composure, but Dirk laid into her again before she could respond. 'What? You thought I'd just forget that a stone dog came to life and attacked us? How much more footage did you take?' Something clicked, his mind went into overdrive. 'Yes, how much footage did you take?' He narrowed his eyes; his tone was now inquiring. 'Especially when all the museum's security cameras were turned off. How did you take this footage?' He gestured at the TV. 'How did you persuade the museum to put your camera in? Donation perhaps? Money talks, doesn't it? Especially in your world.' He hesitated. 'Or did they know?' He asked himself aloud. 'The fear trap… That was set up as protection as well, wasn't it? But the museum wouldn't have believed you, especially about a spell. They would've thought you were a right nut job.' He looked away. 'So, if you sneaked that in, you must've sneaked in the camera too.' He looked back at Ms Jenson. He quickly took several strides forward, wrenched the remote control from the desk, pressed play and then fast forward, while taking several steps back as he did so, just out of reach of Ms Jenson's protesting and swiping right hand.

Dirk could see the camera footage fleeting across the screen, watching Semyon in man-tiger form attacking the stone dog, while Ru Mang could be seen, but only his back was facing the camera. Dirk pressed play as Lin entered the room. Ms Jenson tried to respond angrily, but Dirk calmly intercepted her. 'The zooming on the camera footage, you couldn't have done that remotely. The wi-fi was down! And the footage, it's wobbling, so it's not secured. So, someone must have been holding it, a servant maybe!' A loud squawk could be heard, and the little monster appeared on cue from under Lin's cloak; it glanced around before it stared directly at the camera. Dirk paused the film, and his eyes widened as it finally dawned on him. 'It was a servant. The imp. That's why I didn't see it that night. And that's why there was a hole in its plinth because that's where the camera was hidden. And that creature, he sensed your imp, and that's what it was hunting in the room. That's why it ignored everything else. The squawk I heard was your creature. Not Lin's.' Dirk pressed play again. The camera footage became a blur as it was continuously moving. The sound was the only recognisable thing.

'Enough, Dirk.' The voice was again commanding, but this time it was a male voice that spoke, not Ms Jenson, who was just standing there staring at Dirk, mouth slightly open.

Dirk looked around quickly to see a man walking out of the shadows near the door where Ms Jenson had entered and didn't know how long he'd been standing there, as the door was still shut. He was probably in his late seventies, wearing a grey suit, his pallor skin tone blending with his short-cropped silver hair. 'Leave us please, Amanda,' he said politely. And Ms Jenson, without objection, walked out of the room.

'OK, who are you? Her father?' responded Dirk. His confidence was still evident.

'Something like that,' replied the man, the corner of his mouth just giving away a hint of a smile. 'This is why I chose you, Dirk, because you're a clever man.' He walked past Dirk, gently took the remote from his hand, and pressed stop before seating himself in one of the high-backed chairs opposite Dirk, just five feet away, making a hand gesture for Dirk to sit back down.

Dirk could just make out a hint of an accent as he spoke but couldn't quite place it. 'You have me at a disadvantage.

You know me, but I don't know you. As Amanda's now left the room, I presume you're the one in charge!'

'Careful, Dirk, politeness goes a long way from where I come from. It would be a great shame to spoil it now.' He rested his elbows on the arms of the chair and steepled his fingers.

Dirk took his seat again. 'And where is that exactly?' inquired Dirk.

'Scandinavia,' replied the man. 'And my name is Aric Jensen. But you can call me Mr Jensen.' Dirk could sense Aric was measuring him on the type of man he was.

'OK... Mr Jensen. Can you tell me what all this is about?'

'Well, with what I've heard already, I think you've guessed correctly with most things, except the dog and the fear trap were not for the statue's protection. They were there as obstacles, to test those trying to take them, as were you and your team.'

'What... Say that again... As was I?!' Dirk was caught off guard by the remark.

'Yes. You were to become an obstacle, keep going no matter what, and even die trying. And I must admit, it was difficult to organise everything so that you would all be there on the same night.'

'Hold on... You mean to tell me, we were hired to fail?'

'Yes.'

'Ms Jenson hired us... To steal her own statues!'

'No, Dirk. I 'hired' you. Amanda has to do as I say.'

'You! And you knew these teams were after the statues!'

Dirk suddenly became dumbstruck and couldn't find the right words to respond, trying to make sense of what Aric had just said.

Aric was amused more by Dirk's response and chuckled as he continued. 'Oh no, Dirk, I knew one group was after the statues, but four! No, four was just the frosting on the cake. You see, I knew about the team led by the Asian woman, and in our circles—'

'Your circles!' interjected Dirk.

'Yes. The supernatural here doesn't know much about our supernatural brethren in the East... The Shen. Imagine the renown I'll receive for discovering some of their secrets.' And he smiled at Dirk, basking in what he'd achieved before continuing. 'Now, I didn't see what happened to the Jamaicans. But no special abilities, just fear and parlour tricks, and I can see they gave you no bother. Though I find it fascinating you've started using firearms again.' He halted the beginnings of Dirk's response with just another simple hand gesture. 'Quillon! Let's just say most of his secrets are already known to us, so again, there is no real interest. Quite boring, really. Though I must admit, it was nice to see him using zombies, and I commend you and your team on how you dealt with them and for not damaging my pieces.' Aric became serious again. 'My clean-up crew managed to take some sound samples of the corpses of the Shen. Unfortunately, we didn't get much footage of the team led by the Asian woman and their pet chasing poor old Zex.'

'Zex! That thing has a name?'

'Haven't you ever given a name to a loving pet?' Aric verbally made a clicking sound, and Zex flew across the room from the shadows and landed on Aric's shoulder before nuzzling against the side of his head like a loving cat. Dirk looked around for any more surprises.

'You see, Dirk, imps are excellent at hiding, except when others of their kind are around, like the demon they brought along. So, the footage he got only gave us a morsel of information.' He stopped to give Zex a fuss with his hand before continuing. 'No, the real prize was your tiger friend. No one ever knew they existed. Werewolves, yes, but weretigers... now that was incredible... and the footage Zex got was outstanding.' Aric chuckled as he still fussed the creature. 'And all for some worthless statues.'

Taking in Aric's last sentence, Dirk became hesitant before replying. 'OK... But why am I really here?'

'Well, we do want you to go to Crete, that is true. Though, as you now know we set you up, we seem to be at a disadvantage.' Aric just smiled courteously.

At that moment, the door opened, and a figure walked in, carrying a tray.

Dirk, his full attention towards Aric, just responded, 'What do you mean when you say, 'we seem'?'

Aric was distracted, his eyes closed while smelling the air. 'Ah, my evening aperitif.' And he again smiled before reopening his eyes. 'Where were we? Ah, yes, seemed.' He took a tall, ornate wine glass with a silver rim from a silver tray being held with white gloves to Aric's right, filled with what looked like a full-bodied red wine.

Dirk then received a flashback to the night of the first meeting. The glass was the same one used by the old man in the restaurant. He could now see the reflection of Aric in the restaurant window, looking back at him against the pitch black of the stormy night. He looked at Aric with an unnerving new focus.

'You see, you and your team have always worked for me. And you always come through for us.' He paused again as he took a sip from the glass and looked at his servant. 'Perfect, you've heated it to the perfect temperature. 96.6 Fahrenheit. Thank you. You may leave.' And he let Zex lap up some of his drink before taking several savoured mouthfuls while talking. 'It never ceases to amaze me. You always find something is amiss. Though admittedly, this was much more evident than other jobs we've given you. You always want to retire. But I always 'turn' you around, so you can keep working for me.' Aric twirled his finger around and around as he stated, 'Ignore the bonus, do it right, and live another day.'

But Dirk instantly became confused, as he couldn't recall meeting Aric before. 'What are you on about?!' exclaimed Dirk before asking, 'What are you?'

'And there's the $64,000 question, Dirk. I am a creature of the night. And yes, this is blood.' Aric even lifted the glass slightly and swirled it as he continued talking. Most of the contents were gone, too thick to see through, but it clung to the glass like warm syrup. 'I get what I want without even showing myself. Did you think what happened after New Jersey was an accident?'

Dirk was lost for words, feeling the colour drain from his face.

Aric kept smiling, content with allowing Dirk to stew in his discomfort for several moments before finally adding, 'You know, I like our little chats. We don't get to tell many people we exist; having you is like having a personal counsellor. But before I reveal much more, I think it's time to explore your memory for what Zex missed at the museum before I wipe it again. We need to keep our pet thief in check, don't we?'

A sudden thump disrupted Dirk's emotional thoughts as Zex had fallen limply to the floor. Aric looked at Zex in shock before resting back in his chair. He looked at his glass, eyes widening, before throwing it into the fireplace. The butler, who had not gone away as instructed, launched an attack on Aric, placing something around his neck before he could react. Dirk was still trying to take it all in, but when he finally focused on the butler, he stated aloud, 'Ru!'

'Hi, Dirk,' he replied through gritted teeth and tensed muscles. 'Can you give me a hand?'

Dirk hastily stood up to help Ru Mang and hesitantly began to wrestle with Aric's hands, which were trying to grasp the rosary beads around his neck. The strength of Aric was formidable, but there was a listlessness about him. Dirk could see the beads were causing terrible blistering around Aric's neck and fingertips, where he struggled to take them off. Aric's eyes were now red, his mouth widened, hissing loudly in pain, as the long canine teeth became visible, the trademark of a supernatural apex predator: a vampire.

Aric's hand grabbed and slowly snapped off an arm of the high-backed chair he sat on before dropping it, and Dirk could see the seat of his trousers becoming increasingly wet.

'Quick,' snarled Ru Mang. 'Before he purges the sedative from his system.'

Dirk was temporarily mesmerised, recognising that what he thought was urine was actually blood. Dirk was beginning to feel panicked. 'What do I do?'

Straining, Ru Mang replied, 'Pick up the piece of wood and stab him in the heart. Then drive it in, for all your worth.' Dirk did as he was told, and with the initial hit, Aric screamed in pain. He then pushed with all his might, and the piece of wood began to drive inwardly.

There was a sudden bang as doors opened. Armed guards and Ms Jenson ran in; they began to level their weapons, preparing to fire, while Ms Jenson was screaming obscenities at them.

As the wooden shaft pierced Aric's heart, his body froze solid instantly. The hissing was no more. 'Finally,' shouted Ru Mang, and the beads began to shatter, sending them bouncing and rolling their way to the floor, revealing a thin metal wire. Ru Mang pulled the wire with one swift final action, cleaving Aric's head from his shoulders, leaving it to harmlessly roll onto the floor.

Several more thumps quickly followed, and as Ru Mang and Dirk promptly looked around, they could see the guards' weapons had dropped to the floor. They and Ms Jenson had become dazed and confused and were either leaning against a wall or slumped on their knees. Even Dirk himself began to feel giddy.

'Let's go. Follow me,' stated Ru Mang.

Dirk staggered after him, feeling befuddled. 'What's happening?' stammered Dirk.

'Later,' said Ru Mang with a sense of urgency in his voice and guided Dirk out of the room, leaving Aric and Zex rapidly turning to ash. Everywhere they looked, guards, servants and even the dogs were in different states of bewilderment.

Ru Mang led Dirk to a parked car, opened the rear door, and helped him onto the back seat. He pulled out the confused driver and lay him on the floor, leaving him staring up towards the stars. Finally, Ru Mang started the car and raced along the drive, smashing through the main gates. Dirk slumped as he passed out in the back seat.

Chapter 42

Several hours later, Dirk found himself waking up in his apartment. His mind's fog had cleared, yet he still felt like he was coming out of a dream. His bedside light was on, and with squinting eyes, he looked around to see Ru Mang looking out of his bedroom window before softly speaking. 'What happened? Was that real? Are we safe?'

Ru Mang walked over and handed Dirk a glass of water from the bedside table.

'Yes, it was real. Here, drink this. How do you feel?'

'Strange… like a weight's been lifted.' Dirk took the glass from Ru Mang.

'That's a good sign. Do you recall everything that happened at the mansion? Do you remember what was said?'

'How could I forget! But what happened afterwards? Did I pass out?'

'Yes. You did. Luckily, in the back of the car. Please, drink some water.'

Dirk took a sip of water; it felt refreshing, but he still wanted answers. 'Why are we here? Won't this be the first place they look? And how come you were there?'

'You're like a child wanting a bedtime story.' Ru Mang paused to chuckle briefly before continuing. 'We should be safe here. Semyon should be handling the situation now…'

'Semyon's here as well?!' Interrupted Dirk.

'Are you going to let me finish, Mr Davis?' said Ru Mang firmly. And with Dirk now put in his place, he continued.

'As soon as we arrived here, I called Semyon. He has a warrant to search the mansion and will shortly be entering the grounds without much resistance as they'll still be affected by Aric's death. In doing so, Semyon will find the statues, arrest Ms Jenson and charge her with fraud. Now we've vanquished her benefactor, there will be nothing to save her. The building will be put on lockdown, where they will find other stolen items, most likely collected by you and your team. Any artefacts of special interest to us will be catalogued, made inert and may be reunited with their owners, depending on their nature. The stolen objects will be added to the charge, and Ms Jenson, along with anyone else involved, will go to prison for an exceptionally long time.'

'OK,' replied Dirk, but he was still perplexed and took several mouthfuls of water, trying to hide his expression of confusion, questions slowly beginning to creep into his thoughts.

Ru Mang, noticing Dirk's inquiring mind, spoke again. 'Let me explain. Do you remember when we exorcised the spectre from its statue? That the other statue helped us?'

Dirk just nodded.

'When I spoke to the statue after, I gave him something to swallow, do you remember?'

'No,' said Dirk shaking his head. But he remembered looking into Sharyn's eyes and the warming feeling he felt towards her at that point.

'Well, before I exorcised his spirit. I requested him to swallow a tracking device; we wanted to know who else wanted the statues. We are always finding new groups crossing our path. Some good, some bad. Anyway, I digress. Several days later, the statue's trail led straight back to Ms Jenson's mansion. Semyon went through his usual channels and found the insurance claim for the statues. The heist was suppressed by the authorities.'

'But what about the museum guards?' exclaimed Dirk.

'The official line was the theft never happened, and the time frame for the attack with Mbundu was altered to clash with the guards' death. They all just happened to be in the same car and caught in the crossfire of the turf war on the way to work. The driver lost control and rolled the car. Two died instantly, the third suffered a broken jaw and severe concussion, and…' he paused briefly. 'He has no recollection of what happened.'

Dirk's eyes widened in surprise, but his cheeks also flushed with anger. 'They covered it up? And people say we're crooks.'

'Remember where you've just come from, Dirk,' Ru Mang responded decisively. 'The handful of people Semyon spoke to, who we knew had arrived on the scene after we left, gave the same story, they all believed emphatically in it.

For Semyon and me, it meant other forces were at play. We know how to keep our heads down. If we asked too many questions, we could find ourselves being used and end up like you: controlled.'

Dirk just stared at Ru Mang in silence for several moments. He understood what was being said but was still going through things in his head. He then asked, 'Why did they wait so long to contact me if they had the statues after a couple of days?'

'Most likely for effect. Let you get used to spending the money you earned. Less likely to just hand it back. But I'm only guessing. You don't need to worry about it now. Semyon will ensure there'll be no evidence to tie you and your team to the theft. And I strongly believe that Ms Jenson's mind will be severely muddled over what has just happened. Plus, no one will believe her if she starts claiming she was being manipulated by the supernatural. And the supernatural who knew won't be in a rush to help. Do you remember what Aric said tonight? Where you had met before?'

Again, Dirk nodded without a word.

'Well, as you found out tonight, Aric Jensen was a vampire, and vampires control people with just a stare and a suggestion. When we destroyed Aric tonight, the hold over those he controlled died also. As you pointed out, when you awoke, you felt like a weight had been lifted off your shoulders. The same would have happened to all those at the mansion tonight, and I'd dare say several high-ranking officials in the city are also feeling the same effects. It affected you less because those at the mansion were so heavily controlled, their lives were not their own. Everything they did was set up by Aric, even for Ms Jenson. And that's the only reason we escaped unhindered. You were allowed to keep your freedom of thought, Dirk; you wouldn't make a good thief otherwise. From what I can see, only your memories have been altered, maybe some commands like not befriending too many people, not wearing religious symbols, that type of thing, but I'm not certain about that.'

'I see. But what about the dogs?'

'Even the dogs, Dirk.'

'And how did you get into the mansion?'

'After we found that the statues had gone back to the mansion, we knew we had to go in and find out more. So, I applied for a job at the mansion, and surprisingly enough, I got it. However, I soon learned that all the staff were single and had no social life.'

'But didn't they click you were the guy in the film? And aren't the supernatural supposed to be able to sense each other or something? And how come you weren't controlled?' queried Dirk. He was beginning to find his stride again, his words becoming enthusiastic.

'As far as sensing other supernatural beings, in most cases, that is true. But I am not a supernatural, Dirk. I am a man, just like you. The only difference is I know some simple forms of magic and have an understanding of supernatural lore.' Ru Mang showed Dirk his neckless with an eye pendant. It was like the one he'd given him when they last met. 'Do you remember the one I gave you?'

'Yes.' But Dirk's voice was mumbled, as he hadn't been wearing it and didn't want to hurt Ru Mangs' feelings.

Ru Mang just chuckled. 'Don't worry, Dirk. As I said, a suggestion was most likely implanted in your mind to avoid wearing such items.' He calmed himself before he continued. 'It protected me, as I said it would. With my studies of the supernatural, I faked being controlled. And to some degree, it was probably a good thing you weren't wearing it.'

'How so?' Dirk looked confused.

'Because when Aric would've tried to clear your mind this time, it wouldn't have worked. He most likely would have killed you.'

As Dirk remembered the fangs that appeared when Aric was attacked, he swallowed and shuddered, then quickly finished off the water to quench the dryness now present in his mouth.

'When I first saw the video of the heist, I thought I'd been had, or as you'd say, rumbled, and it was a trap. But fortunately for me, the camera angle only got the back of my head. While I was at the mansion, I was able to piece together most of the events leading up to and beyond the theft we were involved in. As Aric said earlier, it appears it was just an elaborate stunt to gather information on the Shen from the East. Though speaking to Lin—'

'You caught her then!' interrupted Dirk.

Ru Mang paused to answer the question. 'Yes, we caught her.'

'What will happen to her?'

'Rehabilitation. Hopefully, Lin will be able to help us in future. But as I was saying…'

'Yes, sorry. Go on.'

'Thank you.' Ru Mang gave a wry smile. 'Lin told us she used the Terracotta Army exhibition as a front, directing the exhibition to cities where their investigations found strong rumours of where other pieces resided. She arrived in Chicago to hold talks with the museum to hold her exhibition, allowing her to continue her investigation. They found evidence of the two at the mansion and planned to steal them from there. With certain elements of the discussions I picked up while working at the mansion, it appears Aric somehow found out he was being targeted and decided to set his trap. Though I suspect that great age also comes with great paranoia. He wouldn't want someone to violate his sanctuary, either through fear of other prized possessions going missing or fear of his decisive death.'

'He also said the statues were worthless! And he thought I'd gunned down Mbundu!' countered Dirk.

'The sad part is, he didn't know what the statues could do. He most likely acquired them years ago, believing they were something special. Probably heard all the stories that they were keys to the underworld and not to be damaged. But with not knowing where or how to look, they became nothing more than a treasured possession. And looking at the coroner's report, which showed the involvement of gunfire and fire killing Mbundu and his posse, he's assumed you took on Mbundu and needed desperate measures to resolve the matter.' Ru Mang sighed.

Dirk mulled the information over in his mind. Satisfied that all his questions had been answered, Dirk spoke again. 'What happens now?'

Ru Mang smiled. 'You're now free to do whatever you want. You can finally retire if you want, no longer feeling the need to put it off. Enjoy your time with Sharyn. Relax on that boat of yours. Go fishing with Willkie and Cody or meet new friends.'

'And what about Semyon and you?'

'As soon as Ms Jenson is charged and the paperwork completed, we will leave the city. Aric did say that he'd shown his community, but supernatural beings like to keep things to themselves, as I have said before. So, he would've made sure he kept hold of the physical evidence. But just to be sure, we'll lay low for a while before continuing with our work.

'Now rest, Dirk. Get some more sleep. Later, we'll leave and meet with Sharyn and the others. We'll tell them what's happened, and you can all be left in peace.'

Acknowledgements

For the art in and on the book cover: **Glenn Badham**

For reading my first 12 chapters and telling me to keep going: **Mandy Consentino**

For her knowledge of first aid: **Donna Dwyer**

For her knowledge of writing / publishing E-Books and blurb: **Claire Huston**

To the Beta Checkers. For giving me their truthful opinions, so I could improve the original draft:
Victoria Keys, Kathleen Mawby, Kevin Murray, Helen Tucker

A big thank you to **Jen Parker** at Fuzzy Flamingo, for her fantastic assistance and support with publishing my book.

To the **Terracotta Exhibition** and the **British Museum**: The exhibition wouldn't have given me the spark for this story without seeing it.

A Note
from the Author

I created this story in a way of therapy for my mental health. An avid role-play gamer and history buff, the original story was created as four pages of bullet points for one of the games I played after seeing the Terracotta Army exhibition in 2008 at the British Museum.

Throughout my life, I've suffered bouts of mental health issues, and during a rather bad episode in 2016, with the support of my loving wife Jacqueline, I decided to convert the four pages of bullet points into a full-blown novel, in a way of tackling my overactive thought processes and depression. And, seven years later, here we are. Ready to release it upon the world.

Leaving school with an 'E' in English GCSE, improving it twenty years later to a grade 'C', I'm releasing the book for a sense of achievement, and hopefully, no matter how dimly, a beacon to others to show there is light at the end of the dark tunnel when dealing with their own mental health problems.

I hope you enjoy the story.

Printed in Great Britain
by Amazon

33973793R00165